Sophie Duffy has an MA in Creative Writing from Lancaster. Her first novel, *The Generation Game* (Legend Press) was published August 2011. It won the Yeovil Literary Prize (2006) and the Luke Bitmead Bursary (2010).

This Holey Life (Legend Press) published August 2012 was runner-up in the Harry Bowling Prize (2008).

Sophie has also published short stories in a range of literary journals and anthologies, including *Momaya Press*, *The View from Here*, *Dark Tales*, *Arvon* and *Your Cat*.

As well as teaching in primary schools in inner-city London (1991-98) with a specialist interest in early years and emergent writing, Sophie now leads life writing workshops at Teignmouth library. She is a book reviewer for *Serendipity Reviews* and has been a judge for many competitions including The Yellow Room, Retreat West and the Hysterectomy Association.

Visit Sophie at sophieduffy.com
Follow her @sophiestenduffy

For Niall

We are bought and sold for English gold. Such a parcel of
rogues in a nation.
Robert Burns

Christie Armstrong cordially invites you to the
launch of her family's new Niagara Icewine
at The Burlington Suite, The Ritz
150 Piccadilly,
London W1J 9BR
Friday 13th December 2013
From 6 pm

RSVP info@armstrongkingestates.ca

Lancaster University, 1985
Ball

I always wanted to be a hero. A superhero with super powers. My favourite film was *Superman* starring Christopher Reeves, the only man to attempt the whole tights look and pull it off. (The look, not the tights.) You need a proper outfit to be a superhero. A cloak. A mask. A belt.

I had a kilt. The Brown tartan. (Which is actually red, not brown. And which is my mother's name, not my father's.) I would wear the red Brown kilt to the Freshers' Ball. I would draw strength from my ancestors, confidence from my clan. The kilt would be my disguise. My armour. I would go to the Ball and be proud of who I was.

I just hoped I wouldn't spend the evening on my own looking like a saddo.

I did spend the first half of the evening on my own looking like a saddo. But the second half was different altogether. I saw this girl at the bar. She was tall, as tall as me and I am five foot eleven in my socks. She was as thin as me too. I was technically skinny whereas she was what Granny Spark would call 'rangy'. She had this dress on. It was old-fashioned, like it might have been her mum's. Sixties style, Twiggy style, crazy colours, short. But she had these thick black tights and

Doctor Martens. She looked strong. But maybe a wee bit fragile too. Maybe those boots were her superhero disguise. Because girls can be superheroes too.

My mum was a superhero. Brown by name, but not brown by nature. She'd fought and fought that cancer, tough as Maid Lilliard (I'll come back to her) in bloody battle on her horse. In the end, the legion cells beat Mum's body into submission. But not her spirit. Never her spirit.

Mum was there with me that night, at the ball, urging me to be strong.

I stepped out, walked over to the bar.

'Nice kilt,' she said, the student, before I had a chance to speak.

'Thanks.' I took a deep breath. It hurt. 'Would you like a drink?'

'Let me get you one,' she said. 'What'll it be?'

'I was just on the lemonade.'

'Is that what you want?'

'No, I'll be daring,' I said. 'I'll have a Lilt.'

She raised her eyebrows at me, flung back her head and laughed this snorty laugh, her long wild Kate Bush hair shining red-green-and-blue in the disco lights. 'Want a vodka in that?'

'No,' I said. 'I'm all right.'

And she didn't push it like people usually did. She bought me a Lilt, plus a packet of salt and vinegar crisps. She had a pint of cider and a packet of prawn cocktail. Which she assured me were technically veggie. She was a staunch veggie. She was staunch in all her beliefs.

'Come on,' she said. 'Let's move some of those stupid bourgeois name cards and sit next to each other.' And so we did. Well, she did. I merely followed her around like an already unquestioningly loyal dog.

Her name was Rebecca Stone but she was called Bex. She changed her name card, writing in a thick marker pen that she blagged off a barman. This was the first of many times

10

I would see her change things. Over the next few weeks she would daub blood-red paint outside Barclays. She'd rip down posters that propped up the patriarchy. And off campus, out in the field, she'd run with the sabs, locking gates, spraying scent, holding up the hunt. Always fighting the cause of the underdog. She was a superhero. And I was the underdog of underdogs.

I fell in love with Bex that night in the Great Hall with the Indie music and the crush of hormone-charged teenagers and the flashing disco lights.

Over the next week we would become inseparable, me the Scottish lad from Edinburgh, her the Devon lassie from Dartmoor. We would play pool, go to the library, ride the bus into town. Share confidences, secrets and dreams. We would become friends.

I dared hope that maybe perhaps in time she might become more than a friend. Once she got to know me. Once she saw that I was a good man. But before I had the chance to prove myself to her, someone took my place. She still wanted to hang out with me, still wanted to be friends, but she gave her heart to someone else.

But she had my heart, unknowingly grasped in her hand.

I will say it fairly, it grows on me with every year:
there are no stars so lovely as Edinburgh street-lamps.
Robert Louis Stevenson

Edinburgh, November 2013
Boxes

There's no such thing as ghosts. You get that a lot from our visitors. The stag-weekenders in their ginger wigs and tartan caps are the worst – they only believe what they want to believe – and yet they're the ones who have palpitations when they are taken down into the dark, cold, breathy vaults under the Old Town. They blame it on their asthma.

There's no such thing as ghosts? I don't believe that. Not for one minute. You can't walk in Edinburgh without being tripped up by the limboed body of a plague victim or a soggy-footed witch.

It's not the ghosts I'm afraid of.

Twenty-three years ago, I was lucky to get a job. So I didn't mind putting on a costume and telling stories of Edinburgh's murky past. I didn't mind listening to loud American youths and skittish young English women. I was being paid. I could dress up, be someone from another time and put my own history behind me. Of course, history is always behind us. It has gone as soon as it has happened. But there are always repercussions. One act of recklessness, one ill-formed decision, can echo down the years. If you stop for a moment, you can hear it.

Boom. Boom. Boom.

So who was I to complain about dressing up in a cloak? This was my new disguise, stepping into someone else's clothes. Someone else's tights.

Walking tours is the name of our game. History tours, ghost tours, paranormal events for ghostbusters. Around the Old Town, the kirkyards, the prisons, the underground vaults. Candles flickering in the shadows. Health and safety. No Ouija boards. No dogs. No scaredy-cats allowed.

We bring history alive. We make money from the horrors of the past. We try not to blur the lines between history and myth, but if people want to believe in ghosts, that is their choice.

I believe in ghosts.

Today it's the ghost of my younger self that's pestering me. As well as Myrtle, Dad's daft barking machine of a Dachshund. I've managed to park the car in the bus stop outside the old family home, a granite three-storey terrace in Newington. I can see Myrtle on the back of the sofa, crashing against the window panes as she defends her house. Dad's house. My house. I'm back.

I take a deep breath.

Hazards on, boot open, all hands on deck. Not that the hands are particularly helpful. Dad's are arthritic, as are Mrs Paterson's from next door. But between us we manage to empty the boot and the back seat of my Vectra. Cardboard boxes and plastic stackers line up in the hall, the sad contents of my life to date. I'm tempted to set a match to it all in the back garden. But I won't do that. Bonfires are frowned upon these days and anyway, fire won't kill ghosts. Ghosts will haunt you through the flames and ashes.

'Shall I put that kettle on?'

'Thank you, Sheena.' Dad gives Mrs P a smile, sheepish and knowing.

Sheena, is it now.

'Cameron, would you like a cup?'

'That would be grand.'

Mrs Paterson – Sheena – shuffles down the hall, to the kitchen at the back. Mum's scullery. The place of family meals and board games, homework and arguments.

Dad watches after her for a moment, wistfully, but I don't know who his wist is aimed at, Mum or Sheena.

'By the way, son...' We continue lurking in the lobby, Dad chinking coins in his trouser pockets. 'A letter arrived for you yesterday. I've put it on the mantelpiece.'

'The mantelpiece?'

'That's what I said. The mantelpiece.'

I follow Dad into the front room, praying it's not a letter from a divorce solicitor. Surely things haven't gone that far with Amanda?

Myrtle is ensconced on Dad's armchair watching a football match (it keeps her occupied and when she's occupied she's not barking). She looks at me briefly, decides I'm not about to kill her, and returns to watching the ball fly around the screen.

Dad moves over to the fireplace, the fire itself unlit as it is not yet December and we are hardy Scots. The mantelpiece, a beautiful Victorian marble affair, is the keeper of important stuff: pools coupons, cheques, postal orders, invitations, Hearts season tickets. A letter is important enough to put on the mantelpiece.

'It's not often you get a letter from abroad now, is it?' Dad chimes in. 'Usually an email is all you get.'

'Abroad, you say?'

'From away across the ocean.'

'A letter from America?'

'Comedian,' Dad says. 'Not America, no, but you're getting warmer. Or should that be colder?'

'Canada?'

He nods, shrugs, chinks more coins, looks like Dad always does when he is unsure of himself, when we both wish Mum were here to put things straight. Not Sheena.

My heart at this point does actually thump. Like when I

15

used to hear my name called out in class. Or when a shadow shifts in the vaults when everyone's gone home at the end of the day and you're last up the stairs with the keys to shut the ghosts in for the night.

Thump. Thump. Thump.

Maybe Mum's ghost is here somewhere, hiding under the sofa or behind the curtains, watching over us. Spying on Sheena.

I hope she's gone. A bright star shining in the universe. Not a lost soul in the underground world.

So the mantelpiece is where I go, walking that weird walk you walk when you know someone's watching you walk and it could be a memorable moment at the end of your walk.

Standing by the mantelpiece in my old home, separated from my beautiful wife, worried about the investigation, holding a letter that is making my hand quiver. Foreign stamps. Bears and other big animals. Canadian.

It feels heavy. Nice quality stationery. And there is my address, my childhood address, Dad's address, c/o Mr Andrew Spark, my address once more, hopefully temporary, written by a flourishing hand. And on the reverse?

Her name.

Seeing it there, in black and white, solid and real, is unnerving, like it's rattling my bones and I might just topple over and shatter into hundreds of tiny pieces.

Christie Armstrong.

How did she find me?

And why?

I didn't expect to see or hear from her ever again.

It was Mum that gave me my love of history. She read to me every night, here in this room, me tucked up in my bed, brushed cotton tartan pyjamas and flannel-wiped face, Mum in her baffies and dressing gown, sitting in a wicker chair with a mug of Brooke Bond.

It was always history books. Jacobite risings. Battles and

16

clans. Bannockburn. Culloden. Flora MacDonald. Myths and legends and historical events all entwined so you didn't know what was real, what was fiction. She loved her bonnie Scotland. She would've been putting a big tick by the Yes in the referendum. A Yes for independence.

That's why I chose to study History at Lancaster.* You have to study the past to make sense of your present and to navigate your future. But I never finished my degree. Instead, I ended up in a place I never expected to be, my freedom snatched like a rug from under my feet. I ended up playing cloak-and-daggers in locked away, dark and lonely places.

I've always been grateful to have a job, don't get me wrong. It's been a good job, usually interesting, often varied, depending on the punters, and the fickle spectral residents. And I've worked my way up from tour guide to manager. Not exactly Duncan Bannatyne, though not bad considering.

But the ghosts still haunt me. They are chasing me even now as I write my story. My own history, as I see it. Others will have a different opinion, their own narrative. But this is mine. And nobody can take it away from me.

And my story brings me back here to my childhood bedroom, where I lie now, still in my single bed, still with my orange eiderdown, still in my brushed cotton tartan pyjamas (somewhat bigger), but without my mother, without my wife and maybe without my job.

And the letter, the letter. Unopened, still on the mantelpiece amongst the photographs and the sports trophies and the bills. Waiting.

I'm not actually writing an historical memoir. This is actually supposed to be therapy, getting the words down on the page and out of my head. My counsellor, Jeremy, suggested it. Jeremy says it will help me come to terms with what happened

---

*You might wonder why I didn't choose a university in Scotland? It was a matter of grades. I got my place through Clearing. Lancaster squeezed me in at the eleventh hour. Enough said.

in the past if I write my account of it. Jeremy says it will help me work through my feelings for Amanda. Jeremy says it may help me work out why I did what I did last month.

'Are you not away to work today?' Dad asks me as I help myself to some tea and cornflakes.

'I've got some time off.'

'Oh, right.' Dad looks surprised. He knows I never take time off. I haven't mentioned the investigation because there's no need to worry him. What I did was not particularly professional but it'll get sorted and life can carry on.

'So... the letter?'

The letter now sits on the table between us, clean and smart against the crumb-infested, stain-attacked pine surface.

'I haven't opened it yet.'

'Are you going to open it?'

I nod. My mouth is full of cornflakes.

'When?'

Before I realise what I am doing – though I think it's because my mouth is still full and I can't speak without spitting – I make this action. My palm is flat on the table and I realise that the reason it is stinging is because I must have slammed my hand down with some force. I swallow my food. 'Dad, stop fussing.' I don't remember saying this but it's ringing in my head.

He's up now, refilling the kettle, footering around the kitchen.

'Sorry, Dad. It's just, well, I know who it's from.'

He sighs and I can detect a wheeze from his chest. Been smoking since he was ten years old. It's amazing he's still upright and breathing.

'It's from her, isn't it? The lassie.' He turns on the tap, splashing water everywhere and I can't see his face. 'You don't have to open it,' he says quietly, but loud enough. 'I can put it on the fire and we can forget all about it.'

He reels round to look at me now, soft grey eyes washed out with years of work, widowhood, worry over four sons.

'You don't have to return to that place.'

'What place?'

'1986,' he says. 'You can leave it back there with Thatcher.'

'We can't escape Thatcher, Dad. You know that as well as anyone. Her legacy's all around. And so is Christie's.'

'You cannae do anything about Margaret Thatcher. But you can do something about this letter.'

'You mean I should do nothing.'

'I mean you should put it on the fire.'

'Let me think about it, Dad.' I finish the last of my cornflakes and carry the bowl and spoon to the sink. 'I'll take Myrtle out for a walk, shall I?'

'She'd like that.' Dad smiles at me. He has a wet patch on his trousers, which makes me see him as an old man, incontinent, prostate problems.

'You should get that tap looked at.'

'The tap?' He examines his groin area and wipes at it with a tea towel.

'I meant a plumber not a urologist.'

He lunges at me with the tea towel but for once I am quick on my feet. I swipe the letter from the table and join Myrtle who has heard the 'W' word and is waiting by the front door, hopeful eyes, tail flapping, short stumpy legs barely holding her stomach up from the ground.

Myrtle's legs work fast, taking me for a walk around Newington, streets where I grew up, played out with my brothers who thought it hilarious to tranny me up in girls' clothes and push me around in the old big pram.

Myrtle addresses every lamp post with a cocked leg. She is a confused dog in many respects. She strains at the lead, pulling my arm and throttling herself, inhaling every whiff of canine urine along the pavements and against garden walls. We end up in a café that allows well-behaved dogs. Myrtle wouldn't win any awards but she has done her business, which I scooped up in a bag, warm and somehow comforting

19

in my hand, though I was glad to get rid of it in the poo bin. We never had poo bins when we were young, piles of turds everywhere and always one of us treading dog dirt in the carpet, so in the end Dad ripped them up and sanded the floorboards.

It was by the poo bin that I opened the envelope – a strange juxtaposition, I'll give you that.

It was from Christie as I knew it would be. But I wasn't expecting an invitation. I had to sit down.

We find a window seat and a waitress – young, dumpy, metal threaded through various parts of her face – takes our order. I go for a large cappuccino. (No Brooke Bond in this establishment.)

I need to think now.

The date. Next week. An email address to RSVP.

And I do what I've resisted doing ever since I first heard of search engines.

Google.

She's everywhere, quite the famous one, surviving against the odds, a thriving businesswoman running her family's winery, heading up a charity. She's navigated her way into her future.

And the images. The blonde hair, maybe slightly shorter, sleeker, paler. The big smile with the white teeth. The perfect skin. She hasn't changed. Still beautiful. Still youthful. You can't tell at all.

But why Britain?

Why would Christie ever want to set foot – oh God. Why would she ever want to come back?

The be-metalled waitress delivers my cappuccino to the table with a slickness I could never attain. I am one of those men who always manages to catch an elbow on a door frame, who invariably kicks a table leg as he sits down, who can be relied on to spill the milk, the beans, the dirt. To tread dog poo into a carpet. That's me, dyspraxic loser that I am. If I was a ghost, I wouldn't even be able to walk through walls.

The waitress gives me a smile that I do my best to reflect, but she's already turned away.

I'm not so good at smiling.

Mum always made us smile at the camera. It felt false; I didn't know how to do it. But I tried my best for her.

There's a photo on the mantelpiece – that mantelpiece – of the four of us brothers, smiling. We are standing in order of size from left to right, me the bairn, being on the far right. Andy has his arm around a shorter, younger Gavin's shoulder, Gavin has his arm around a shorter, younger Edward's shoulder and Edward has his arm around the shoulder of a much shorter, younger me. We all have someone to lean on, except of course for me. My arm is clutching a teddy bear. I am five years old. I am wearing a school uniform as it is the first day of school. Soon that teddy bear – Frank – will be left at home and I will have nothing to clutch and no one to lean on. I will have to rely on myself. I actually cry all morning, leaving my poor teacher tearing her hair out. Eventually I puke all over the Ladybird books in the reading corner.

I am Peter. I am Jane.

I am sick on Peter. I am sick on Jane.

The sudsy coffee is making me nauseous now. I can smell the sick congealed on those Ladybird books, dried up and crusty on my hand-me-down bobbly jumper.

Myrtle sits on my foot. She's the weight of a small dinosaur rather than a ridiculous stumpy-legged, wee-and-poo machine.

Good boy, Pat. Good girl, Myrtle.

I push my coffee away, scan the interior of the café, its arty photos on the shabby chic walls, reclaimed shelving stacked with packets of Fairtrade tea and coffee, students on their iPhones and Macs, nothing like our day of anti-Thatcher protests and phone cards and chips and gravy.

My phone. Dad. Should I answer? I should answer.

'Dad?' Deep breath. 'Are you okay?'

21

'I'm fine, son.' His usual reply. 'I wondered if you were on your way home. Your brother's bringing back his new girlfriend and I might need some help.'

'Edward?'

'Aye, Edward, being that the other two have wives.'

'I know that, Dad. I mean, Edward has a girlfriend?'

'A lassie from work. English.'

He says that last word with difficulty.

'So you need back-up?'

'I thought you might want to meet her…' His voice trails off, leaving that suggestion of family loyalty lingering in the ether between us.

'I'm coming back now.'

'Oh right… that's good… so I'll be seeing you soon.'

And in that breath between him speaking and me responding, I make a decision. 'But I'll be away next week.'

'Away?'

'London.'

A pause.

'Why?'

'I've been invited to this event.'

'Event?'

'A launch of a new wine label.'

I let this sink in for a moment, wait for the inevitable question.

'By the Canadian lassie?'

'Aye.' Now I've said it, I'll do it. I'll go. 'I'm on my way back now, Dad.'

'Right, son. See you soon. Don't forget that dog.'

I can't forget that dog. Right now she is licking her privates. I pull her further under the table so she can do her ablutions unseen. My younger self would have been mortified, blushing with embarrassment. But now I don't care so much.

It's the ghost of my younger self I'm more bothered about. And Christie. And what if the other two are included in this, whatever 'this' is? The four of us back together is something

I never thought would happen. I parcelled up Bex, Tommo and Christie in a box many years ago. I never wanted to open that box ever again so I secured it with string, tape, padlock, a label marked DANGER: DO NOT OPEN. CONTENTS WILL CAUSE HARM.

But what do you do when you are forbidden something? Do you ignore the warning? Or do you do as you're told? When I was small, maybe three or four, Mum told me not to touch the oven because it was hot. So what did I do? I touched the oven. It was hot. I got burnt. I never touched the oven again.

So Edward isn't the only one who has a girlfriend. Sheena is 'walking out' with Dad. Her words. Dad's words are 'she cheers me up'. I don't delve into the hows and whys of this cheering up as that would be too much information.

We sit around the kitchen table, Edward holding hands with his girlfriend, Katie, Dad not holding hands with his girlfriend, Sheena. And me. The one whose wife has kicked him out, who said she couldn't live with him anymore, not with everything that's going on. She wants a baby. How can she bring a baby into such an uncertain world? Meaning, she places great importance on the investigation, as if it's something to be ashamed of.

And your wife, who promised you it didn't matter about your past, it was a long time ago, your wife suddenly decides you are obviously a criminal at heart, and that there is no smoke without fire.

'Will you have a piece of fruitcake with your tea?' Sheena prises the lid off Mum's Tupperware container to reveal what looks like the *Blue Peter* birdfeed cake. She saws us a wedge each. It's not how I remember my mum's, but it's nice to have something home-made nevertheless. Amanda's never baked anything in her life. Nor have I for that matter, so I shouldn't be sexist. What would Bex say?

Bex.

And what would Bex have to say about ghosts? She'd

scare them away. Boo.

'What's it like down in those vaults?' askes Katie, her posh English voice, a lecturer at the university, who can see into my mind or so it seems. A witch. She would've been drowned in the Nor Loch for sure.

'I'll get you some tickets so you can see for yourself.'

'You've still got a job then?' This is Edward, joking, not funny. I confided in him about the incident and he finds it all amusing. It's not amusing.

'I have still got a job.' I eyeball him. 'There's just a health and safety matter to sort out, that's all. I'll be back before you know it.'

'And what about Amanda?'

'Really, Eddy, not now.' This is Dad, not knowing what's going on but not liking the way it's going, certainly not in front of guests (and English ones at that).

'Have a piece of cake, Katie,' Sheena urges. 'And I'll fetch us some more tea.' She's out of her seat like a whippet.

Katie accepts another piece of cake and nibbles at it obediently. Eddy squeezes her hand and this gesture almost brings a tear to my eye.

Dad meanwhile has got up – making that old man noise as he struggles to his feet – to switch on his spaceship of a CD player. Barbara Dickson. The sound of my childhood that has become his passion. Some might say 'obsession'. There's nothing that can't be put right by listening to Barbara. Apartheid, the Taliban, Independence, all put to rights by she of the husky voice and fine head of hair.

We sit and listen to a very loud rendition of 'January, February'. I know all the words. Before it is over, Edward and Katie have made their excuses and slunk off upstairs. He doesn't live here anymore but like our other two brothers, he still lays claim to his bedroom.* And soon enough no doubt

---

*'His' bedroom is actually 'our' bedroom. We had to share, being the youngest. But now, as an otherwise homeless adult, I am claiming it as 'my' bedroom.

Edward will be laying claim to Katie. Like a teenager. When he's nearly fifty, for goodness' sake.

I make my excuses too and escape to the front room, leaving Dad alone with Sheena and Barbara who is now belting out 'MacCrimmons Lament'. Myrtle scampers after me, claws clicking on the boards like a tart in high heels.

What's it like down in those vaults? Is it normal to see things out of the corner of your eye? Am I in tune with the spirit world having mixed with several of its members for such a long time?

It's more than imagination. I do see ghosts. I hear them. I feel them, the cold swirling around me, kissing my cheek as I pass from one vault to another, a drop in temperature alerting me to recent or current 'activity'. I'm not a paranormal investigator. I'm a historian. I tell the facts as I know them, I dispel myths where I have the evidence but I am open-minded enough to know that this is my version of events as I believe them. Not everyone will agree with me. Amanda, for example. She thinks I'm to blame for what happened in the vault that day. But really it was a silly mix-up. I could have handled the situation better, granted. I could've reacted differently, but there you go. None of it was intentional. So I see the investigation as a positive thing where the truth will out.

Hours later and I am jolted awake by Myrtle licking my face. She has the breath of a dragon. It is dark outside; the streetlamp beams a light across the rug and up the wall. My left arm has gone to sleep and feels like it will drop off. When the numbness becomes a fizzing pins-and-needles, I gather myself and stagger down the hallway, wondering why Dad hasn't woken me up.

He's been hard at it in the kitchen, piles of paper strewn across the table, but he's nowhere to be seen now. A stew has been abandoned mid-construction on the draining board. Hacked up chunks of carrots, onions and peppers. A chicken carcass, its skin puckered like a scrotum.

Myrtle sits and looks with determination at her empty food bowl. It's past her suppertime. Dad must've wandered off and forgotten what he was doing.

Just as I am contemplating the possibility that he might've had a stroke or a heart attack, the front door opens and there's the familiar sound of Dad's heavy gait down the hallway.

'Is that you, son?' he calls out.

'No, it's a robber.'

'Help yerself. We've got it all boxed up and ready for you to sell on e-amazon or whatever it is.'

Ever the joker.

As he enters the kitchen, he blinks in the light, claps his hands together, rubs them, warms them by the radiator, surveys his abandoned meal and paperwork. Gives me a shy look.

His hair is dishevelled.

'I'll get back to this chicken stew,' he says. 'I got distracted. Had to call in next door for something.'

His hands are empty.

'I've been hankering after chicken stew all day.'

'Okay, well, I'll let you hanker away while I get sorted.'

'Stay and have a beer with me, son. I'll get this in the oven and clear the table.'

'Why don't you use the dining room, Dad? As a study. Or any of the bedrooms.'

'I'm happy here.' He surveys the hillock of correspondence on the table.

'You could get a laptop. Go paperless.'

'Her fans like writing letters.'

'They could write emails.'

'Maybe some of us like the old ways.'

'You're not that old.'

'We're a different generation. Even Barbara is back to her folk roots.'

Yes, my father, who runs a Barbara Dickson fan club. The

other woman he has loved all his adult life.

'I'll skip the beer, Dad. Maybe later. I should make a start on those boxes. And I have some emails of my own to send.'

And some more digging to do.

So.

Back to my wee bedroom, the wicker chair, laptop balanced on my legs, fighting with the dongle to get a signal in this pre-historic house. Finally back to Google. This time Tommo. A shoddy website. A band. Based in a hippy town in Devon.

An email address.

How do you write to someone you haven't seen since *Cagney and Lacey* were on prime-time telly? Especially when the last time you were together was in a prison.

Dear Tommo?
Hi there, Tommo?
Dear Ptolemy?
How's it going, my old mucker?
I hope life is treating you well.
Are you and Bex still together?
Why have you never got in touch to see if I was okay?
Sincerely, Cameron.
Best wishes, Cameron.
Yours, Cameron Spark.
This is pathetic.
Hi Tommo
Been a while. Wondered if you were going to Christie's launch in London. If you are, I will see you there. Is Bex going too? It would be good to catch up.
Regards, Cameron
Send.

A week and maybe I'll finally know if I made the right decision back on that cold starry night in 1986.

♦

Lancaster University

The main architect was Gabriel Epstein of Shepherd and Epstein. On a barren hilltop on a windswept day in 1963 the two architectural partners surveyed the future site of the university. Peter Shepherd recalled that day. 'We went up there on a windy day, and it was freezing cold. Every time we opened a plan it blew away. And we said, Christ! What are we going to do with these students, where are they going to sit in the sun and all that? Well, we decided, it's got to be cloisters. All of the buildings have got to touch at the ground. We then devised this system and it had an absolutely firm principle: it had a great spine down the middle where everybody walked. That led everywhere.*

---

*'Building the New Universities', Tony Birks, David and Charles, 1972, p.115.

Edinburgh, Michaelmas Term, 1985
Trunk

The old steamer trunk was right at the back, deep in the cobwebby recesses of the attic. Dad was going to drive me down from Edinburgh later, when we were ready, whenever that might be. If Mum had still been here, she would have had us organised days before but, as with everything else in this family, it was all last minute.

It took four of us to ease the trunk down the ladder. At one point Edward let it slip and I thought it was going to crush me, ending my life as an undergraduate before it even began. But Gavin saved the day, with his body-building muscles, and caught it, holding it up one-handed, like he was Popeye. That's what his friends at school had called him. Popeye. I would've settled for that. I'd had much worse. But that was all behind me now. A new start. A new life. Hopefully some new friends. Some friends full stop would be nice.

We heaved the trunk into the kitchen, crashing into the door frame and chipping some paint, to add to the other scars that marked most of the woodwork in our house. The trunk itself was bashed-up, its metal dented, various old names and addresses scrawled and scratched out and replaced with new ones, among them, my mother's. Annie Brown and her childhood home, in the heart of Glasgow.*

Gavin and Edward skulked away, back to their weights and dartboard. Dad had that pained expression on his face so I knew he'd also read the name of his dead wife.

'She'd be proud of you, son,' he said. Just like that. He rarely talked about her. I so wanted to say something, build a conversation, make her alive for a moment, back in our kitchen, cooking bangers and tatties. But the words got stuck and all I could say was 'Thanks, Dad.' And she was gone like a magician's trick. Pouf! And it was me and Dad alone in the kitchen, only her name to remind us she'd once been there.

I opened the trunk.

Old baby clothes. Romper suits. Woolly jumpers Granny Spark had knitted, way up on the Mainland of Orkney, in her croft by the Churchill Barriers, itchy and scratchy but each stitch looped and purled with love, the intricate Fair Isle pattern, proud and rich in its heritage. I was a Spark. And Granny would never let me forget it.†

'Look at this one.' Dad held up a tiny navy and red affair. 'One of your own, I seem to remember, instead of a hand-me-down.' He sniffed the jumper, his litmus test for laundry. 'She's always had a soft spot for you. Wanted to be here to see you off. But... well... She did send something. It came in the post this morning. I'll away and fetch it from the mantelpiece.'

He returned after a minute, waving an envelope, handed it over. Gran's old-school handwriting on the front. I got a knife to slice it open cleanly.

A card. A twenty pound note. I held the money reverently between my fingers, held it up to the light, that's what people did. And a brief message: *Make the most of your time in the big wide world. Be proud of who you are.*

I recited those words for the rest of the day, all through the rushed packing, grabbing socks from the airing cupboard,

_____

*A weegie. I didn't like it when people called her that.

†But my maternal grandmother wouldn't let me forget I was a Brown. Hence the red Brown kilt.

hunting down jumpers, scouting under beds, gathering pens, books, antiperspirant, everything I could think of, shoving them in the trunk, saying awkward goodbyes to my brothers, Andy having called back briefly from work to see me off, which was almost enough to send me over the edge, tumbling into the waiting sea of emotions – my oldest brother never did anything like this. Andy was the hard man. The tough one. The one who lived closer to the dark side than I would ever dare. (Or so I thought.)

Be proud of who you are.

I was the first and only one of the brothers to go to university. My mother had started a history degree, here in Edinburgh, but never finished – she'd fallen with Andy, having met Dad, recently down from Orkney, in a local pub.*
But they'd worked hard, my parents, bought a large tumble-down terrace for us brood of boys, bought it cheap in the Seventies and with help from both grannies. They nurtured our talents, our passions. Bikes, exercise equipment, golf clubs, drum kits. For me it was books. Christmas, birthdays, treats, rewards, encouragement. I couldn't have asked for more – except, of course, I could ask for my mum back.

Time to leave. My brothers lugged the trunk to the old Volvo estate, pushed the seats down, loaded it up. I had this brief image – a coffin, a hearse – but I blinked it away as they patted me on the back, extra hard and manly, hands and arms and deep booming voices coming at me from all directions. I got in with Dad, belted up. Clunk click. Dad wound down the window, shouted, 'No parties, no boozing. Mary's checking in on you, remember.'

Then we were away, leaving Edinburgh behind, the city of my birth, childhood, schooldays. The grand Georgian buildings, the old crooked tenements and cramped dark closes, the looming volcanic rock holding up the ever-present castle, softening in the dusk now, dimming. Away to

---

*This was appropriate as Dad was employed by one of the breweries in town. One of several alcoholic connections in my story.

live a new life down south, England, the city of the red rose: Lancaster.

'Open those travel sweets will you, son.'

I opened the travel sweets, the icing sugar puffing over my face. Dad lobbed a yellow one in his gob. And a Rothman's. My brothers at home, me and Dad on the road. The Lost Boys.

Be proud of who you are.

Lancaster University, Michaelmas Term, 1985
Damp

It was your typical student accommodation. Cell-like, stripped back, bare. A basic desk, a built-in wardrobe with an ill-fitting door that rattled in the draught, metal coat hangers clinking like chains. The constant, persistent, relentless drone of the M6, even in the dead of night, cars, trucks, juggernauts trundling north and south while I lay in my bed, my hard monastic bed, shivering under my inadequate sheet and blanket – shivering even though I was a hardened-off Scot, bred in Edinburgh's granite-cold climate. Even the haar off the Forth had nothing on this Lancashire damp that seeped through clothes and shoes, crept through windows, walls and closed doors, and hung in the air like the breath of a ghost.

We'd left it so late, been so disorganised that Dad had to stay over that first night, in a guest room close by. The following morning, before heading back home, he took me into town. We found a sad wee carpet shop and Dad haggled down the cost of an off-cut that would do as a rug on the cold lino floor. He got me slippers too as I'd forgotten mine. And he picked up an alarm clock in the indoor market. 'So you've no excuse for being late for those lectures of yours.'

At least the tick distracted from the M6.

As Dad made to leave, I found myself getting weepy and I

33

didn't want to upset him or let him down somehow. I was the bookish, quiet, weak, young son. I wanted him to see me as independent and grown up. I couldn't cry. But I felt a trickle of snot bubble out of my left nostril.

'Thanks for bringing me, Dad. And for the rug and the slippers and the clock.'

'Take this too.' He handed over another twenty pound note. I held it up to the light.

'You can do it, son,' he said. And he was gone.

That night I focused on the tick as I tried to sleep, as I tried to keep my thoughts from jumping on that runaway train that would take me back home, to a time when Mum was waiting there for me after school with a batch of biscuits. A no-hope destination.

My room was at least my own. No more sharing with Edward who breathed like an old miner and whose socks smelt of fertiliser. My own space. I could walk around naked. I could sit at my wobbly desk, doing my coursework naked. I could do press-ups on the cold, unforgiving floor, naked. I could.

I lay in bed, listening to the boozy shouts of other Freshers that the sad wee clock had no hope of drowning out.

The Wednesday of Freshers' Week I took myself to a poster sale in the Great Hall. It was like Athena on acid. I only had money for one poster so I took my time to consider. Did I want a band? The Smiths? The Cure? The Cult? Did I want to wake up to a Hollywood legend? Marilyn? James Dean? Marlon Brando on a motorbike? Or did I want to go political? If so, I could have CND, Greenpeace, Anti-Apartheid. I went political. I bought a three by four of Che Guevara. I wasn't entirely sure who Che Guevara was (I was yet to meet Bex who idolised him) but I knew he represented something heroic, anarchic, the anti-thesis of whatever it was I represented.

Be proud of who you are.

Rule-keeper, safe plodder, head-down Cameron.

Lying in bed, listening to the traffic, to the clock, to my thoughts squelching around in my brain like feet in a peat bog, I would gaze at that poster, gaze and gaze, and imagine myself a rule-breaker, a rebel, a man at whose feet women fell. Only I'd need new shoes. Clark's Commandos were very practical and hard-wearing, not to mention incredibly comfortable, but let's face it, they were never going to fell women.

My room was on the ground floor of Block 4, Fylde College, the Oxbridge ring to 'Fylde College' barely balancing the Stalinist Gulag clang of 'Block 4'. I shared a kitchen with ten other lads. Hygiene levels soon plummeted to those of the Nor Loch during the Plague, where the contents of the Old Town's slop buckets ended up. I stuck with Pot Noodles, which I could prepare in my room. Steak and tatty pies from Birkett's. Chips.

I was on nodding terms with one or two of the others as we bypassed each other in the corridor. I'd endured a conversation with Jim from Hull, an engineer who wore the same Black Sabbath T-shirt for days at a time. Groups were already forming – Sport Billies, Dungeons and Dragons, Christians – but I was reluctant to ease myself into any of these. I was clumsy and cack-handed, not quite a nerd, and my faith was seriously damaged having seen my mum die a drawn-out, painful death. My Calvinist, all-boys' schooling didn't believe in Sport for All, or fantasy, and my mother's time on earth had been predetermined before she was even knit in my Granny Brown's womb.* So, I remained those first few days, on my own.

It wasn't until the Thursday night – actually the early hours of the Friday – that I met Tommo. I was in bed, drifting off, when there was this knock on my window. I tried to ignore it, guessing it was either the wrong window or a drunken

---

*Not a Fair Isle pattern, but an intricate and beautiful one all the same.

prank. The knocking continued. I should have ignored it. But I switched on my light, opened the window and let this man in. I've often wondered what would have happened if I had been more persistent. If I had put my fingers in my ears, my head under my pillow. Would he have given up and knocked on the next window along? We would no doubt have met at some point but the point would have been different. Things would have been different.

'Let me in, will you? I've locked myself out and the porter's lodge is closed.'

I glanced from my clock – ten to two – to Tommo who at this point I didn't know was Tommo though I recognised him all right, as the poseur whose room was next to mine. I'd only seen him the once, Billy Idol but with black hair, on his way out the door just as I was coming in. He'd nodded his head at me and his towering quiff didn't move. He said all right and I said all right back and that was the end of our interaction.

And now here he was, one skinny leg hooked over the sill, the other lagging behind, fag gripped between his teeth and a guitar strapped to his back.

'You're a gent. Cheers, squire.' He looked around for somewhere to stub out his roll-up. 'A kettle. You gonna offer me some tea?'

Tea? Was he teasing? Surely his type only drunk Jack Daniels or lager.

'Tea? You want tea?'

'Sorry,' he said, finally acknowledging my pyjamas. He lobbed his fag butt out into the night, smiled one of his charming smiles at me. 'Did I wake you?'

'Aye, but not to worry,' I said, shutting the window, shutting out the cold and the noise. 'I'll make you that tea, shall I,' I said. 'I'm awake now,' I said.

That's what I said, when what I should have said was get lost, get out of my room, and never trouble me again. Because trouble was Tommo's middle name. If I had demanded to see his birth certificate right then, it would have been there in black and white. Ptolomy Trouble Dulac.

'Milky with two sugars, cheers.'

I busied myself, making his tea while he made himself at home, shedding his black pointy boots on my rug and flinging his black leather jacket across my bed. I couldn't bring myself to make eye contact because I half thought I was dreaming. Why was this creature in my room at ten to two of a morning? I didn't know whether to be flattered or annoyed. I suppose I was both of those things. And that would become the pattern of our relationship: Tommo taking me for granted, me being both flattered and annoyed.

I should have stuck my fingers in my ears, my head under my pillow, gone la-la-la-la-la, and ignored the rapping on my window until Tommo gave up and chose someone else.

Ball

I had my ticket. I made myself buy it because I knew I had to start meeting people. The only person I felt drawn to so far was Tommo. He'd 'slept' over in my room that night, spouting his all-over-the-place political beliefs, not a moment's respite till the dawn chorus. I knew he'd never be friends with shy, quiet, boring me.

Maybe that's why I put on my kilt.

I'd packed it in my trunk, on the off chance, not really thinking there would be an opportunity to wear it. But I thought, hell, why not? I'm a Scot and this is my clan.

I didn't go for the whole regalia. Just the kilt, sporran, hose, flashes, brogues. A black ghillie shirt on top. I checked myself in the mirror above my sink, balancing and contorting myself on a chair to get the full effect, wished my hair would do something other than curl and that my legs would look something other than spaghetti-like.

I'd never be cool. But I could be different.

I felt like fetching up my tea.

Be proud, be proud, be proud of who you are.

They called it a ball. I'd not been to a ball before. We didn't have balls in Scotland. We had ceilidhs in the country and at school we had discos, where girls* and boys lingered in

---

*Invited from the girls' school

the dark corners of the gym, snogging and groping until disengaged by a passion-killing teacher. There weren't any ball gowns here, in the Great Hall, though there were puffy dresses with shoulder pads and gold buttons. The lads were for the most part wearing suits, or Farah trousers and tucked-in shirts, thin ties with the smallest knots possible. One or two bucked the trend and wore jeans and Docs and leather jackets. Actually just one. Tommo. I saw him chatting up some hapless girl who was laughing at everything he said. He was smoking and drinking a pint and still managing to gesticulate everywhere.

But he was soon eclipsed by someone else.

I was standing on my own, trying to avoid Jim from Hull who was yet again sporting his Black Sabbath T-shirt although, to give him his dues, he had ironed it, and then this girl – woman – comes towards me, why me, I have no idea, well I do. It was my kilt. It gave me super powers. It made me different.

And she bought me a drink and we had a laugh and we sat together, ate together, danced together and that night when I went back to my room, I shut my eyes and I didn't hear the motorway. I didn't hear my clock or the drunken shouts of first years having a better time than me. I heard the sound of Bex's loud throaty laugh and I saw her wild hair and her long legs and I felt like the world was an okay place to be.

Flexible Study
Lancaster prides itself on having a flexible approach to undergraduate study, particularly in your first year, and is one of only a handful of universities within the UK that allow students to study additional minor subjects alongside their major subject.*

*http://www.lancaster.ac.uk

Library

The world never stops still. It keeps on spinning, shifting, nauseatingly and dizzyingly. Tommo wanted to be friends with me for some reason. I made him look better, I knew that, but Tommo didn't need me to reflect his shine. He glittered enough on his own, with his dark, brooding looks and with – what would be referred to in the talent shows of the future – his 'star quality'.

It turned out we were both studying English as a minor subject. We were doing British post-modern literature. *Lucky Jim. Memoirs of a Survivor. The Spire.* And although Tommo didn't seem the studious type, he did turn up to the first lecture.

I was sitting maybe halfway down the Faraday lecture theatre, next to Bex,* relieved to have someone I knew beside me, ecstatic that it was her. Week Two of Term One, the first week completed and Freshers' Week a memory, and I had someone like Bex to go to lectures with. Bex whose long legs were close to mine, whose hair dripped onto her notepad, who chewed her biro in a way that made me quite, quite dizzy.

The lecture had got underway, Professor Proctor was

---

*Bex was also doing English as a minor. But social work was her thing. She was born to it. And also possibly rebelling against her father who thought all social workers were do-gooders.

introducing the major literary theories, getting into the flow, talking about the death of the author when there was an almighty bang followed by a 'crap' and a 'sorry'. Everyone turned round. Professor Proctor glared, sighed, tapped her fingers on the rostrum. Tommo. He put his hand up in a gesture of what was presumably apology, although you might not be mistaken in thinking it was a wave to his adoring fans.

And did he sit down in a nearby seat and get on with it? No. We had to wait for his prolonged entrance of the Queen of Sheba, mincing down the steps until he draped himself over a chair next to, of course, Bex. He leant forward and saluted me then proceeded to make a fuss out of finding a notebook and pen.

'Rather than trying every zip in those trousers, I suggest you ask your neighbour to lend you a pen.' Professor Proctor paused to allow sniggers.* 'Then perhaps I may continue?'

Bex released the biro from between her teeth and handed it over with a sour look. Tommo ignored the sour look, gestured to Professor Proctor that she may continue and began writing with a flourish Oscar Wilde would have been proud of.

'Wanker,' Bex hissed.

'Why, thank you,' he replied.

I could feel the burning coming off her cheeks, the wound up tension in her body. At that moment I wished my brothers were here to sort him out.

Tommo was waiting for us after the lecture. He made it look like it was chance that we were heading the same way, but I knew full well he was trying to cut in on Bex.

She didn't like him. Either that, or she was pretending

---

*Professor Proctor had quite possibly seen that episode of Not the Nine O'clock News where Rowan Atkinson is in a public lavatory wearing similar punk trousers with many zips and he cannot find the right zip to be able to relieve himself.

she didn't like him.

By the time we'd made it back to the JCR*, he was beginning to win her round. Did you read that article in the *Guardian* yesterday? Did you hear about the student union meeting? Are you going to Glastonbury this year? Will you sleep with me, I've got a massive bagpipe?

He didn't actually say that last thing but I know he was thinking it. He might as well have said it. If he had said it then Bex would've wiped the floor clean with him, the filthy dirty floor, shiny shiny clean.

As it happens, she did wipe the floor clean with him. Once in the JCR, he offered to buy her a coffee and she said she'd buy her own, thank you very much.

'Don't be like that,' he said.

'I'm not being like anything.'

'It's okay for a bloke to buy a woman a coffee, you know.'

'What if she doesn't want him to buy her a coffee?'

'Then she's a silly bitch.'

'A silly bitch?'

'Just kidding. Lighten up.'

'You think that's funny? You think I should think that's funny?'

He shrugged, nonchalant, but I could see a glimmer of fear lurking in his eyes. 'Prick,' she said. Not her most articulate of speeches but she made her point quite succinctly.

Tommo laughed, one of those I-don't-care laughs that no one actually believes, not even the person actually doing the laugh. I thought she was going to hit him. I really did. But she spun round and stormed off, me following in her wake, ignoring Tommo's jibes about lapdogs.

I went to the library the following week, stood in line for a short-loan book. They were like gold dust. I needed the book overnight so I could get on with my essay. I'd been distracted. It wasn't like me to leave my work to the last

---

*Junior Common Room.

minute.* This English unit was harder than I thought it would be. There was so much reading and the reading was mostly re-reading and re-re-reading as the texts were so dense with meaning and metaphor and metonymy (whatever that was) that I couldn't take it all in. I was muddling my Structuralists with my Russian Formalists and getting in a tangle that left me unable to wield a pen and make letters and words and sentences come out of it and onto the page. Frustration and angst and a shedload of Tippex.

The librarian stamped the label with an authoritative clunk, reminding me it had to be returned by nine o'clock the following morning. I clasped the book to my chest, showing the old walrus I'd cherish it like a bairn. I could be trusted. I was dependable.

'Fancy a pint?' It was Tommo, as out of sync with the environment as he was in the lecture theatre.

'Me?'

'Yes, you. Just a drink. It's not a marriage proposal.'

So I followed him, clutching my book.

We went to Fylde JCR, waited for the bar to open. I had tea; he had black coffee, three sugars. Jim from Hull in the Sabbath T-shirt was loitering with his Weeble-like girlfriend who he'd somehow recently acquired. Apart from that, the place was pretty empty.

'I can't stay long. I have to get this essay finished.' I brandished the book. 'I have to fetch it back in the morning.'

'I guess I should've borrowed one of those too.'

'This was the last one.'

'Good for you. I'll have to blag it then. Bat my eyelashes and beg for an extension. That Professor Proctor fancies me

---

*I was never late handing in my essays at school, always focused despite the constant distractions from my litany of brothers. Band Practice. Arguments. Punch-ups. Raging hormones floating round the house like a party of poltergeists. Rows with Dad over money and motorbikes and the odd visit from the police. None of this was me, you understand. I was the good one.

anyway, so it'll be fine.'

Tommo then went on and on about the ins and outs of Rousseau and Saussure and I couldn't follow his train of thought, distracted by his eyelashes. Was he actually wearing mascara?

Then suddenly Bex was there, breezing in, commandeering our attention. 'There's a hunt in the morning.'

'Oh?' Tommo seemed interested.

'A hunt?' I asked, wondering where this was going. Did she mean foxes? She must mean foxes. Surely she didn't want to go out and kill foxes. She was a vegetarian.

'Up the valley.' She looked around, discounted Jim from Hull (and his Weeble-like girlfriend). 'I'm a sab.'

'A sab?'

'A hunt saboteur, you idiot,' Tommo said.

I was none the wiser. Didn't say anything.

'We've lost a driver to mushrooms or something,' Bex blethered on. 'Which one of you can drive?'

We both shot up our hands, school boys trying to please Miss. Ms.

'Wow, that's great,' she said. 'We can use Dodger's van, no problem. I've got his keys.'

Keys. 'What does the driver have to do exactly?'

'Just drive us round.' She looked at me, considering. 'Don't worry. I've done this loads before. All the time back home. And I've done two up here already. Signed up during Freshers' Week.'

'What about insurance?'

'Car insurance?' Bex looked at me. 'A fox's life is at stake here.'

'Yeah, and what the hunt represents,' Tommo added, the smarmy weasel.

She ignored him.

'Okay, I'll do it,' I said. 'I'll drive.'

They both stared at me, like they'd already discounted my efforts. I felt this bubble of pride rumble round my belly.

Or maybe it was sheer terror at the thought of being out in a strange place with strange people with absolutely no idea what was going on.

'What do I have to do exactly?'

'Drive us up there early tomorrow and stay in the van.'

'I can do that.'

'That's great, Cameron, thank you.' She touched my arm and gave it a pat.

But then Tommo ruined the moment. 'So how can I help?'

Bex thought about this. I wanted her to say get lost, you're not helping. But instead she sat down between us, shook off her back pack and rummaged inside, discreetly revealing the contents. Sprays of some kind. A pair of binoculars. An OS map. A camera. 'Are you in?'

'I'm in,' Tommo said.

And Bex gave him this enormous smile.

It was only later, after she'd talked us through our tactics, after Tommo and Bex had left the JCR to meet up with the other sabs, that I realised my book was missing and that I wouldn't be finishing my essay that night.

Fox

Tommo owned plenty of black clothes so I borrowed a jacket off him, and I had my woolly hat. I was to stay in the van but Bex had said to dress dark.

'You need to keep a low profile,' she'd told us, looking at Tommo. 'It'll be hard for you but this is serious.'

'I know that, Bex,' he said. 'I might come across as flippant and facile but I do care about animal welfare.'

'It's not just about reading the *Guardian*. It's about doing stuff.'

'And I'm doing it. With you.'

I don't think he meant the double entendre but it didn't exactly help his seriousness.

Bex walloped him. 'You'd better not bloody louse this up.'

'I won't, I won't.' And he did actually seem serious, like he wanted to do something important. Or rather, he wanted to please Bex.

But she wasn't going to cave in so easily. 'It's not about animal welfare, by the way,' she said. 'It's about animal rights.'

I was a careful driver, passed my test first attempt. I could handle the van well enough as I'd been allowed to drive our hearse of a Volvo a few times, manoeuvring it down narrow streets and up steep hills, Dad with his hands clutched to the seat, smoking as if it were his last cigarette.

We drove for twenty minutes or so, heading into countryside, through the early morning darkness, a mist clinging to the hedgerows and shrouding the distant woodland. Me, Bex and Jules in the front, Tommo and Bob lolling around on a grubby mattress in the back. I was glad Bex was next to me but she made me nervous too. She was kitted out in camouflage trousers, bomber jacket and boots, her hair shoved into a black woolly hat. She looked the business. She looked amazing, all sinew and strength and energy.

Jules on the other hand was tiny, barely five foot, but with this granite force field around her, rather than the soggy puddle I had. She was a veteran, a local, a third year Philosophy student and all round activist. She knew this area inside out. Every hollow, every covert, every tree.

Jules showed me where to park up then she briefed us like a firebrand preacher keeping us out of hell. Tommo was to shadow Bex as it was his first time. A virgin. Bob was staying with me (another virgin). Bob was reassuringly bulky, with a scar across his face and dirt under his fingernails. Well, under nine fingernails as one finger was half missing, like Dave Allen off the television or the Professor man in *The 39 Steps*.

Jules indicated the other van, parked up across the valley with two other sabs. Both vans were rigged with CB radios so we could keep in contact, move on if necessary.

'You'll get hunt supporters trying it on. Don't let them intimidate you.' Bex was worried about me, hoped I could handle it. 'Just stay here until Bob gives you the nod.'

'Right,' I said. 'Okay,' I said. 'I'll be fine,' I said.

She gave me the thumbs up and headed off into the gloaming with Tommo and Jules. Tommo turned around before they were out of sight, saluted me. He'd better not screw things up and put Bex in danger. I'd heard some nasty tales of the terrier men. And now Bob was telling me even more nasty tales with grim attention to gruesome detail, sitting up front with me now, a right harbinger of doom. And a vegan. With vegan hair like a scant bird's nest. But a fellow Scot, a Highlander, so I felt some comfort hearing his voice. Tried to listen to the rhythm of it, rather than the things it was saying.

'Will the girls be okay?'

'Are you referring to Bex and Jules as "girls"? That's wrong on so many levels.' He shook his head and laughed. 'Don't *ever* let them hear you call them "girls". He said the word 'girls' like Miss Jean Brodie, driving home the point so that it struck me through the heart.

And he laughed some more and the laugh filled the van, swamping me with a shame I didn't quite understand, like being back in school, like I hadn't grown up at all. 'I just don't want Tommo messing things up for Bex?'

'For Bex or for the hunt?'

'Well, both, but especially Bex. I only came here cos she asked.'

'Someone's got it bad.' He laughed again, a right comedian. 'You'd better concentrate. Don't want you getting distracted.'

'Please don't say anything.'

'Course I won't say anything. Us Scots have got to stick together, right?'

'Right. So what happens now?'

Bob sighed expansively, put his muddy boots up on the dash, rummaged in his coat pocket for his tobacco tin, rolled a fag with great skill, dexterity, and perfect uniformity, hours of practice waiting in a van. 'There's a chance the hunt will be called off if Jules' phone calls work.'

'Phone calls?'

'Yeah, she'll be in the village phone box ringing the local pubs to tell them it's off.'

'The hunt's off?'

'No, it's not off. We're just spreading the word so hunt supporters *think* it's off. That way it might get cancelled if not enough turn up. It sometimes works.'

It didn't work. The meet went ahead, gathered outside one of the pubs Jules had hoaxed. The hunt knew now that the sabs would be out. They were always out.

We took turns watching them, the sabs, through Bob's binoculars, a ramshackle legion, dark clothes, boots, hats, striding out northwards across the washed-out fields, through a fragile sunlight that cast feeble shadows on the bumps and crevices of muddy grass. They closed and locked gates, they stooped low against the ground, they moved forward. Bex had checked the wind direction and Jules told them where she thought the hunt was likely to go. They were organised. Nothing ramshackle about the 'girls'.

My thoughts were shot through by the wail of a horn.

'What does that mean?' I asked Bob.

'The bastards have found the fox.' He stubbed his fag out in the ashtray, sat up, alert.

'Look.' He handed me the binoculars and took control of the CB.

I didn't hear what he said because I spotted it, up close, so close I thought I could reach out my hand and grab its tail, its brush, a creature so breathtakingly beautiful that my heart pumped faster and the adrenaline kicked in.

The fox was pelting full speed across the adjacent field, headed towards the covert, as Jules said it would, close upon the sabs now. They let it go past, then began to spray, extra sabs appearing out of the dawn light, spreading out along the line, quickly as they could.

The horn got louder. They didn't have much time. I could make out Bex, pulling Tommo along with her over the rough sodden ground, towards the copse where the fox had darted.

Then I couldn't see anymore. Bob grabbed the binoculars back, ordered me to drive.

'Put your foot down. We've been spotted.'

I checked the mirror, saw a looming group of men with dogs. 'Who are they?' Pathetic question. I already knew the answer.

'The terrier men.'

It happened so quickly. The rock. The smash. The broken window. Glass on my head. Blood in my eyes. I put my foot down, following Bob's shouted instructions, and we got away, the van swerving and lurching as I struggled to see, leaving the shouts and the anger behind us, the smoky exhaust cloaking them like a moorland mist.

'You all right, mate?'

I barely heard Bob above the beating of my heart. We'd found another lane by this time, pulled into a passing place. I only had part vision out of one eye. There was the crackle of the radio as Bob gabbled to Bongo, the other van driver, over the airwaves, using unfamiliar words, a mystifying language.

He handed me his drinks canister, one like Edward's old Action Man's. And a grimy rag. 'You need to rinse that, mate.'

It stung. I had a cut above my eye but it wasn't too bad. The bleeding had all but stopped. My vision began to clear. Bob handed me back the binoculars.

'Look at those scumbags,' he said. 'The spray isn't working. The wind direction's changed. They've got his scent.'

'Is that it then? Is it all over?' I had the covert in my sights, but no fox and no Bex.

'Not yet,' he said. 'We're one step ahead. Jules and Bongo unblocked the earths in there so he's got somewhere to hide. But if the hounds get in we'll have our work cut out.'

'What can we do?'

'Hope they call the hounds back from the draw. Jules will use the horn, her voice, any tactics she has. I just hope that tosspot Tommo doesn't cock it up.'

I don't know why but I laughed then. A small nervous laugh that I covered with a cough.

Bob didn't notice. He carried on. 'They need to call the hounds in the opposite direction to where the fox is headed.'

The hounds were baying, an eerie sound. I wasn't overly keen on dogs, especially ones flying towards you with one thing in mind. Flying towards Bex who would stop at nothing.

The pack disappeared into the covert, yelping in some awful chorus, mournful and haunting. Then I heard this voice. A tough, scary, firm '*come-come-come*'. And then a horn. And then clapping and shouting.

'What's happening?'

Bob was out the car now, had the binoculars back off me, standing up on the gate so he could work out what was going on. 'The guys are making a racket, getting the hounds off, confusing them.' Next thing he was punching the air. 'They've led the hounds out the copse!'

I didn't need the binoculars. The sabs were running breakneck downhill towards us, hounds following, hunters behind them, confused as their dogs, but a determined huntsman was ahead of the game, catching up on the sabs, a splurge of blood red, the thud of hooves and a whip-crack cutting through the cold air.

'Back up the van, mate. We need to let them through.'

I did as I was told, my hands shaky, head spinning, while Bob opened the gate. A few seconds later, Jules was through, effing and blinding, panting and angry. Then Bongo and a few others scrambled after her onto the lane. But Bex... Bex had stumbled in the field. She'd caught her foot in a hollow, a rabbit hole or something, and gone flying onto her face. The thud of hooves was louder, the whip cracked. Bob had to slam the gate shut, before the hounds ran into the road, they were everywhere, chaos, then I saw Bex on her knees, hands to her head, blood escaping through her fingers. Tommo lunged towards her, heaved her up, dragged her along and somehow got her over the gate, Bob and Jules hauling her by the shoulders.

And then the police turned up.

We, the sabs, were the good guys but the police didn't see it like that. Even when they clapped eyes on Bex with her bloody face and ripped jacket, they were distinctly unhelpful.

'They're upper-class tossers,' Tommo informed the sergeant. 'See what they've done to her?' He put his arm around Bex, protectively. Possessively. She shrugged it off.

'It looks to me like the lass slipped and cut her head.'

'It was that bastard with the whip.'

'Are you alleging one of the riders whipped her?'

'No, but it was pretty close. He was chasing her.'

'I think maybe you'll find it's you lot that were trespassing.'

'I told you. They're bastards.'

'Are they, sir? And who might you be, sir?'

'I'm Tommo. Tommo Dulac.'

'Short for Thomas?' The sergeant took out his notepad and began scribbling. The other copper was standing behind him, arms folded.

'Short for Ptolomy.'

'And how do I spell that?'

Tommo spelt it clearly, a pronunciation Miss Jean Brodie would admire, brashing out his name, his background, his class.

'A 'P' you say, sir?'

'It's Egyptian.'

'Egyptian are you, sir?'

'No, I'm British. My parents liked the name. Don't ask me why.'

'I'm sure they had their reasons, P-tolomy.'

Bex was trying not to laugh. She couldn't help herself, maybe the bang to her head, the tension of the day, the relief of escape, the hunt that was now disbanding, successfully sabbed.

'And what about Doolack? Is that Egyptian too? Or Ancient Greek?'

'D-U-L-A-C. It's French.'

'French. I see.' He scribbled some more, slid his pen back into his pocket and gave us all the once over. 'Farmers get very angry about this sort of caper. But if you lot clear off, we'll say no more about it.'

'What?' Tommo was agitated, strutting his stuff.

'And the tax disc is out of date, sarge.' The other officer was shaking his head, facetious bastard, and Tommo looked about to lose the plot.

'Leave it, yeah, Tommo.' Jules gripped his arm and pushed him towards the van. 'We've done what we came to do.'

Tommo paused for a moment. 'You're right, Jules.' And he put his arm decisively around Bex and squeezed her. She winced in pain but didn't shrug him off this time. Maybe she was concussed.

'As long as you're all right, Bex,' he blethered. 'And the fox gets to live another day.'

She smiled weakly and let him lead her to the car, limping and shivering.

'I've done something good,' Tommo said. 'I didn't know I could do that.'

We piled in the car, bloodied and weary. I turned on the engine and revved up, pulled away, held my dignity together. We were off, turning the corner, the worst of it over, but then I stalled.

'Never mind, mate,' Bob said. He gave me a reassuring smile and I wanted to punch his teeth out.

Rib

I was between lectures, didn't want to trudge back to my room where I'd only brood over recent events: the hunt and the library book. When I confronted Tommo about it (the library book, not the hunt), he said he'd picked it up 'by mistake'. He said he'd return it to the library. He said he'd pay the fine.

I forked out for a mug of tea in the Nelson Mandela coffee bar, an extravagance, as money was tight. My grant had to last the term as there'd be no more. Dad was struggling, Edward told me. The roof was leaking and there was no such thing as savings for a rainy day, not since they'd stopped his overtime. And he'd hinted at something else too, some debt, but I didn't quite work it out and didn't ask as my head was already full to bursting.

Tommo didn't have to think about money, his dad was minted; he could splash it around on clothes and records and massive library fines. He even had a portable television in his room and a video recorder. He was the only person I knew with a video recorder – anywhere, let alone university. And there I was worrying over a cup of tea.

That was when I saw Christie for the first time. In the coffee bar. She was sitting on her own at a table and she was coughing. I soon realised that she was actually choking, her cheeks flushed and her eyes watering. It was clear no one was going to help, they were all busy or embarrassed or in

55

their own hungover world. I knew all about the Bystander Effect – I had a Higher in Psychology – so I knew it was up to one individual to do something or nothing would be done until it was too late. So I went over and gave her a pat on the back. Only it wasn't hard enough, I'd held back, not wanting to appear like a violent mad man. Christie grabbed my arm with both hands and looked pleadingly into my eyes. I took this as a sign to try again, only this time with more force. So I walloped her. A sultana flew out of her mouth and hit the far wall, sliding down it like a swatted fly. But then she screamed in pain. Evidently, as I'd walloped her, the force had sent her forward with some momentum so that she whacked into the table where she'd been sitting drinking a Pepsi.

'It's all right. You're all right,' I said. 'Don't panic.' Corporal Jones from *Dad's Army*.

In between gasps of air, she managed to breathe the terrible words: 'I think my rib's cracked.'

I laughed.

'My rib's cracked... and... you're laughing?'

She was joking. Had to be. I wasn't that strong. I was the weakling of the family. The lightweight girly swot. But then I noticed how there was no colour to her cheeks and she was still struggling for breath and it was clear that she was definitely hurting badly and that this wasn't funny at all.

'Oh my God, no, really?'

'I've done it before... skiing...'

'I'm so sorry. I thought you wanted me to hit you hard.'

By this point there was a wee crowd gathered, finally the rest of the customers taking an interest in the beautiful blonde woman getting beat up by the Scottish weed.

'Everything all right here?' asked the manager, a spaced-out relic of a former era, an ex-student who'd never managed to leave.

'What does it look like, asshole?' Christie was quite abrupt when she wanted to be, for a Canadian – said it came from her American mother. Her dad was a big old softie, or so she said. I didn't believed that. Though I never met him, not even at the court case.

I somehow got her to the Infirmary in town, by taxi, where they confirmed a cracked rib. The staff eyed me with some suspicion. Her injury, my black eye. Was I her boyfriend? (No.) Had we had an argument? (No.) Had I been drinking? (At two o'clock in the afternoon? I don't think so. No.)

They told me to wait outside the cubicle while they asked Christie how she'd sustained her injury, even though they'd already been through that with me. She said loudly and clearly for the whole casualty department to hear: 'I am not a victim of domestic violence. Now will you fix me up with some drugs and let me get the hell out of here.'

So they did. They fixed her up with some drugs and they let her get the hell out of there.

For now, I had a good excuse to keep on seeing her. While she was incapacitated, I took it on myself to be at her beck and call. I ran errands for her, got her messages. Every day for the next week I'd drop by her campus room, as messy as my brothers' rooms all put together, bearing presents of pies – steak and tatty being a favourite – and chocolate that was *so much better than the crap we call chocolate at home.*

One day she said: 'You don't have to keep bringing me gifts, Cameron. Don't feel bad about my rib. You did stop me from choking, remember.'

'It's no problem,' I said. 'I like coming round here.'

'I'm feeling much better now so I can take care of myself.'

'Of course, I'm sorry,' I muttered, not sure what either of us was saying.

'Listen, Cameron. Let's get something straight. Nothing is going to happen between us.'

'I know that.'

'Sorry, I just thought I should get that out in the open, then we can be friends.'

'That's what I want. I want to be friends. That's all. You're way, way out of this wee Scot's league. As my brothers would say, you're Liverpool, I'm Stenhousemuir.'

She looked at me questioningly so I just carried on and I told her.

'Besides which, I like someone else.'

'You do?'

I nod.

'Then she's a lucky girl.'

So we were friends. I was a safe pair of hands. The lads on my floor couldn't believe my luck, Christie drifting in and out of my room as if it were normal. I was a gay best friend, only without the gay bit.

'You got the golden ticket,' Jim from Hull said. And his Weeble girlfriend nearly flattened him, nearly fell over in the process.* I didn't put him right. He could make up his own filthy mind.

That afternoon changed my life. The coffee bar, the wheezing and gasping, the trip to the Infirmary, spending that time with Christie in unplanned circumstances. I was drawn to her otherness. She was so sure of herself. Although I rescued her from the raisin – hardly a pack of braying hounds, but nevertheless life-threatening – it was more like she'd rescued me from the depths of something I couldn't even describe. But I didn't know if she'd be strong enough to keep me from falling back in. That was down to me.

The hunt, the library book, Bex. Tommo always got what he wanted. Maybe he would get his hands on Christie. Maybe that way Bex would be free to choose me.

---

*But she didn't fall over because, aye, you know what I'm going to say but I'm going to say it anyway: Weebles wobble but they don't fall down.

Shards

When Thursday came around, the three of us – Tommo, Bex and I – planned to go into town to the Moghuls, then on to the Sugarhouse. Curry followed by dancing. Bex persuaded me. 'Go on, it'll be fun.' I didn't feel so sure but gave in pretty quickly.

Bex called round, waited on my bed while I sorted myself out, changing my sweater twice and searching for my room key that wasn't in its usual place. I told her about the rib incident. How guilty I felt putting Christie out of action, what with her being an exercise junkie. So Bex suggested Christie come along.

'I don't think so.'

'Why not?'

'She's got a cracked rib.'

She leant down, showed me her bald patch with the scab and stitches. 'I've got a cracked head. I win.'

I couldn't argue. I should've argued. But no. We called round for Tommo and then on to Bowland, to Christie's room.

'So how do you know this Yank?'

'She's Canadian and don't be so flipping racist,' Bex reprimanded Tommo.

'Well?'

'She's the one whose rib I cracked.' I told him the story.

Tommo started laughing, a wild cackling, thrashing his

arms around, that way of his that made you both worried and annoyed. He eventually took a deep breath and calmed himself. 'And now we're taking her into a provincial northern mill town for a curry.'

'That's right.' Bex was getting irritated. 'We're extending the hand of friendship. Do you have a problem with that?'

'No. No problem with that.' And then he sniggered and she whacked him in the stomach, hard enough to make him stop.

Christie answered the door, holding her hand oddly in front of her, protecting herself from further injury. She looked amazing – and slightly terrifying – in her tight blue jeans and a sports top. Baseball or something.

'We're taking you out,' I said, in charge. 'An Indian restaurant in town followed by the Sugarhouse.'

'What like a gingerbread house?'

'It's the students' union club,' Bex explained. 'In an old warehouse. It used to hold sugar. You know, way back, in Lancaster's shameful past.'

'Shameful?'

'Slavery.'

'Oh, yeah, right. That's shameful, for sure.'

We were waiting in the corridor, this posse, and Christie was in the doorway of her room, standing her ground. She looked Bex and Tommo up and down. 'Are you gonna introduce me to these guys, Cameron?'

'Your room's a pit,' Tommo cut in, off piste as usual, the attention span of a puppy, peering over Christie's shoulder.

'Gee, thanks.' She somehow made herself wider, to stop him being nosey, like she had something to hide. 'You must be the asshole I heard all about.'

Tommo looked at me.

I shrugged. 'I didn't actually use those words.'

'Anyways, I've never had an Indian meal, so let's do it.'

'Never had a curry?' Bex was shocked. 'How come?'

'We don't really have them where I come from. We're all

60

burgers and beaver tails.'

'Really?' we said in unison.

'No, not really. We have moose and bear as well.'

We headed into town, wincing along with Christie as the bus bounced over potholes and swayed round corners, swapping general details, hometowns, subjects, families. Christie was from Niagara-on-the-Lake. Her parents owned vineyards.

'I've never had Canadian wine,' Tommo said.

'That's cos we keep it all to ourselves.'

'Nice one.' Tommo laughed. 'And hey, Niagara... that must be pretty cool.'

'It's just water falling off a rock.'

Tommo laughed some more. Bex looked put out, fiddled with her hair.

Once seated in the restaurant, already rowdy with students filling their stomachs for the night ahead, we tried to explain the menu to Christie as she couldn't make much sense of it. 'All I know is I want a beer. And not one of those warm ones.'

'We call it lager,' Tommo drawled and I could see it grating on Bex's nerves, the way Tommo was acting around Christie.

'I know you call it lager but that's just weird.'

'Have a vindaloo,' said Tommo, the evil bastard.

'No, Christie,' I said. 'Ignore him. Go for a chicken korma. Ease yourself into this and we'll harden you up as the year goes on.'

As the year goes on. It was me saying those words – words that resonated with a sense of permanence in a temporary world – that somehow bonded us together. But at that moment, of course, we had no idea how those bonds would be tested.

Tommo was already a devotee of Thursday nights at the Sugarhouse. Bands, indie music, cool kids. And now me.

Tommo wanted to be a rock star. He played the guitar. He sang (in his own inimitable way). He was a performer. So far it had only been in my room – the singing, the guitar playing, the performing – but he had ambitions. He was going to get a band together.

So while Tommo planned to be a star, I was but a moon reflected in his brightness. Tommo was trying to sort me out. Despite marching me to the barber's and Burton's, I still managed to look like a sixth-former, but he was warming to my company nevertheless. I had no pretensions, he told me, and where he came from, he wasn't used to that.

'Where do you come from?' I'd asked him one day in the Assembly Rooms, checking out vintage jeans. (You paid a premium for the most ripped and faded. I said I'd stick with my Lee Cooper's.)

'I come from Middle Narnia,' Tommo said. 'I mean Middle England. Well, actually Hampstead to be more specific.'

'I've heard of Hampstead. That's posh, isn't it?'

'Almost as posh as Edinburgh.'

'But I don't come from the posh bit of Edinburgh.' He waited for me to go on. 'I mean everywhere has its posh bits and its crap bits and its somewhere-in-between bits. The somewhere-in-between bit of Edinburgh is where I come from.'

He'd laughed and said, 'I always knew you were suburban.'

I wasn't entirely sure what he meant but it felt like an insult. So I stuck up for my home. 'It is a capital city, you know. Like London. Only stronger.'

'Stronger?'

'Well, Edinburgh was never an outpost of the Roman Empire, was it?'

He didn't look convinced.

And now we were in the Sugarhouse, in the quiet room as Christie didn't want to get shoved around in the crush of the bar and the dance floor. She and Bex were talking about Christie's passion: cheerleading. Bex was on at her, her Feminist radar alert and glowing, which Christie pushed aside saying cheerleading was about acrobatics and fitness and courage. Bex wasn't so sure. They were obviously wary of each other.

'Aren't you going to watch the band?' Bex asked Tommo.

'Nah, they're crap. Drummer's all right though.' He looked pensive. Or was that drunk. 'Bassist's not bad either but they need a decent frontman.' He coughed. 'Or front woman.' He mimed breasts for some reason, as if we didn't understand what a woman was. Bex glowered and he continued quickly. 'Fergal Sharkey. Lemmy. Bob Geldof.' A pause. 'Debbie Harry. Chrissie Hynde. They might not have the best voices, but they all have energy. This bloke needs to lie down on a chaise longue and have smelling salts administered. He'd be far better off singing chamber music in a cathedral.'

'You'd be better off reading *Spare Rib*,' Bex said.

Tommo changed his mind about the band. Decided they were worth seeing after all. Decided to take Bex with him. He grabbed her by the hand. 'Come on, let's do some moshing.'

'All right,' she said, trying not to sound too keen but not resisting. 'You coming?' She looked at us, Christie and me, didn't wait for an answer, let herself be pulled along by a maniac fuelled with curry and lager and music and lust for her, my friend, Bex.

'You go too, Cameron,' Christie said. 'I'm okay, sitting it out here, assimilating all this English culture.'

'I'm Scottish so it's awful strange for me too.'

And she laughed. And I was pleased that I had made her laugh. But I said I'd go and watch the band nonetheless. I wasn't a complete square. I liked bands. I liked Aztec Camera and The Skids and of course I liked Big Country who were hugely under-rated. I'd watch this band for a few minutes, see if they were any good. The Shards they were called. She said, go, just go, and there was a cluster of lads hanging around waiting for my departure, including Jim from Hull with the Black Sabbath T-shirt, though tonight he had pushed out the boat and was wearing a Motorhead one.

'Will you be all right?'

She raised her eyebrows.

So I went.

It was loud and hot in there. I hovered on one side, towards the back, leaning against a pillar, watching Bex dance. She was wearing her usual black mini, a Housemartins T-shirt, monkey boots. Where had she learnt to move like that? Did they have clubs in Devon? Wasn't it all farms and cows and caravans? I'd asked her that at the ball, joking, and she'd come back with, 'Yeah and we all marry our cousins and have six fingers on each hand.' And those big eyes with the spider-leg lashes had flashed at me, catching the lights and sparkling, but she'd given me a smile that made my heart shout.

And now here I was, a few weeks later, leaning against a pillar, on my own, my head banging in time to the bass, my lungs filled with smoke so I could hardly breathe, like I was too close to a bonfire, Bex out there on the packed dance floor, contained but separate, leaping up and down, shaking her head so her hair was everywhere, Tommo flailing around her.

I watched Bex. I watched Tommo. I watched Bex and Tommo orbiting each other like stars. I watched.

Filofax

Since the hunt, something had changed between Bex and Tommo, some kind of respect and understanding. There was this friction between them but friction makes things move and it moved their relationship to another place, where I couldn't follow. Maybe it was because they both had a passion. Bex's commitment to her causes motivated Tommo to commit to his music. He was fired up, writing songs, practising every waking hour. And now he was holding auditions.

He'd commandeered a room in the music department, put an advert in *SCAN*, the student paper, and spent a fortune photocopying flyers in the library which I helped him plaster around the college JCRs and on the concrete pillars of the North and South Spines.

We waited now, Tommo sitting on a table with his guitar, early for once, riffing and tuning, Bex and me playing cards though she was distracted by Tommo. I began to wonder if they had done it. The deed. The nasty, as Christie called it. They were definitely an item, even if they hadn't named it as such. You don't have to name something for it to exist.

First to audition was a Welsh lad with a mullet and Rambo muscles shown off by his wife-beater vest and red dragon tattoo acquired after a bar crawl in Carmarthen. Billy was excitable as a kid, fidgeting and whooping, and I actually wondered if he was all there. But Hyper (as we'd know him from now on) could play the piano, Grade 8, classical, jazz, with gigs in restaurants and weddings to his credit.

Then in walked two guys I recognised from the other night. The Shards, minus the feeble, foppish frontman. So basically the drummer, Dave, and the bassist, Carl.

'You come to check out the competition?' Tommo asked, as laid back as he could manage.

'Something like that,' Carl said.

'The Shards are no longer,' Dave said.

Tommo sat up straight. 'Musical differences?'

'Something like that,' Carl said.

'Richie was crap,' Dave said.

'I know.' Tommo gathered himself. 'So far we've got Hyper, fantastic pianist. And me.'

'You?' Carl and Dave both said.

'Me and my guitar and my enormous aura.'

While Bex and I continued to play our game of Racing Demon, they blethered on about Fenders and The Fall and the *NME*, moving on to debate which bar to go to.

But then in walked Christie.

Every one of those lads straightened up and smiled like kids. Except for Tommo. Tommo stayed where he was, sitting on the table. He laid down his guitar, folded his arms, casual gestures maybe, but I could see the stiltedness behind them. I could see through his actions, right through to his cold, dark heart. 'What are you doing here?' he said.

'Your ad didn't specify only men need apply, 'cause that would be sexual discrimination, right?'

'Right, no, I didn't mean anything like that, I just didn't think you'd be interested in my band.' He was faltering, aware that the others were staring with their gobs open, ogling the cleavage-show popping out of her baby-pink cashmere jumper. 'Are you here about the band?'

'Sure, I'm here about the band.' She smiled her toothy smile. 'You're going to need a manager.'

'We are?'

'You'd be stupid to miss this opportunity. Give me twenty per cent of your fees and I'll get you far more than you could ever manage on your own.'

'Okay,' the others chanted in unison. (Which was one of the few times they ever agreed on anything.)

'Woah, hang on a minute.' Tommo put his hands up, Canute trying to control the waves. 'We haven't even jammed.'

Christie ignored him, whipped out her yuppy Filofax. 'Let's book the first band practice. I need to see what I'm dealing with.'

Tommo stood there, silent, staring. Then he pulled himself together, trying to impersonate a man in charge.

'All right,' he said. 'But fifteen per cent.'

'Sure,' she said, like she was expecting him to say exactly this. And she shoved her hand towards him and he had no option but to shake it.

Bex persuaded me to go along with her to band practice, for a laugh, like a pair of groupies, to see what they sounded like, if there was any potential or if it was a non-starter. We left it a while, had a few games of pool in the JCR, before heading up to the music department.

We could hear the jangly guitar and funky drummer beat from down the corridor as there was no soundproofing and the amp was cranked up. A porter was sure to come along soon and put a stop to the racket. They needed a proper practice room and Christie was on the case.

Bex opened the door and stuck her head round. No one noticed so she beckoned me to follow and we crept in, hunkering down in a corner, amongst the guitar cases and discarded denim jackets, shuffling to get comfy, trying not to be noticed.

The 'band', as yet unnamed, moved onto a cover of Teenage Kicks. Dave and Carl were good musicians. Hyper was really good on the keyboard. But Tommo... well, Tommo... he was something else.

Bex knew it too. Her eyes were wide and her mouth open. Tommo winked at her.

She smiled back.

I felt sick.

Then the door swung open and the rhythm of the music stumbled, went to pieces, slurred into a mess of noise and discordant notes that grated and brought Les Dawson to mind.

'Guys, guys, what the hell was that?' Christie stood there, arms spread wide in a gesture of despair. 'Get it together or there's no way you'll be ready for a gig. I've only got till June remember, then I'm back home.'

Hyper actually apologised, blushing up to his mullet, Dave and Carl stood like scolded schoolboys, but Tommo's eyes darkened and sparked and Christie held his gaze all the while till he put down his guitar, turned away and shrugged on his leather jacket. Then he lit up a fag, which hung out of his mouth while he zipped up his case and left the room. Not a word. Not a look in Bex's direction. The door slammed.

'What's eating him?' Christie asked innocently. 'Right, guys, show us what you've got. And you there.'

'Carl.'

'Carl, quit with the slap bass. You sound like a jerk.'

Fylde bar. Bex dragged me along with her to find Tommo, knowing we'd probably locate him in his habitual spot and yes, she was right, there he was, leaning back against the counter, a pint in one hand, roll-up in the other, two packets of crisps already demolished and scrunched up in front of him. 'Drink?' he asked, trying to be cool, barely glancing at us.

'Half a shandy, ta,' I said.

'Pint of bitter, Ron, and whatever this beautiful woman wants.' He twitched his quiff at Bex.

'She'll have a pint of bitter too,' said Bex, torn between having a go and accepting a compliment.

For some reason, Ron, the grumpiest barman known to

mankind, didn't mind Tommo. After all, he was not only Ron's best paying customer, but he never threw up on the carpet. A win-win situation even if Tommo was a spoilt southerner.

I, on the other hand, could stand at a bar for an age waiting to be served, barmaid after barmaid studiously ignoring me as if I were an inspector or the taxman. Ron occasionally took pity, deigning to take my order but, seeing as how I drank shandy, what did I expect?

'Sometimes Christie can be a right cow,' Tommo whined. 'We didn't take her on as manager to have a say in our music.'

'Then why did you take her on?' Bex was trying to sound neutral, an arbitrator, but I could tell she was getting irritated with Tommo.

'We took her on to book gigs and that. To negotiate our fees.' He shook his head. 'Not to get involved with the music.'

'Stop stressing. Just go with it.' Bex was cajoling him now, the big bairn that he was. Stick a dummy in his gob and suck on that. Tommo, ten years of age, not getting his own way with the au pair. 'For some mad reason, she believes in you.' Bex glugged back her pint, froth round her burgundy lips.

I remember thinking how far away London was from Edinburgh. How far I was away from Edinburgh. How I longed to be back. How I longed to be with Bex. Tommo was cool. Tommo had money. Tommo was a spoilt English bastard.

I made my excuses.

'Sorry, Cameron?'

'I said I'm going to have a game of darts.'

'Okay, you do that,' Tommo said. He didn't look at me. Nor did Bex. They gazed at each other with doleful eyes and she took Tommo's hand in hers and gave it a squeeze.

Edinburgh, November 2013
Deaf

I wake with dead legs. Myrtle has somehow opened my door, scaled my bed and sprawled herself across my shins. She barks good morning to me, growls when I try to shift her so I give her a helping nudge down the cliff face of the bed. She scuttles off.

Dad appears in the doorway a few moments later. 'Morning, son. I've brought you a cup of tea.' He holds it aloft, as if I don't believe him, his favourite 'Blood Doesn't Show on a Maroon Jersey' mug, puts it on my bedside table then sits down, to catch his breath, on Mum's wicker chair. No bedtime stories. No Jackanory. No Ladybird Readers. But a copy of the *Scotsman*.

'I've been thinking,' he says.

'Sounds serious.'

'Aye, it's been bothering me.'

'Go on.'

'I've been wondering whether to maybe get one of those electric collar things for Myrtle. I've tried all that positive rewarding. It's just making her fat.'

'Right.'

'Well, what do you think? Her barking's playing havoc with my ears.'

'I don't know. Seems a bit drastic.'

'You don't have to live with her. Well, now you do. Maybe you'll change your mind.' He shakes his head. 'I have tinnitus. Just like Barbara. I'm lucky I don't have to rely on my voice. She's a saint the way she carries on.'

'Saint Barbara of the Two Ronnies?'

He swats my legs with the *Scotsman* but I have no feeling from the waist down thanks to his wee dog.

'There's porridge downstairs if you want it,' he says.

Dad has been trying to get me to eat porridge all my life. I hate porridge. It makes me gag. This can be emasculating for a Scot. I used to decant it from my bowl to my trouser pockets when Granny Spark was visiting, scooping it in with a teaspoon when her back was turned so I wouldn't let her down. And while Mum complained about the sludgy mess in the laundry, trouser legs stuck together like they'd been Superglued, she never let on to Granny.

'Don't worry about me, Dad. I'll get some cornflakes then take Myrtle for a walk if you want.' I feel guilty about the Saint Barbara comment.

'She's already been out with me to fetch the paper but she won't turn you down,' he says, softening. 'Just make sure you put on her coat. It's cold today and she feels it.'

Myrtle gets to have a coat. We don't get to have the heating. Not until tomorrow, 1 December. Unfortunately Myrtle's coat is tartan. I have to walk the streets of my home, a place where I was teased and ridiculed for being weak and feeble and prone to tears, wielding a tartan sausage dog who cocks her leg and barks at anything that moves. Even anything that doesn't move. She's not particular. All fur coat and no knickers, as Granny Brown would say.

I keep my head down and slink into the café. The same waitress serves me. She's actually quite friendly once you get over the menacing metallic battle dress. She's called Gina and she is the granddaughter of Massimo who owns the

71

place. She tells me she's doing a PhD in some kind of Italian literature, a reminder not to judge someone by their looks.

Once she's delivered my cappuccino, a heart etched on the froth, I check my emails, Myrtle warm and heavy on my feet, snoring. There's one from work which I'll get to later. And there's one from a certain P. Dulac.

Tommo has replied.

I hear Jeremy urging me to open it, to face my past. But I can't. Not just yet. I'll get to that later too.

Dad is at work at the kitchen table amongst a pile of newsletters and envelopes, three half-drunk mugs of tea and an ashtray of stinking butts.

'Ah, you're back,' he says, taking off Myrtle's lead and defrocking her. She makes for the dog bowl, splashing water all over the discoloured lino. 'Give us a hand with these envelopes. It's taking an age to stuff them.'

'Okay,' I say. 'If I can put the heating on.'

'It's the middle of the day.' He sounds outraged and appalled.

'I'll fetch another jumper then, shall I?'

'Now you're talking. Fetch another jumper.'

He sighs but I sit down next to him, keeping on my coat and scarf, and flick through the newsletter. Barbara's latest adventures. Tour dates. New CD. Fan features.

'Emailing this lot out would save you so much time.'

'What do I need time for?'

Dad is in one of his philosophical moods, I see. So I decide to ask him a question that I have wanted to ask in a long time. 'Have you considered maybe downsizing?'

'Aye, I have considered downsizing.'

'And?'

'I like it here. It's my home.'

'But it's so expensive, Dad. It needs money spending on it. Wouldn't you like to free up some capital? Go on holiday maybe?'

72

He looks at me blankly. A holiday to him is a week in Orkney at Granny Spark's croft. Or a Barbara Dickson convention. He wouldn't swap either of those for all the cruises in the world. 'I can't leave. Not after everything you did.'

'Is that what's stopping you?'

'Well, you sacrificed a lot for me. And then there's your mum. I couldn't leave her here.'

'She's not here, Dad. I don't know where she is, but it's not here. And I thought you didn't believe in ghosts.'

'It's not ghosts,' he says. 'It's memories.'

'Your memories follow you wherever you go.'

Dad ignores my own attempt at philosophy. 'And you live here now.'

'Temporarily.'

'Hopefully.'

'What do you mean "hopefully"?'

'I mean hopefully you'll work things out with your wife. She's a great girl. Despite being English.' Dad, oblivious to his sexist-racist comment, gets out his fag packet, stands by the open back door in a gesture of consideration, though when he turns to speak, the smoke blows inside, swathes me. He uselessly wafts, as if this will help, but it just serves to further smother me. 'And Myrtle would hate to move,' he says. 'She's very sensitive, you know.'

'So you think electrocution is the way forward for a sensitive dog?'

'It would only be a few volts. Nothing to make her jump out of her skin.' He puffs and blows and wafts again. 'So what did you do about your letter?'

'I read it.'

'And?'

'I leave next Friday, for the weekend.'

'Next Friday?'

'Next Friday.'

'London?'

'London.'

I take the invitation from my coat pocket and show him. He reads it. Is quiet a moment. 'Be careful, son,' he says.

'I will, Dad. I will.'

Dad tootles off to the Post Office with the newsletters. He used to be the hard man. Trade Union rep, football coach, brewer. Now he has one of those old lady shopping trolleys and dresses up his wee dog.

At least I have the kitchen to myself so I can read that email.

Dear Cameron

I would be grateful if you could attend a meeting at 0900 on Thursday 5 December with myself and Fiona McCabe, the Human Resources Manager of Skeletours Inc. The purpose of the meeting will be to discuss a very serious complaint against you, lodged by a Mr Sanderson, of Guildford, Surrey, relating to an incident that took place on a history tour conducted and led by you on 14 November. If his allegations are true, this is clearly a serious matter and a breach of health and safety regulations with the potential to be of great embarrassment, and potential expense, to the company.

I should warn you that the meeting will take place under our Disciplinary Procedure and that a range of sanctions are available to us if we find that your actions have fallen short of the expected standards of the company. Because of the seriousness of the allegation, you may, if you wish, bring along a friend or representative with you to the meeting.

Yours sincerely,

Daniel Cooper
Assistant Director, Skeletours Inc.

Well, Daniel Cooper, I did what I thought was right at the time. I was responsible for the tour. I was provoked.

You'd better be ready for me, Daniel Cooper. I won't be walked over by an Englishman ever again.

Fee-fi-fo-fum
I smell the blood of an Englishman.
Be he alive or be he dead
*I'll grind his bones to make my bread.**

It was another of those stag parties. We all hate leading those tours. Things can kick off if you're not quick-witted. These men, they don't take history seriously. They try to spook each other. They heckle and make a nuisance of themselves. We never let them on a tour if they are intoxicated but they sneak in their hipflasks of whisky bought on the Mile. Mix that with a dram of unbridled testosterone and the breathless atmosphere and it can go to your head, the dark, the ghosts, the energy. It only takes one of them to overstep the mark.

I don't often do the tours now but on this day we had two of our staff call in sick. I didn't want to put Charlene through it – there was quite a queue snaking along by the skeleton key rings and plastic pencil sharpeners in the gift shop, where the tour starts and finishes. They were all men. I had images of being back at school, running up and down the football pitch, not a clue what was going on, trying to keep warm and out of trouble, dodging the mud and the jibes and the chants. Like I said, I'm dyspraxic. Clumsy. Especially in an awkward situation. I can panic if I'm bullied. This should be taken into account. What happened can partly be blamed on this and on my state of mind which wasn't good at the time, having had a row with Amanda that morning. And there was Charlene. She was the only other person available but she's young and pretty, a Kiwi backpacker who ended up here, and I just didn't think it a good idea. So I stepped in. I put on

---

*Though I'd much prefer multi-seeded granary bread from that nice baker's in Leith.

a velvet cloak and knee breeches and I led them down the vaults and back in time.

Jeremy says it's important for me to write this all down so I can understand why I did what I did. He is of the opinion that I was out of line although of course he wouldn't couch it in those terms, being a non-directive, non-judgemental counsellor. Jeremy says it's important I get the facts clear in my head before I can move forward. But all I want is to go back. To my job. To my flat. To my wife.

I don't want to go back as far as he is making me but that is what I am doing.

Lancaster, Lent Term, January 1986
Return

It was strange going home for the holidays. A whole month back in Edinburgh with my father and my brothers in the old house, with its leaky roof and rising damp, its familiar smells and mess and stuff I'd not ever considered until I'd been away and returned with fresh eyes. The sunburst clock above the mantelpiece in the front room. The Ercol coffee table with Mum's cork coasters (chaos everywhere, but no tea rings). The brushed cotton sheets on my bed, washed in my absence, the fluffy feel of them, rough and soft at the same time, like being a child again. Edward in the other bed, sleeping for Scotland.

And then a letter from Bex, just after Hogmanay. I'd been convinced she'd forget me once down south but she wrote six sides of A4 in her slanting scrawl, squashed between the narrow lines, circles for dots over her i's which seemed artistic and exotic to me, an all-boys' school education behind me, brothers, and a father. She only referred to Tommo fifteen times. Obviously I'd had no word from him. Or from Christie, who'd flown back to Canada for the holidays. But Bex's letter heralded a good start to the New Year. I was surprised at how much I was looking forward to us all being together again. Apprehensive too, like the first day in a new class after the long summer holidays.

I waited in my campus room, hashing out my history essay, due in at the beginning of term, for the tutor with the bushy eyebrows who terrified me, especially as she was a woman. I'd caught the train a couple of days early; studying at home was a challenge, the usual mayhem plus boozy relatives dropping by for seasonal cheer, itching to see how I was getting on with university life. *We're so proud of you, Cameron. Are you eating properly, Cameron? Do you have a girlfriend yet, Cameron?* I loved my family but I was loving my independence more.

I wanted to see my friends.

A quote from *Brideshead Revisited* flitted into my head. I hadn't read the book but I'd seen it on the telly. Charles Ryder's pompous cousin, visiting him when he arrives at Oxford. 'You'll find you spend half your second year shaking off the undesirable friends you made in your first.'

I swatted it away.

Christie hunted me down on her return, battering my door. 'Are you in there, Cameron?'

I opened up to see her standing in the corridor, in her coat and boots, not quite her usual tidy self.

'Christie? You're back. Is something wrong?'

'Is something wrong? I've travelled thousands of miles, I'm exhausted and stressed, and I can't face my damp, depressing room on my own.'

She still had her suitcase with her. A suitcase the size of my wardrobe at home, far away and empty now except for my ghostly school uniform and some old gym shoes.

'Do you need a hand with that?'

'No, I don't need a hand with this. I've got bigger muscles than you, idiot. I want your company.'

So I followed her meekly, gratefully, up the Spine, across Alex Square and along to Bowland, to her room. People nodded, smiled, said hi to her. She was Ms Popularity. I was a nobody. Mr Nobody. But I was a somebody with her. Well, the friend of a somebody. And I was dead chuffed.

After she'd unpacked – tipping the contents of her suitcase onto her 'totally crappy single bed' – she announced: 'I need some liquor so I don't go crazy.'

We headed back to Fylde bar.

'Two pints, please, Ron.' She beamed years of expensive orthodontic treatment at him and Ron morphed back into the boy he'd possibly been all those years before. Two pints were speedily placed delicately in front of her, alongside a rare smile.

'Thanks, Christie,' I said. 'I'm not sure I can manage a pint of this stuff but I'll give it a go.'

'Sure you can, Cameron. You're a big boy.'

'And you're an angel. You rescued me from an essay on Science, Reason and Enlightenment.'

'Just call me the Ice Princess,' she said. 'No, scratch that. Call me the Ice Queen. Because I will be one day, you know. Call me the Queen of Freaking Everything.' Then she sunk back her warm, frothy beer. 'I hate to say it, but this stuff is kind of growing on me. Like a nasty rash.' She smiled her beautiful smile and I missed Bex in that moment more than anything. More even than Mum, though I didn't want to think like that.

We sat companionably in the JCR, catching up, comparing Christmas traditions, stuffing crisps and steadily drinking till I felt my shoulders relax and Christie's smile slipped sideways across her bone-white, glossy teeth. We cracked bad jokes and laughed a lot and I felt I could do this whole student thing, even though the work was already creeping up on me.

'So when are you getting out that kilt of yours?' She raised her pale, groomed eyebrows. 'I've heard all about it…'

I shed my scarf.

'I'm not teasing.' She tried to reassure me, put her hand on my thigh.

I shed my sweater.

'I have Scottish ancestry and I'm proud of it. We even

79

have a Scottish shop where I live in Niagara-on-the-Lake. It's really neat. I just love tartan.'

'Did you know your Armstrongs were reivers?' I had to focus on our conversation, to sound like I was present there in that moment, in those words, in those sounds escaping from her foreign, moistened, blushed lips.

'Reivers?' She looked puzzled.

'Raiders,' I informed her, waiting for her reaction.

'Really?' she said. 'Like me?' And she grabbed my packet of crisps and scoffed a handful. Then she flexed the biceps on one of her arms and made me squeeze them. Rock hard. Strong. Arm strong.

'Wow,' was all I managed. Then I pulled myself together; I could do better than this. 'Do *you* have a kilt?' I asked her.

And she looked at me in what I believe was a flirty way and said no, but she intended to put that right. Then before I could respond, she'd leapt up and bought more drinks.

Christie was telling me about the time she lost her virginity at a party in the basement of her friend's house when she was sixteen. I was mortified. Partly because I was still waiting for that particular rite of passage to happen, naturally. Mainly because I'd never talked about this stuff with a girl. Or anyone for that matter. Especially someone who wanted to maintain eye contact throughout.

My modesty was saved when Bex staggered in, ruffled and pale, wild hair cascading over her old man coat, dragging a body bag of a rucksack.

'Eight hours on a stupid, wee-stinking, sick-inducing coach. Newton Abbot. Exeter. Bristol. Birmingham. Manchester. Preston. And everybloodywhere in between.'

She slumped down next to me, right next to me, stretching out her long legs and resting her boots on her bag. Christie leant over and gave her a hug – squashing me back against my seat so I couldn't breathe – then strutted to the bar to fetch more drinks.

I couldn't think of anything clever or witty to say, so I said nothing. Nor did she. I wasn't anything as quick in life as I was in my daydreams. I felt sick. I felt ecstatic. Then Christie returned with our drinks.

'Slàinte,' Christie said, raising her glass.

'Slàinte,' I said back, impressed.

Bex gave us both a look. 'Cheers,' she said. 'So how was Canada?'

'Cold.' Christie took a sip of her Barcardi and coke.

'Okay... so how was Scotland, Cameron?'

'Also cold.' I glugged back my pint and wiped my mouth as some of it dribbled out the side.

'How was Dartmoor?' Christie and I asked at the same time, egging each other on, so Bex looked put out. The odd one out. Over and out.

Bex crunched her knuckles. 'Dartmoor was cold. Obviously,' she snapped. 'A damp, clingy, miserable cold. I spent a week in bed with flu and another week recovering and I'm still not over it.'

I didn't know what the hell I was doing. I was being stupid. Here was Bex and I was teasing her because no better words could find their way out of my big fat gob. I felt awful. So did Christie. She fussed around Bex, saying we'd help her back to her room. We'd make her a cup of tea, some beans on toast. And Bex cried because she said it had been such a long time since anyone had wanted to mother her like that. Because Bex was motherless too.*

'Dad left me to it,' she said. 'Worked overtime as it was Christmas, to give families a chance to spend it together.' She sniffed a snotty sniff. 'So what are we?' she asked. 'Aren't we a family?' And she cried some more. Tough, forthright Bex.

Christie – the only one of us to have a full set of parents, alive and under the same roof, albeit thousands of miles away

---

*Tommo was pretty much motherless too. She lived in the south of France but he hadn't seen her in five years because he hated her new husband, the Knob.

at that moment – held Bex's hand and steered her towards the door. 'Grab her bag, Cameron,' she called over her shoulder and I did as I was told, determined to make it look easy though the heaviness bent my spine in two like a pipe cleaner.

Back in Bex's cold room, Christie ordered her into bed while she turned on the heater and I made a hot water bottle. Once we were done with faffing around her, we squashed together on the bed, limbs overlapping, sipping tea and eating our way through a packet of Rich Tea.

'Thanks, guys.' Bex smiled. 'You've really helped.'

'You're welcome,' Christie said. And then, more thoughtfully: 'So what does your dad do?'

'He's a prison officer.'

'Oh, wow, cool.' Christie looked impressed. 'We call them correctional officers back home.'

'That's a nicer name,' Bex said. 'A better ethos. The hope that criminals will somehow be made better before they're allowed back into society, rather than just punished, the key thrown away.' A pause. 'God, do I sound like a middle-class do-gooder?'

A shiver shimmied up my body, a ghost walking over me, stepping up each vertebrae of my crushed spine. They carried on talking but I didn't want to think about it, being locked up. I busied myself making more tea.

Bex put on a Lloyd Cole tape and we chatted, Christie explaining the ins and outs of wine-making and then I ventured an Edinburgh ghost story, which had them hooked only then there was an almighty, unmistakeable knock on the door.

Tommo.

And Bex whispered, terrified and in awe: 'I think I love him.'

I think I love him.

I thought my brittle heart would snap and crackle into tiny, tiny pieces.

'Christmas was shite. Always has been ever since I can remember but I've learnt the hard way to keep my expectations low, that way I don't get flattened with disappointment.' Tommo took a breath. We said nothing. Waited for him to carry on which he did at some length, my ghost story all but forgotten.

'It's not just the presents – they're usually pretty good, no expense spared, though obviously bought and wrapped by someone other than my parents which would be all right if Christmas day itself was all about family but my mother's in the south of France with the Knob and my father thinks having business colleagues round for caviar and Champagne is a good substitute, expecting me to dress up smart and make small talk, picking at the disgusting nibbles, hankering after Wotsits, until it's finally time for lunch.'

Another breath.

'One thing about being an adult is that I can say no to all that crap. So this year I did that, I just said no.* Instead, I stayed in my room, played records, wrote a song, smoked and drank.'

'Doesn't sound like shite to me,' Bex said. 'Better than being in bed with flu, on a wind-blown moor with just a shaggy dog for company.'

'Poor you,' said Tommo and he pulled a sad baby face that made Bex blush. 'I should've come and seen you.'

'Why didn't you?'

'I'm scared of your dad.'

'Really?'

'Of course I'm scared of your dad. I come from Hampstead. I wear mascara. He's a screw. I'm in love with his daughter.'

I'm in love with his daughter.

And I was bereft.

Tommo slurped the tea that Christie made him, wincing.

---

*He was possibly quoting Nancy Reagan's tagline from her anti-drugs campaign. Grange Hill was yet to produce their pop song of the same title. That would come later in the year.

'You make crap tea.' He heaped in more sugar, leaving a trail over the floor, then finally he looked at Bex who was lying back on her pillow, all blocked up and snotty, her dark hair shrouding her porcelain face like a consumptive Victorian, taking in the words he had just uttered. Bex blinked at him with those cow eyes and it hit me how much I'd missed her and how little she'd missed me. She only had cow eyes for Tommo.

'Time we were making tracks, eh.' Christie escorted me out of the room and the door clunked shut behind us.

Tutorial

It was a coat-hugging day, a pathetic sun hovering behind clouds up in the wide sky above campus. I was wearing my Fylde scarf, a naff accessory, but it annoyed Tommo. Annoying Tommo was becoming a wee game so I reckoned I might as well play it properly.

I was meeting Christie for a coffee in Bowland JCR before our Marketing lecture.* The warmth hit me as I stepped inside, smoke all but asphyxiating me. I tried to pick out that bright blonde hair through the fug, found her at a corner table, a scowl on her face.

'You okay, Christie? Can I get you something?'

'Sit down.'

I sat down. 'What's up?'

'Act like we're deep in conversation.'

'What?'

'Just do it.'

I did it, forcing myself not to work out who she was avoiding.

'You can relax now. They've gone.'

'Who's gone?'

'It doesn't matter who.'

· 'Right, well, shall I get us a coffee then?'

_____

*As well as taking English and History as minors, I was also doing Marketing along with Christie.

'Sure, go ahead. That would be great.' And she changed that scowl to a smile.

But I was getting to know her now. There was something going on. I might not be the sharpest knife, but that kind of look usually involved someone of the opposite sex. And it clearly wasn't me. It would never be me. I didn't want it to be me.

I went to get the coffee, elbows at the ready. When I glanced back at Christie, the scowl had returned and looked all set to stay. But whatever was wrong with her right now, she would sort it. She'd get what she wanted. True to her ancestors, she was a reiver.

We stayed there drinking coffee after coffee until Christie was whizzing and I was stuck on the dirty ceiling and the lecture was all but forgotten. She had the band's progress all mapped out, she said. She'd found a practice room and penned in two evenings a week. Hyper would have to forget his pool league, Dave would have to shear his Brian May hair, and Carl would have to quit his nasty habits. She might have been freaked when she'd first heard them, but not as freaked as she'd made out. She could see there was talent.

I nodded. Wondered where she was going with all this.

'They're solid musicians and Hyper's awesome on the keyboards. But...' She bent a beer mat in half for dramatic effect. 'Tommo is our weapon. He might be a jerk but he has it all going on. The looks, the presence, the voice, the technical ability.'

I neither agreed nor disagreed.

'But does he have the stamina and perseverance?' She continued, as if she were addressing a studio audience or a courtroom. 'He'd better pull himself together when it's time to perform. It's kind of like cheerleading. You have to train and train but it's only in competitions, when the adrenaline's cruising through your blood that you peak. You perform to your potential and I know Tommo will respond to a crowd of girls screaming and making eyes at him. But he has to keep his stick on the ice.'

'His what?'

'His stick on the ice,' she repeated.

I must have looked baffled. I was baffled.

'Geez, Cameron. Keep up. It's a hockey term. Figure it out.'

I tried to figure it out. But something was distracting me, bothering me. 'Christie, it might sound intrusive but... can I ask you a question?'

'Sure.' She looked at me expectantly, ready and willing to field this question from the floor.

'Do you like Tommo?'

'You mean like-like?'

'Yeah, I mean like-like.'

'No. I don't like-like Tommo. He's an idiot. An ass. I mean, I can see his appeal to other girls and all. Though I'm kind of surprised Bex is so into him. I wouldn't have thought she'd go for a pretty boy like that.'

'So...' I tried again. 'Do you like-like anyone?'

'Sure.'

'Who?'

'Let's just say he's a man, not a boy. A lecturer in the Marketing department.'

'You're having an affair with a lecturer?'

'Geez, Cameron. Pipe down.'

'Sorry.'

'I wouldn't say an affair. A fling, maybe. Whatever you want to call it. He's pretty cute for an older guy.'

I was shocked, I have to admit. Shocked. But intrigued, like when you drive past a road accident and you don't want to peek but you can't help yourself. 'How did you get involved?'

'He touched my butt when I bent down to pick up some papers I'd "dropped" on his office floor at the end of our initial getting-to-know-one-another tutorial. It wasn't an accidental brush-up. It was a full-on handful.' She paused long enough to give me an image of this handful. 'And I looked up at him, into his hazy green eyes, and I thought, hell, why not? This is a year for experience. And yeah, I know, I'm living a cliché but I'm in control. I'm always in control.' She sleeked down her hair with her delicate fingers. 'This is what Bex's feminism is all about. I don't get why she hates Mrs Thatcher. Your prime minister is a woman in control. She gets what she wants, whatever the cost.'

'Was that who you saw just now then?'

'Mrs Thatcher?'

'Your lecturer.'

'No. That was his wife.'

Shiver

The inaugural gig of The Lunes was in… drumroll… Fylde
JCR. I was actually almost quite looking forward to it a wee
bit. I'd heard my brothers' bands often enough but this was
different. I felt privileged, I suppose, to be allowed into the
Inner Circle of Coolness, nerd-boy that I was. But I needed
a role within that Circle of Coolness so I agreed to act as
roadie. Bex was hoofing equipment around too.

'No way am I being a groupie,' she'd said to the band,
striking her standard pose of hands on hips. 'There won't be
any knicker-throwing, so don't get your hopes up.'

(That had made me feel peculiar, thinking about Bex's
knickers being thrown. Thinking about Bex's knickers full stop.)

The pair of us worked like dockers while Tommo took an
age in the men's bogs, preening and doing stuff I didn't want
to think about. Hyper helped out, eager as a Jack Russell.
Dave Drummer got stuck in as he was used to lugging round
his kit. Slap-bass Carl claimed a dodgy back and grunted
instructions in his Accrington accent. Bex was strong. She
manoeuvred the amp like a weight-lifter, her slim arms packed
tight with muscles that she said came from her summer job
on a farm hurling around bales of hay.

(And then I had a Benny Hill vision of Bex in a checked
shirt tied at the waist, chewing on a wheat sheaf, a rosy glow
to her cheeks.)

The bar was filling up, the usual Friday night crowd, plus some less familiar faces curious about the new-look band. We'd slathered posters all over campus. Christie got an interview on Radio Bailrigg, the university station. A feature in *SCAN*, the student newspaper. The Lunes were coming to town and they were going to rock Lancaster's socks off.

But pride comes before a fall. And Tommo was not the most humble. Didn't know what humble meant. Right on cue, he strutted out the gents, his hair a riot of colour and spiky architecture. Tight black jeans. Doctor Marten boots with yellow laces. Flowery shirt. And he'd dared mock me for wearing a 'skirt' at the Freshers' Ball. My dad and brothers would've lined up to Glasgow kiss this nancy English boy if they'd heard that comment, if they could see Tommo now, doing the soundcheck, one-two, one-two.

I knew it wasn't nice of me but I kept having this thought. I tried to push it away and enjoy the event but the thought burrowed under my skin, deeper and deeper, impossible to ignore. It was a bad thought. A nasty thought. My mum would've hated it. She would've scolded me and sent me away to my bed. But I was free to think what I wanted to think, so I lanced that bad, nasty thought and I let it ooze.

I hoped the band would flop. I hoped the gig would be a disaster. I hoped with all my heart that Tommo would reap the fall from grace that was surely coming his way.

Smoke, sweat, heat, lager fumes. The audience loved them, loved Tommo, fed off his charismatic performance. His voice was hitting the right notes. Dave was sweating like a pig and likely to lose a drumstick. Hyper was nodding his head so hard it might drop off. Carl was in his own world but thankfully no slap bass, sticking to the agreed style. It looked like they were going to pull it off. Two amazing songs that hit the mark and smashed it.

Only then I realised things weren't quite right. Jim from Hull in the Black Sabbath T-shirt was lurking by the pinball machine with his Weeble girlfriend, holding her hand, watching Tommo with a curious expression. I watched Tommo too. Saw the sweat on his face, felt his energy sizzle, caught Bex's expression. She was standing still, not dancing, not even swaying. And Tommo, he was leaping and pogoing and letting it all go but he was out of rhythm, sync, whatever you call it. I'm not a musician but I appreciate music and he was speeding up, too fast, too quick, like he was somewhere else, not with this band at all. Like he was tumbling through space, slipping through a crack in time, falling from grace.

And poor Bex, just stood there, dumbstruck, appalled, scared.

'What the hell was that, you jackass? You've been doing drugs, you idiot! Your first gig, you screw-up! You've no idea how hard everyone's been working, you selfish jerk!'

'Don't reckon much to your team talk. Call that a motivational speech?'

'Shut the hell up, you asshole.'

This exchange was taking place in the gents while I sat, unnoticed, in one of the stalls. I'd gone in there to have a moment to myself, the way I used to at school when it all got too much. And now I didn't dare come out, had to put up with the smell of pee and lager and old fags for a while longer.

There was a beat when all I could make out was the sound of Christie chewing gum.

'It's all right for you, Miss La-di-da, in your rhinestone designer jacket, your tight blue designer jeans, standing there, tall and Amazonial, set against a blank canvas of pissy urinals.'

'What did you take? Was it coke?'

'Wish I could afford that.'

'Tell me, you idiot.'

'Speed.' Tommo sounded like the worst kind of schoolboy.

'Speed?' She was the head teacher from hell.

'You know, amphetamines.'

91

'I know what speed is. I'm not the loser here.'

She was pacing the floor now, I could picture her, stepping over dodgy-looking puddles in her baseball boots. She stopped. Took a deep breath. Started again, more calm, more measured. 'Why?'

'I was tired. I needed to get fired up. I didn't want to let you guys down.'

'Cut the crap.'

'Okay, okay,' he whined. 'I messed up but please… please don't tell Bex, Christie. Please.'

I thought Christie was going to shout again but she took another of those deep breaths, like she was about to start sprinting, and I could almost hear her brain working, hurdling from thought to thought.

'I must be sick or something cos I'm gonna keep quiet this time. But I've got this on you, buddy. One more foul and Bex will know. One more foul and you're off, you hoser.'

'Off?'

'Out.'

'You can't sack me.'

'Watch me.'

'I am watching. You're fit when you're angry.'

Then I heard a slap and a gasp. Footsteps, the door slam shut.

I stayed where I was, not sure what to do.

A creak, a rustle. Tommo was still there, outside the cubicle. Just inches from me.

'Did you get all that, Jock?'

Bex was mad at Tommo. Said she'd have it out with him but not now. Said she couldn't face him yet. Didn't know whether she would cry or shout. She wanted to shout but she was too tired. Too down.

I'd caught up with her outside, in the rain, in the quad that was nothing like the quads of Oxford I'd seen in *Brideshead*. I'd left the bar, left the students who'd jeered as Tommo had launched himself in a ridiculous attempt at a stage dive, crash-landing amongst the plastic pint jars and scrunched-up crisp packets. They'd not even got halfway through the set.

'There's something I think you should know,' I said.

She slowed, let me come alongside her. 'What's that then?' she asked. 'What do I need to know?'

'It's Tommo.'

'Speed? He's been taking speed? I assumed it was booze. He wouldn't do that stuff.' Bex was sitting on my bed. I'd persuaded her to come back for a cup of tea so I could talk to her. She needed comforting but she also needed to know the truth about Tommo. Believe me when I say I didn't want to grass him up. I had no choice. My conscience wouldn't let me hold anything back from her.

She took a breath, gazed at me with big Bambi eyes and I wanted so much to console her, to wrap my arms around her. Tommo was wrong for her. Tommo was all wrong. But I just sat there, rubbing her shoulder gently, her woolly jumper bobbly under my fingertips.

'Bex…'

'What?'

'I wondered if maybe you should rethink, you know, your relationship with Tommo…' I trailed off. Maybe I'd said too much. But I was only looking out for her. 'I don't want to interfere. I mean, I know it's none of my business but I am worried for you.'

'You're worried?' Bex shuffled away from me, made some space between us and I ached for it to be closed up again. Me and Bex side-by-side, no one else, on my bed.

But she was annoyed. She'd crossed her legs, folded her arms and her voice was escalating.

'What are you saying, Cameron? That I can't make my own decisions about Tommo? He's been stupid, yeah, but he isn't going to hurt me. I can handle Tommo. Don't worry about Tommo. Don't worry about me.'

'I know you can look after yourself but he could really throw your life into turmoil if he's into drugs.'

Bex shrugged off that idea but I was sure she stiffened as if she knew there was truth in this. 'It was probably a one-off, to get him through tonight. It went wrong and Tommo will learn from that.'

Tommo wouldn't learn anything he didn't want to learn. But I wasn't going to push my point home now. She was obviously tired.

'Let me get you that cup of tea.' I made myself useful, put on Radio Bailrigg, fiddled around. She began to relax and I felt the anxiety lift from my heart to see her there, in my room, on my bed, with the clean sheets.

'You can stay over, if you want.' I hadn't planned to say this. I couldn't actually believe those particular words had come from my mouth. Here I was, asking Bex to stay over. Beautiful Bex. Just to give her a refuge for the night.

She said yes, all right, without even looking at me, took off her jeans and jumper and stood there in her thick black tights and long baggy Free Nelson Mandela T-shirt. 'Do you have a spare toothbrush? My mouth's like the bottom of an ashtray.'

'Sure,' I said. 'I always keep a spare toothbrush.'

'You ladies' man, you,' she teased. But she was wondering all the same. I could tell. I knew Bex better than she knew herself. She thought she was hard and tough and, yes, she could save a fox and push the law but inside her heart was fragile. She shouldn't give it to Tommo. She should give it to someone who would take care of it. She should give it to me. I would keep it in tissue paper and bubble wrap. I would cushion it in rose petals. I would treasure it always.

She crept off to use the loo and when she came back with fresh teeth and a pink face, I was already in the bed, in my boxers and T-shirt.

'Top and tail,' she said. 'More room that way.' And she took a pillow off me and got in the other end of the bed.

94

There was a blast of cold air as she flapped the bedding. And then I felt the warmth and length of her legs in those tights and wondered what I would do if she got hot in the night and took them off.

The cold made me shiver.

Song

'Where the hell were you last night?'

There she was, Bex, bedraggled, panda mascara, yesterday's clothes, her hair wilder than ever, waiting outside Professor Proctor's room for a seminar, the one all three of us shared. She'd not had time to go back to her room, which Tommo could clearly see.

She opened her mouth to speak and then shut it, changing her mind. But then she changed it again and I knew this was going to blow up. 'It's none of your bloody business where I was last night.'

'So you were with another bloke?'

'Yes, I was, actually.'

'You were?'

'Yes.'

I felt I had to speak up at this point. 'She stayed with me.'

Tommo stood very still. And then he smiled. He turned to Bex and apologised, made himself stare deep into those puppy eyes and mean it. He was sorry. He should've known.

The apology slammed into a brick wall and slid down onto the floor and then she stamped all over it with her boots before storming off into the tutor's room, sitting at the far side of the table between two geeks and busying herself with her notebook and pen.

Tommo followed her in, pushing past me, chose the empty

seat next to a pretty girl and started making witty comments to her, making her laugh. Couldn't help himself. Such an arse, sneaking schoolboy looks at Bex while she ignored him, scribbling all over the white space of her notebook, filling its lines with her erratic, exotic handwriting. He wouldn't give up. He'd pester and pester her.

After the seminar, Tommo caught Bex by the arm. She let him hold it while he made his excuses.

'I looked everywhere for you. All over campus. I even went in the Chaplaincy Centre and asked the God Squad if they'd seen you.' And then, when this failed to move her. 'I wrote you a song. The bloody great song we've been waiting for.'

He had her attention now.

'I wrote it in my head as I walked back under the stars. I walked down along the Spine, past the same old tattered posters, theatre productions, union meetings, Nightline, drink-driving, drugs, and one I'd somehow missed before. Battle of the Bands. The Sugarhouse.' He managed a quick smile, carried on. 'I went back to my room and I wrote the song – an advantage of being an insomniac – and I cried when I thought of you and I vowed I'd put things right.'

I'd heard enough. I hurried away, leaving Tommo with his muse. I didn't have much choice as Professor Proctor was on the warpath, about to rugby tackle me for my elusive essay. I vanished into thin air. Pouf!

Kilt

The pubs were kicking out and the queue outside the Sugarhouse was swelling. Inside, it was filling up fast. What had been a trickle at first was now a flow of bleached ripped denim, baggy T-shirts and big hair.

'You Brits have such weird fashion sense.' Christie had to shout at us to make herself heard at the bar. As ever she was served straightaway, the barman drooling. 'I mean look at that guy's shirt. What the hell is that?'

We looked at the guy's shirt. It was a hybrid of Miami Vice and Noel Edmonds.

'Come on, they're not all that bad.' Bex pointed out one or two guys who were half-decent but Christie remained to be convinced. 'What do you wear in Canada?'

'To be honest, I'm usually in sports gear so I guess I shouldn't comment.' She handed Bex her pint of cider, me my lemonade. 'Anyway, cheers.'

We clacked plastic glasses and moved out into the quiet room; the blast of Guns N' Roses in there was overpowering – though Christie was into that kind of soft rock middle-of-the-road music. But Christie was also proving that her taste was versatile. She liked the stuff Tommo was writing. She liked the sound The Lunes were making. Now was the time for stripped down indie bands with loud guitars and big drums, she said. Instead of the high-production synthesised sound, she said. They were on the money, she said.

'How you feeling?' Bex asked. 'Nervous?'

'Sure,' Christie said. 'A little nervous.' She flicked back her hair. 'Hoping your boyfriend doesn't mess things up.'

The word 'boyfriend' hung there in the smoky atmosphere.

'He's not my boyfriend.'

Christie paused. Ploughed on. 'They'd better step up tonight. They only have to ride out two songs. Surely even Tommo can do that.'

Bex wasn't offended by this comment. Didn't seem bothered about Tommo right now, not after the Fylde fiasco. Christie deserved some respect. She was a great manager; unknowingly to Tommo and the rest of the band, she had already entered them into this competition. She was always one step ahead.

And tonight The Lunes were third up. Third out of six acts. Each with a two song set. Judged by the SU president, the manager of the Sugarhouse and Andy Kershaw.

Yes, Andy Kershaw from the radio and telly. Another drumroll.

They had a chance. If Tommo stayed on track. Okay, he should be allowed to veer off here and there, but he had to stay with the others. Be tight. That's the word Christie kept using: tight.

We finished our drinks then went out to watch the first band. They were crap, it was clear from the outset. The second band was marginally better but too derivative, all Johnny Marr guitars, gothic lyrics and dreary, hammy performances. Top marks for effort. The lead guitarist/singer had spent hours on his sculpted hair and knew exactly where to place himself, where to look, how to look. But his style didn't reflect the content. It was insubstantial.

The audience was revving up though. 'So long as Tommo does what he does best,' said Christie. 'I've no worries about the rest of the band.'

Tommo was the loose cannon.

I didn't want to hang out with Bex and Christie anymore. I moved away, lingered at the back, not sure how to feel, uneasy. I'd had several swigs of vodka on campus earlier. The swigs were swirling round my empty stomach now, making me want to fetch up.

Then there was this change in the atmosphere, something electrical, right there in my head, like a storm was on its way, over the horizon. A tautness. A pressure behind my eyes. The smoke didn't help. The lack of air. I leant against the wall, tried to breathe.

A drum beat. Dry ice. The crowd clamouring. Dave, emerging as if from a misty loch, the drums slow and steady, then faster, faster, louder, louder. Hyper on his keyboards, minus his mullet. Carl on the bass, adding depth and pulling the audience in further, into this strange land that I couldn't navigate. And then on strutted Tommo, a dazzling light shining on his chiselled face. He was singing now, words I'd seen written on scraps of paper, drifting around the practice room, his bedroom, the JCR. Tommo was doing more than singing the words out loud; he was performing them, meaning them, living them, putting emotion into his voice that wasn't there before. He was leaping round the stage with the energy of a punk, the sounds of the Skids, Big Country, Scotland. But as the dry ice cleared, I could see the bloody bastard was wearing a kilt. My kilt! The one he'd mocked. The one I thought was hanging up in my press, in my room. He was using my culture, stealing my heritage. What did I have but my family, my ancestors? And there he was, Tommo, prancing around, lapping up the attention, screeching and howling and grating his guitar which was louder than guitars should be, like there was a whole clan of them, and the heavy drums banging and banging and banging like a call to arms.

Bex was leaping around down the front, elbows jabbing, hair flying, Christie giving her the thumbs up, the Ice Queen giving her royal approval. The audience loved them. They loved Tommo. And I think in that moment I actually hated him.

By the end of the song, I'd slid down the wall, was slumped on the dirty fag-strewn floor, cross-legged, head in my hands trying to stop the small monkey pogoing around inside it. I was back in the classroom, the boy on the edge, listening to the popular kid reading out his work. I didn't know why, but I was on the verge of tears.

If only I drank like the other students. If only I drank like a true Scot. If only I drank properly, idiotically, paralytically, so I could reach that haven of oblivion. But I couldn't even do that.

Then silence. Tommo filled it with his faux Cockney accent, cracked some joke about men in skirts and introduced their second and final song, their weapon. 'Bright Star'.

'Bright star'. The pain and joy of love. The sweet unrest. Simple, poetic and really, really catchy. 'Bright Star'. Keats. A love song. About Bex. The bloody great song they'd been looking for? They'd found it.

And it was clear the judges had found their winner. It might only be a poxy Battle of the Bands but it was judged by someone who mattered, a bloke who knew what he was talking about, who had influence, and the prize was to support The Damned at the Great Hall on campus, following in the footsteps of T. Rex, Queen, Pink Floyd, Thin Lizzy, The Ramones, The Clash, The Stranglers, Ian Dury, Blondie, Madness… Tommo was fast becoming one of the bright stars. And I was the random piece of space dust drifting in this new orbit, blinking feebly while he shone.

We don't support or endorse training techniques using pain, fear or dominance and we strongly believe that the (electric training) devices are unnecessary for treating behaviour problems in animals.
RSPCA

Edinburgh, December 2013

Btw

It is time to open the other email, the one from P. Dulac.

Cameron! Great to hear from you, mate. Good to know you're alive and kicking. As for next week, yep, we'll both be there. Looking forward to putting on the Ritz.
See you then!!!
Tommo

Btw. We're bringing our twins. They're 16, one of each. You might have to duck the flying sarcasm in their presence.
And another btw. The other half is now Rebecca. Has been for a long time. Weird to hear her called Bex again...

Rebecca. That suits her much more than Bex, reflects the softness within her that was always hiding just beneath the tough skin.

Jeremy says I should think carefully before I go to London. I will be in a place that has bad memories with people who have a traumatic shared history. Although he wants me to explore the events of my past – hence this lengthy, wordy journal or whatever it is – he's not sure I should actually encounter the people who were key to these events. My behaviour is somewhat erratic, he says. Perhaps he is right. Am I sure this is really what I want?

Lancaster University, 1986

Trip

I was sitting in Alex Square eating a cheese and onion pasty from Birkett's, sipping penny-brown tea from a polystyrene cup. A blustery day but I was protected with my bobble hat and college scarf and warm inside my duffle coat, the one that Tommo said made me look like a boffin. I liked being a boffin. It was safe being a boffin. At least I wasn't a show-off. He was a show-off. A great fat bagpipe of a show-off.

Problem was, I hadn't been much of a boffin lately. I had three essays to do in a week. I'd let things slip. I'd always handed my work in on time at school but now I was struggling. I'd been to nearly all my lectures, every one of my seminars, understood pretty much everything, but I couldn't concentrate. I'd tried working in my room, in the library, even in the senior common room, but my mind would wander, not towards anything specific, just a general meandering, a sense of being adrift. I was used to being apart from those around me, never anything like my brothers, my classmates, but this was a more fuzzy feeling, like I wasn't quite in my body. I was displaced, a drop of oil in a sea of water.

It was something to do with Tommo. The last couple of weeks were a blur of events – Battle of the Bands, Andy Kershaw, a demo tape, and now the gig at the Great Hall just a few days away. I couldn't concentrate because of Tommo.

I ate my pasty, not tasting it, but feeling it heavy and sticky in my gullet.

Campus was quiet, a few students beetling along, heads down, hunched against the cold, on their way somewhere, lectures, the cash point, the bar. The pathetic sun cowered behind a barricade of porridge-grey clouds. The wind was frisky, biting into my cheeks. I longed for my dressing gown and slippers. I might be the bairn but I was born old.

Tommo would never make old bones.

I swiped away the crumbs onto the step below. A pigeon appeared from nowhere, ignoring me, aiming for my leftovers. I couldn't be bothered to shoo him away, carried on sitting there, watching the bird peck, its silly head nodding.

The square was empty now, the concrete austere and sparse as a Scottish heath. Without the bogland. Or the coconut smell of gorse. Or any vegetation. I felt this unease creep over me, as if someone were spying on me, which was stupid. Who would spy on me, Cameron Spark, with my pasty and duffle coat?

I'd go to the library. Put my head down. Be a good boy. Good boy, Cameron.

Only before I'd even made it across the square, Tommo appeared and that put paid to that.

'The Lakes? What do you want to go there for?'

'I need to get away, mate. This place is doing my head in. I can't breathe.'

Always the drama queen.

'Maybe you've got asthma. You should make an appointment at the medical centre.'

'I haven't got asthma.'

'You can borrow my inhaler.'

'I haven't got asthma, you plank. It's this campus. This whole place. You can't move for students.'

'It's a university.'

'I know that, MacCameron. I just need to get away.'

'In case the students harass you for autographs?'

'You've noticed?'

'Where do you have in mind then, Show-off?'

'Anywhere.'

'That narrows it down. And do you want to go on your own?'

'No, not on my own, though I could do with a break from Hyper. How about the four of us go have a daytrip to the Lakes?'

'The four of us?'

'Bex, Christie and us.'

'The Lakes?'

'They're just up the road and we should take Christie else she'll never believe England is actually a green and pleasant land.'

'Since when has it been pleasant?'

'Enough of your Scottish insanity.'

'You didn't think it insane when you nicked my kilt.'

'I apologised profusely for that.'

'Too right,' I said, not prepared to forgive him yet. 'I would've thought you'd be happier on a day out to Manchester. Or Blackpool.'

'You think Christie would like Blackpool?'

We shared a wry smile at this. But then maybe she'd feel at home. From how she'd described Niagara, it sounded just as gaudy. For all her haughty prettiness, she wasn't a snob.

We borrowed Hyper's Cortina on the promise of a payback. I was reticent about this but didn't want to show concern as they'd only call me a Scottish wimp. The Cortina was at least fifty-seven per cent rust with a distinct lack of working seat belts but, on the bright side, it had a few days tax on it. I offered to be driver, but Bex jumped in – a wee bit quickly – and offered her services.

By the time we were through and out the other side of

town, she was used to the sticky gearbox. I was up front with her, nominated navigator by Tommo who said he was rubbish with maps. He was in the back, next to Christie, the pair of them banging on about the gig. The demo tape was blasting from the cassette player – the only thing that worked properly in the car – and they were singing along. I didn't join in. I gazed out of the window at the passing fields, cocooned in my duffle coat, trying not to think of the work I should be doing, the missed deadline and the extension that was zooming ever closer. The A6 blurred into the M6, then off at Junction 36 onto the A590 and then the A591 and then it all got hazy, blurry, hills and fells and bare trees and then finally a loch. A lake. Stretching into the foggy distance, gloomy and grey.

The music stopped just as we arrived in Bowness-on-Windermere with its hotels, boats and jetties. Bex found a parking space overlooking the lake and cut the engine. We watched the wind scuffling the surface of the water, listened to the wind whistling through the rust holes of the Cortina.

'Well, then,' she said. 'What now?'

'Let's take a walk,' Christie said. 'I feel nauseous after that drive.'

Bex was peeved, pulled her woolly hat low over her ears and I could picture the small girl she once was and felt a desire to protect her. And there was Tommo, with all this frenetic energy crackling randomly like fire. It was up to me to keep an eye on him. And be there for Bex.

I followed the others, through a fine drizzle. I couldn't take in the scenery, couldn't take my eyes off the backs of their heads. Bex's dark curls escaping from her hat; Christie's blonde, tidy ponytail; Tommo's black irritating, ridiculous quiff. They didn't even notice I wasn't keeping up. Christie was my friend. I'd found her. And Bex. I'd found her first as well. But I had to share them with Tommo now. The posh lad, the spoilt brat. He would hurt Bex. I hoped she'd never take him back but it seemed inevitable.

'Oi, Cameron, mate. Wotcha doing back there? Come on. Time for a pint.'

I'd have preferred a cup of tea, to ward off the chill, but didn't want to sound like a complete wuss.

So the pub it was. Then maybe afterwards we could go on a proper hike and clear Tommo's precious, genius head.

Tommo pronounced himself better after a couple of pints. Bex was nursing an orange juice, a conscientious driver, asking when we could go and do something.

'Okay,' Tommo said. 'Let's go and do something.'

Christie snorted with laughter. Some lager trickled out of her nose. He laughed at her. She laughed back. A gut-busting laugh.

'Are you drunk, Miss Armstrong?'

'It'll take a whole lot more than a couple of beers to get me drunk, Mr Totempoley-whatever-you're-called. Remember I'm the daughter of winemakers.' She shook her hair like a best-of-show dog, shrugged on her ski jacket and strode out the pub, knowing the rest of us would follow her, the sheep we were.

We mooched along the lakeside, the playground of rich Victorians, with their suffocating class, heavy clothes and frigid ways. At the edge of town, we headed up a footpath, up a hill that disappeared into mist, Tommo wheezing but persevering with his roll-up, just like my dad, so unlike my dad, Christie bounding ahead, Bex doing her best to keep up, a competition, me dawdling behind. I could feel my own flinty face, my mouth in a zipped-up line. I wasn't a violent man, but sometimes I wanted to chin Tommo.

Once at the top, my calf muscles burned and my chest felt tight like I'd outgrown my jumper. The Incredible Hulk, or the Incredible Sulk as Tommo called me when I disapproved of something he'd done, which was quite often. Most days. All the time.

'All right there, MacSparkle?'

I gave him a full-on bruiser of a scowl.

'If it was good enough for the Romantics, it should be good enough for me, right?' He didn't sound convinced. He stood there in the thickening fog, in the sleety chill, as if he were posing for an album cover, Christie nearby scribbling in a notebook like Dorothy Wordsworth.

I searched for Bex but couldn't see her. It was dreich. I was shivering with cold. I panicked a little, so I headed back the way we'd come, stumbling over tufts and rabbit holes. And the relief when I found her, some way down the hill, hobbling, her injured ankle playing up.

'Here, you sit on that rock while I fetch the others. You shouldn't be out in this.' And for once she didn't argue. So I left her there with the promise I'd be quick, and I jogged back up that hill, minding my way, through what felt like clouds.

I found them where I'd left them, only now they were up close, holding each other, Tommo's arm around her, Christie laughing, leaning into him. They pulled apart when I was almost upon them. They could've been two friends having a laugh. Two mischievous cherubs in their heavenly realm. I should've been happy, Tommo away from Bex. But I wasn't. I had a bad feeling.

'You all right, MacDuff? Seen a ghost have you?'

'It's Bex.' I tried to say these words but I was wheezing too much. Christie was beside me now, rummaging in my pockets. She found what she was looking for and put it to my mouth.

'Breathe, you idiot.'

I took a puff of my inhaler, held it in, let it out.

'It's Bex. Her ankle. Can't walk.' And then another puff. 'What were you doing?'

'Stop talking. We'll find her. Come on.' And she grabbed me by the arm, not giving Tommo another glance.

'We were only talking about the band, having a laugh,' he whined but we took no notice, left him there, in his foggy, blowy Xanadu.

We found Bex, sitting where I'd left her, rubbing her ankle, eyes glistening. Tommo was a prize tosser. And there he was, materialising beside us, having followed us after all.

'Come on, you invalid. I'll give you a piggy-back.' She smiled up at him and he hunkered down while she clambered aboard.

And somehow the four of us scrambled back to the Cortina, which of course Bex couldn't drive. So that left me because I hadn't been boozing. Me in the driver's seat with the Canadian as navigator, Bex in the back with her leg stretched over Tommo, nestling against his crotch, him grinning like a kid.

And then the snow came.

By the time we got out of town, visibility was poor.

'Why don't you guys have winter tires? There's no grit on the road.'

'Don't worry. We have snow in Scotland, you know.'

The roads were slippery and it was getting dark. I had to really concentrate to keep the car steady. We'd be okay when we reached the A6.

'You've got your lights on, right?'

'Of course I've got my lights on.'

'I'm trying to be helpful here.'

'I'm trying to concentrate.'

'Sorry, Cameron. You're doing fine.' And she gave my knee a squeeze, which was a bad move, a really bad move, as I swerved, skidded, and somehow, by the grace of God or Fate or pure luck, there was no oncoming vehicle. Christie lurched and yanked the wheel. The car squealed and the noise cut through me so I could hear nothing else, only the noise, only the squeal, and all I could feel was my hands squeezing the steering wheel and all I could see was the whiteness outside. It was only a moment. Then the car was at a standstill, at the roadside, in relative safety.

'What the hell did you do that for?'

'I saved our asses. You should be grateful but hell, no.'

I got out the car, slammed the door, and stormed off into what was now a blizzard. I walked through it, one foot in front of the other.

The thing with snow is that it distorts sound. It can swallow it up or amplify it. I could hide like a ghost and I could hear every word they said, Tommo and Christie.

'What the bloody hell happened there?'

'Geez, my rib. I could've done without that.'

'Will Bex be okay on her own?'

'She'll be fine. She only has a sprained freaking ankle. I'm more concerned about Cameron. He's been acting kind of nuts.'

'He has? More than normal?'

She laughed a not-funny laugh, winced again.

'He could be anywhere. Let's leave the daft bastard. He'll have to hitch back.'

'Seriously? He wouldn't even think of it. And he wouldn't have the balls. He's never even done it at the hitching post on campus because he's afraid of being mugged by those rugby women or something.'

'He should be so lucky.'

'Tommo, concentrate. We can't leave him. Come on, keep going.'

'It's not far back to town. He can get help there.'

'I guess...' Her voice didn't sound certain. 'He might be wrapped up well, he might be from Scotland, but he's Cameron. He's asthmatic. We have to at least try and find him. It's getting cold, even by my standards.'

'He's a hardy Celt, he'll be fine.'

'I'm not so sure.'

Then they appeared, one behind the other, Hiawatha and Minnehaha.

'There you are, Cameron! Thank God.' Christie looked genuinely surprised and relieved to see me.

112

'Let's get you back to the car, MacGrumpy.'

'Sod off.'

'Don't be a plank,' Tommo said. 'It's bloody freezing.' And then, more diplomatically, as an afterthought. 'We need you.'

'I'm not driving.'

'You want me to?' Tommo suggested, knight-in-shining-armour style. 'I should be all right. It was only three pints and that was ages ago.'

'No way,' she said. 'Never drink and drive. I'll do it.'

'You can't.' I had to speak out now. 'You're not allowed to drive over here, are you? And it's the wrong side of the road. And the car's a manual.'

'I can use a shift stick, no problem. We'll be fine. It's our best option. Now come on. I'm half-starved. We can stop off somewhere. One of those Little Cooks.'

'You mean, Little Chefs,' I said. Even to my own ears, I sounded like a small boy in a mood, lured by the offer of sweets. I heaved myself up reluctantly, and we turned to make our way back to the car as if this was all normal. A delightful day out.

'Yes, Little Chefs, that's what I'm talking about. Some of your crappy coffee and a plate of your finest sludgy food and we'll all be fine and dandy.'

Only we weren't all fine and dandy, were we?

Wrecking her ankle at least meant Bex was relegated to the back seat with me. We'd left the Little Chef far behind – paid for by Miss Moneypenny's American Express. Tommo appeared oblivious to Bex's pain, flirting outrageously with Christie. And Christie teased him mercilessly in return – which was flirting by any other name.

'Are you okay?' I asked her, quietly.

'Just trying to get some perspective.' Bex sighed. 'There are foxes being hunted, sabs being attacked. Starving children

113

in Ethiopia and floods in Bangladesh. Horrific crimes committed by men towards women all over the world, every second of every day. I'm not one of them. I'm at university, studying a subject I love. I have friends. Admittedly, one of them is Tommo who's messing with my head in a he-loves-me-he-loves-me-not way. But he sees the world like me. He makes me laugh. And he can be sweet. Sometimes. Unless he's showing off. Or drunk. Or in one of these weird moods. Then I want to commit a horrific crime towards him. Bash him on the head with a big stick. Ram a chair down his gob. Only, violence is never the answer.'

Now, slouched awkwardly in the back seat of the revolting Cortina that smelled of steamed-up breath as well as its usual Hyper stink, she stretched out and let me take hold of her leg in my lap. She even let me touch her ankle, delicately and softly like she was a fragile parcel. Like she might break in the wrong hands. Tommo's hands were the wrong hands.

There was no cassette on this return journey, no sing-song. Instead we had to listen to the tennis match back-and-forth quips from the front seats. Christie was a good driver, despite the snow, the strangeness of the roads. When we finally hit Lancaster, the snow was replaced by sleety rain, the streetlights reflecting on the shiny roads.

Bex moved her leg off me. I was pressing too hard, she said. Her head was banging, she said. Tommo was a prat, she said.

And then the sirens and flashing lights. The police car.

I thought my heart was going to hammer its way through my chest, through my ribcage and tumble onto the mucky floor of the filthy Cortina, never to beat again. We were so close to campus, we were nearly there, Christie's driving was fine, so we had no idea why we'd been pulled over.

'Any problem, sir?' Christie wound down the window and smiled at the officer, all North American charm.

'If you'd like to step out of the car, miss.'

Christie stepped out, slowly, demurely, knowing full well the officer would be checking her out.

'Students, miss?'

'Yes, sir. Back from a day out.'

'The pub, was it?'

'No, sir. A trip to the lakes. They were really neat.'

'So you've not been drinking?'

'Oh no, officer. We've been hiking and my friend here has hurt her ankle so we need to get an ice pack on it.'

He peered through the car window and Bex gave him a small smile and a little wave. I felt myself grin ridiculously, making out this was all great fun. The officer turned his attention back to Christie, sizing her up, then answered a call on his walkie-talkie. Some problem outside a pub in town.

'That'll be more of your student lot up to no good.'

I thought that was it. I thought the policeman would turn around, get in the car with his partner and head back to town. But that's not what happened. Instead, the other policeman got out the car and sauntered over, fingering the truncheon on his hip, like he was Dirty Harry.

'Right, everybody out,' he growled.

We did as we were told. Bex struggled and I tried to help her but my arms were wobbly, like I had no bones. We stood on the verge like naughty children, the first officer keeping watch, while the other did a search of the car. He found nothing other than chocolate wrappers and crisp packets. There was nothing there. Was there? Unless Hyper had left something. Oh no. Please no.

Dirty Harry straightened up, swaggered towards us.

Christie smiled primly. If he asked to see her license she'd be in it up to her neck. It looked like he was about to ask this when he turned his attention to Tommo.

'Evening all,' Tommo said and then the smart-arsed soft southern student idiot did a PC Plod bend of the knees.

The officer didn't appear to be impressed. 'Do I know you, sir?' he asked in a tired drawl.

'I don't think so.' Tommo shrugged.

'I never forget a face,' the officer said. 'You're one of those hippies who like to trespass and cause havoc in the fields.'

Tommo paused. I prayed he'd be sensible.

'You mean I help rescue foxes from being torn to shreds by dogs?'

There was a big moment where no one moved or said a word. Cars swished by on the road. The wind blew. The rain fell. I wanted the dark to swallow us up.

'Empty your pockets.'

Tommo hesitated for a second then pulled out the contents of his leather jacket pockets. Cigarettes, a lighter, scrunched up tissues, chewing gum. Nothing incriminating.

But then the police officer panned in on the chewing gum. A packet of Wrigley's Spearmint. 'May I have that please, *sir*.' It wasn't a question.

Tommo held it out, offering it up like they were best friends. 'Help yourself.'

'Don't be clever with me, lad. Hand over the packet.'

Tommo did as he was told, his fingers quivering. It could've been the cold or it could've been that he was actually scared.

The moon shone down on us. Tommo's face was silver-pale waiting for the officer to do what he was going to do. He slipped out each of the pieces of gum, one by one, then shook the empty packet over the palm of his big fat hand. Out rolled a piece of silver foil. Inside the foil, like an anti-jewel, was a lump of brown stuff the size of a piece of Blu Tack you'd use to stick up a corner of a poster. I'd seen it before in my brother Andy's room, thought it was a rabbit dropping till he told me to keep my mouth shut.

If Tommo kept his mouth shut, was polite, sensible, he might possibly wrangle out of this. Christie was biting her tongue for once. Either she didn't want to draw attention to herself, or she'd had it with Tommo. Maybe both. And there was nothing I could do. But Bex tried.

'Please, officer. It's only a small amount. You could just

confiscate it and I'll make sure he doesn't buy anymore.'

'Are you trying to tell me how to do my job, lass?'

Bex took a deep breath. I could see how hard she was trying to save her boyfriend's neck. The one who'd taken speed a few weeks earlier. The one who was carrying drugs around in his pocket. All she could do was shake her head.

He scratched his bristly chin, took a step towards her so he was right in her space. 'You were there too, miss, the hunt. Up to no good.'

'We saved a fox.' She stared at him defiantly.

He swept his eyes over me. I smiled weakly, stood up straight, hands by my side, rigid and still, boy scout on parade. The officer dismissed me. No recognition. I wanted to scream, *I was driving the van!* But he'd already turned back to Tommo.

'Right, lad. Get in the car. You're coming down the station. The rest of you, I suggest you get back to your ivory tower and stay there.' He adjusted his trousers. 'And keep your nose out of other people's business.'

So that was it. The policemen marched Tommo to the patrol car while the three of us stood on the verge, wet, cold, motionless, watching Tommo disappear inside and speed away towards Lancaster, red brake lights blurry in the sleet, shrinking into the distance.

Edinburgh, December 2013

Lock

I am submerged in the deep old enamel tub of a bath, suds up to my ears, eye mask on, listening to a *Desert Island Disc* podcast, one from the archives, Kenneth Williams. Quite a different experience for this bathtub from when we were bairns, paired up, two out, two in, puddles of soapy water on the floor. I always got Edward and his torpedo bubbles of the kind you don't want to be bathing in. What would his English Katie say if I told her about that?

As for my English Amanda, well, we've shared a bath or two. She'd sit behind me, her soapy breasts pressed against my back, her arms around me. She'd wash my hair. She'd soap my chest. She'd hum a tune in her head, unrecognisable, hypnotising.

She's my wife but she doesn't want me at home with her. I'd sell my soul to the Tory party, to the Raving Monster Loonies, to the Devil himself to have Amanda here in the bath with me right now.

Amanda.

Once my skin is crinkly and shrivelled, I remove the mask. Myrtle is sitting side-saddle on the toilet, staring at me, cold-eyed and menacing, believing herself to be a much bigger and less ridiculous-looking dog than she actually is.

For a stumpy-legged mutt she can scale whatever heights she sets her mind to.

I put my flannel in a strategic position, switch off the podcast.

Barbara Dickson floats up through the floorboards. 'Caravan'. Maybe I should get a caravan. Travel around Scotland, seek refuge on Granny's Orkney croft, wreck that it is, just me and the birds, the sea and the sky.

The door opens.

'Dad!'

'I've brought you a cup of tea, son.' He removes Myrtle from the loo and sits himself down. 'Having a nice soak there, I see?'

'I was.'

'Your phone was ringing.'

'Can't be important.'

'It was quite important.'

'Excuse me?'

'It was Amanda. I saw her name flashing.'

I dip my head under the water, a whoosh inside my head, cleaning it out, purging it, and when I come back up Dad is still talking but he could be saying anything.

'Can you leave me to finish my bath?'

'All right, son. But we're going to talk, okay.'

'Maybe.'

The dog barks. Dad clutches his ears in a dramatic fashion. 'Be quiet, Myrtle. My tinnitus. And mind poor wee Cameron. He wants to be left in peace.'

He goes. My dad who wants to talk to me. And his dog. I don't want to talk. I just want to write it down. Get it out my heid. And buy a new lock for the door.

Lancaster University, 1986
Doodle

Bex came to the library with me. She needed the peace, she said. To be surrounded by earnest students, she said. You're a good friend, Cameron, she said.

We found a free table, organised our piles of notes and stacks of books, highlighters, Post-it Notes and pens. She was writing an essay on Care in the Community, her Social Work unit, trying to focus on something solid, knowing Tommo was across the way in Senate House, in a formal boardroom with faceless men and women who were footering over his future.

'I've made a deal with myself,' she said. 'If he's kicked out, he'll go back to London. He'll start another band and he'll move on. I'll forget him, carry on with my life up here, concentrate on being an earnest student.'

'And if he stays?'

'I'll give him another chance.' She sighed. 'And still try my best to be an earnest student.' She closed her book with a clap. Shuffled through her notes. 'Don't worry, Cameron,' she said, irritated. 'I'll be fine. Either way.'

'Infamy. Infamy. They've all got it in for me.' Tommo tried out the pathetic joke on us. Christie was with him, beaming away that smile.

'Sshh,' Bex said. 'Sit down.'

He'd found us. He'd only been in here a few times to use the photocopier, couldn't even find his library card. But now he was grinning at us, Laird of the Manor, Monarch of the Glen. He was allowed to continue with his degree, he informed us, but had to be on his best behaviour from now on.

'Best behaviour?' Bex snorted. 'Do you know what that is?'

She looked relieved all the same. He had a criminal record but it wasn't like he'd done GBH or robbed the Abbey National.

'Am I forgiven?' he asked, penitent and contrite.

'That depends,' she said.

'On what?'

'On whether you make the most of this second chance.'

Second chance. The university was giving him a second chance. And Bex too. I'd persuaded myself that Tommo would be leaving; now the reverse was true. And as for Bex, well, I was taken aback that she was reconsidering, a strong woman like her. She obviously thought she could handle Tommo. But I didn't reckon anyone on earth could handle Tommo. Except maybe Christie.

Bex might not want me to look out for her but I had no choice. I'd do whatever it took. I loved her. And love was not selfish. Or proud. It was patient. Persistent. Protective. And usually unrequited. But sometimes, for a moment, you could believe in miracles.

'Christie was amazing.' Tommo planted a squelchy kiss on her peach-soft cheek.

Bex bristled.

'All he had to do was say sorry like he meant it,' Christie said. 'They wouldn't kick him out just for being a space cadet. Those professors in there were all graduates of the Space Cadet Academy of the 60s. Geez, you should have seen them.'

'But you gave a convincing witness statement and character reference,' Tommo said gallantly. 'Thank you.' He bowed and gave her a hug.

Bex bristled some more.

'Come on, MacSunshine,' said Tommo. 'Let's push the boat out and get a pint of shandy.'

'Not for me,' I said. 'I've got an extension on my extension to meet. And some of us don't get second chances.'

'Some of us have just got it, mate,' the bastard said. 'Catch you later.'

I gave the weakest smile of acknowledgement, then stared down at my notes. A doodled mess that meant diddly-squat.

The Great Hall

Generations of students graduating from Lancaster will know the Great Hall best for its hosting of the summer exams and the graduation ceremonies. The building remains largely unchanged to this day. The design of the Hall was a compromise because it had to fill a variety of functions ranging from the staging of concerts and dances to exams and degree ceremonies.

During the early days of the university, there used to be student meetings in the building. The hall also played host to a number of popular bands until the student population got too big and concerts became a fire hazard. Bands such as Pink Floyd, Bob Geldof and Eric Clapton played in the Hall before the construction of the Sugarhouse.*

---

*http://www.lancaster.ac.uk

Spin

This was the biggest night of Tommo's life and he was sober and chemical-free. Even the other lads were off the beer. They were nervous as hell and couldn't stomach anything other than jam sandwiches and Lucozade courtesy of Christie who was taking her job as manager to another level, a nagging sergeant major.

I left Bex with them backstage, hid myself in the crowd out front.

A growing cheer blew like a howling gale, gathering force. On they went, one after the other. Dave. Hyper. Carl. Tommo. The stage was dark. Dry ice. No kilt this time. Tight trousers from the vintage shop in town. The hair, the attitude, the desire, the need to shine. Tommo was ready. They hit the ground running and by the end of the second song they were flying, using the crowd, the energy to keep them up there, the mass of students feasting off them, off Tommo.

I watched, mesmerised, standing alone in that mass, heavy bodies pressed alongside me, pushing and shoving and jumping and sweating, until finally a wave of calm rolled over us and we were all watching Tommo, watching him as he sang in that voice that really wasn't a good voice but was different. No long notes because he couldn't hold a long note. Short and sweet. They were good, really good, together and flowing, a proper band who could play their instruments, with their own sound and identity, though they'd swiped parts of my culture, the whole drumming tattoo, the beat, the rhythms.

And then the third number, 'Bright Star', slower but keener, they kept it going, this heat and fizz, the song catching up the crowd to new heights, holding them up there, believing in John Keats, the young, tortured genius, wracked with consumption, separated from his soul mate, never able to consummate their passion.

Tommo had them entranced. Not bad for a support group.

But I couldn't feel any of this for myself. No pride at knowing the man with the swagger and the moves. No happiness at their success. Not even jealously. Or hatred. I was numb, dead inside, like I could be mistaken for a corpse, worms crawling through my eye sockets and mud in my mouth. Why had I ever thought I'd fit in? I'd never belong. I was always found out, singled out, pushed out, used to make other people feel better about themselves.

I was knocked and swayed, against the tide as always, this urge to give in, lie down and be swept away, but the floor was littered with plastic beer cups and fag butts, so I swam my way through the hot bodies and finally made it outside to a place where I could breathe, empty my lungs, and fill them up again.

Then I stumbled back through the Baltic night to my dank, empty room.

Later, much later, unable to sleep, unable to work or read or do anything useful, there was a knock on the door and it was him, surprisingly undrunk, shockingly coherent.

'Guess what, mate? We've only gone and bagged a record deal.'

And I laughed, actually laughed at Tommo's joke as it must be an actual joke, only after a few moments I realised it was serious. Tommo was being serious. He was blethering on, barging in without an invite, sitting on my bed, running his hands with the grimy fingernails through his messed-up hair, thick with gel, glistening with rain or sweat or gob.

'And we're releasing 'Bright Star'. Can you believe it?'

No, no, no, I couldn't believe it. How was this happening so fast?

'Christie did it,' he said. 'What a woman. I'm so glad you broke her rib. I might never have met her. You lot were right, she's amazing.'

I didn't break her rib, I wanted to say. I cracked it. But I couldn't speak, didn't know what I would say if I did. The world was spinning, spinning, spinning and I was barely hanging on, back on that rusty roundabout in the park with my brothers, dodging the dog dirt and fractured glass, gripping the metal bar as hard as I could, lost somewhere between laughing and crying, joy and fear, Edward with one foot on the floor, pushing us round, faster and faster, Adidas trainers skidding on the asphalt that gave you serious grazes if you lost your hold on the slippery handle, the greasy pole. I could remember the feeling of being hurled through the air, that moment before the fall. I was hurling now, hurling through space with no gravity to pin me down, nothing to hold onto, waiting for the painful fall, the cuts and bruises, the tears.

Tutor

I'd just been in to see my tutor. Professor Proctor. She'd summoned me to talk about my work. She asked me if anything was wrong.

'Is there something bothering you, Cameron? Is there something you'd like to talk about?' She looked at me earnestly, sympathetically, and maybe a wee bit pityingly. 'Is it a girl?'

'A girl?' I said, Miss Jean Brodie at work again. 'No, not a girl. I'm just finding it hard to sleep. I can't concentrate and my head's all in a fankle.'

'A fankle?'

'What my granny would say. A muddle. A mess.'

'Would you like me to refer you to a counsellor? Someone to talk this through with. Or maybe see your doctor? Have you registered at the health centre?'

'No. And yes. I'll be okay. I'll work harder.'

'I don't doubt your intentions to work hard. I just think perhaps you'd benefit from some guidance. To equip you with strategies for getting on top of your coursework.'

'I'm fine,' I said.

'Cameron, it's okay to ask for help if you need it.'

'Thank you,' I said. I could feel my cheeks burning up. 'I'll let you know.' I aimed a smile at her, avoided eye contact, gathered up my things.

As I exited that stuffy room, I bumped into Christie, coming out of her tutor's room. That tutor.

'You'll never guess,' she said, breathless and ruffled. '"Bright Star" has got on the Radio 1 playlist.'

'What?'

'It means the song will be played on Radio 1. People will hear it! They'll buy it!'

'How did that happen?'

'Some dude with a beard called John Peel really likes them.'

'John Peel?'

The corridor seemed to be moving, the walls pulsing and the floor rocking, like we were at sea, all at sea. 'You're joking, right?'

'Do I look like I'm kidding? I'm serious. Really, the Radio 1 playlist! Come on. Let's go get a drink. I'm buying.'

'What does your tutor have to say about this? I mean, doesn't he think you should be concentrating on your studies?'

'My studies? Richard isn't interested in my studies. As for the band, he's clueless. Only listens to Schubert and Brahms.' She moved me down the corridor, leant in to me so she could lower her voice, tactful for once, the smell of flowers and summer fruit all mashed up. 'You know, a few weeks ago he seemed like this big, strong, intelligent, powerful guy,' she said. 'Now he's a broken man. I've totally broken him and I didn't even have to try. *Christie... I... think I should find you another tutor...*' She attempted to mimic him in a poor English accent. '*I have behaved inappropriately...*' A scornful snigger. 'As if he's never done this kind of thing before. It's finished.'

'How will that affect your work? Will he take it out on you?'

'Stop worrying about my work, Cameron. Enjoy this moment.'

I must have looked blank. Because she shook her head, confused that I wasn't doing some kind of celebratory dance about the rise of The Lunes. Then she wrapped her arm around me and propelled me out of the department.

As we stood outside in the cold, leaves blowing around us, sleet in our faces, she said: 'Anyways, I'm pretty sure Richard will be giving me a good grade.' And she gave me a lewd wink.

By the time we reached the JCR, Tommo was already high on something. Someone had put money in the jukebox – Echo Beach, a Fylde anthem – and Tommo was dancing with Bex, up on a table, people standing all around them clapping and laughing and being quite ridiculous in their reactions. Bex looked embarrassed, lanky and awkward, but she carried on with it. She went with it. And I knew I'd have to man-mark* her or Tommo would ruin her life.

---

*You might not expect me to use football terminology, but I come from a Hearts family, a father and three brothers with season tickets. Some of it had to rub off on me.

Cardigan

By the time the Charts next came around, 'Bright Star' had actually, astonishingly, made it to number 38. The following morning Christie gathered us together in the practice room. (When I say 'us', I tagged along, the lucky Scottish mascot.)

'The Lunes are going to be on that TV show!' she announced.

'What show?'

'*Top of the Pops*,' she said, pretending to examine her fingernails, like this was nothing important, as if it meant little to her being Canadian, when she knew exactly what it meant. That it was really, really important. 'That's pretty good, eh?'

This revelation was followed by screams and whoops and much back-slapping. Tommo gave Christie a kiss, a big smacker on the lips, but before Bex had the chance to look put out, he'd grabbed her in his arms and bent her backwards, Rhett Butler-Scarlett O'Hara style.

I offered my feeble congratulations then made my excuses. I had a lecture. Which was true. But I didn't go to the lecture. Instead, I caught the bus into town and sat in the Wagon and Horses with old men in flat caps, spit-and-sawdust style, and I downed pint after pint of some noxious brown ale that was served to me, sitting in a corner with a man called Vern, a retired undertaker, and of all the places I could think of right now, this was where I most wanted to be, learning about techniques of embalming and decomposition rates of bodies buried in Victorian multiple graves.

I can't remember all that much about the journey down to London. The borrowed van was stuffed with equipment and Hyper's canary yellow Cortina was joining the convoy. We got clogged up on the M6 through Birmingham but once out the other end, going south, we stopped for fuel and cans of Coke and Mars bars and a pee.

'I want to remember all the details of today,' said Tommo. 'But it's like nailing jelly to a wall.'

The details: the smell of the fir tree air freshener dangling from the rear-view mirror. Sitting in the passenger seat, on a knitted blanket. Dave's cracked knuckles on the steering wheel. Dave's trademark ripped jeans, like Venetian blinds. Dave's sick jokes that made you question how he'd ever got a university place. The taste of Mars bar mixed with Coke and a wee slither of sick in the back of my throat. Nothing important, random memories that when added up hardly come to anything substantial, nothing near to the reality of what was actually ahead of us.

I didn't even know why I'd tagged along. It was just assumed I'd be there, I'd go, part of it from the start. Though I had no idea what that part was.*

By nightfall we ended up, stiff and knackered, at the dump of a hotel that Christie had booked. She said the band would only be getting session fees for appearing on the show so they couldn't exactly afford to stay anywhere swanky. But if they played their cards right...

_____

*Like the non-twin in 80s pop group Bros. Bez in the Happy Mondays. The bloke in Boney M who seemed happy enough to dress in white Lycra and mime. I wasn't even a part of the act. I was a spare part.

It was nothing like the telly. No glitz, no glamour. The rulings meant their performance had to be live so to make sure it was good enough for national television, they did what all the bands did and made a 'live' BBC recording which they would then mime to on the actual show.

While the band did this recording, Bex and I wandered off to a café down the road. I had that weird feeling again that I was being watched. There were so many people, how would you ever know? I didn't like it here. Even the air smelt different and, inside the café, the voices were harsh and grating.

We ordered tea and toast. She nibbled at it, not her usual appetite.

'Sorry, I'm not much company.'

'That's okay,' I said. 'We don't have to talk.'

So we sat in silence but I didn't mind. We knew each other well enough so that it wasn't awkward.

Afterwards, on our way out of the café, she swiped a copy of the *Sun* that was lying splayed open on Page 3, on a table by the door. She ignored the unusual swearing that its Cockney owner sent after us as we pelted down the street. Once round the corner, she rammed it in an overflowing dustbin. She was laughing hysterically. Then she was crying. She told me she'd had some news. But she didn't want to talk about it. She'd tell me some other time. Later.

The studio itself was disappointingly small, sort of shabby, like if you touched anything it might fall over or give you an electric shock. We were there for the technical rehearsal. The band had to know which camera was pointing where and when.

Bex and I watched Tommo prance around, making weird faces at the cameras. He was clearly the front man. The one they were going to love. Or hate.

It was an odd day to say the least. I saw George Michael disappear into the gents and A-ha were hanging out by the fire exit. There was so much to take in, the make-up artists, the technicians, the runners, the entourages, the dancers with Bananarama hair and Madonna rubber bangles. Everyone had a job, something to do, somewhere to be.

Then it was time for the dress rehearsal. Tommo looked the part, leather drainpipes, big quiff, blousy shirt. The Lunes were good. Very good, despite the idiotic miming, a shiny façade which Tommo was only too eager to prop up. A charade he embraced.

During a break, we hung out briefly in the dressing room. The band was talking with Christie, while Bex and I sat together in silence once again, apart from the crinkle and crunch of my cheese and onion crisps. 'You okay?'

'My ankle's throbbing,' she moaned. 'And I feel sick.'

She edged slightly away from me and shoved her hands in her cardigan pockets. She'd bought the cardy in a jumble sale the previous week, a church hall somewhere in town. The cardy had those old man wooden buttons and square pockets to put your Woodbines in. She was searching in them for something.

'What are you after?'

'A letter.'

'A letter?'

'From my dad.'

'That's… nice.'

'No, it's not nice.' She took it out. It was folded over and over so that it was a small, fat rectangle of furry paper. 'I read it in the back of the Cortina, trying to make out the words, what they mean,' she said. 'I almost chucked it away, telling myself it didn't matter, I didn't care. But I've hung onto it; like a pain in my side.' She squeezed the letter in her hand, wrapped her fingers tight about it.

I was about to say something comforting when Tommo butted in. He was standing over us, our huddle on the floor, tall and lean and annoying.

'All right, Bex?' It was a generalised question, not real

concern. He had other things on his mind. Important things. Pop star things. And I could tell she was miffed with how much time he was spending with the Canadian Maid of the Mist. He should've been making more of an effort to involve her. They were meant to be back together, after all. If it was me, I would've said something nice then and there. I would've given her a hug and told her how much I loved her. But no. He said something else. Something you should never say to someone who looks so unhappy.

'Cheer up. It might never happen.'

And that's when she lost it. She cried again. This was so unlike her, all this weeping. I moved to put my arm around her but she shrugged me off, fled from the poky excuse of a dressing room.

'Go after her,' Tommo urged. 'I can't right now. The band needs me here.'

Tommo didn't have to ask, the stupid idiot. I knew he wouldn't go after her now. And anyway I was already on my way out the room to find her, down the corridor, down another one, checking all the rooms on the way, all the places I could think of until finally there she was, outside, leaning against a wall, her eyes clamped shut, breathing too fast. She was hyperventilating. She needed a paper bag. I pointlessly and foolishly checked my pockets, on the off chance, when Tommo was somehow there too, appearing from nowhere as if by magic, the way he always did, a thief in the night, talking to her, saying words that meant nothing, nothing that I could actually understand.

She handed him the letter which he read.

'Wow,' he said. 'Were you expecting that?'

She shook her head. 'No, I wasn't expecting that.'

I might as well have been a ghost, a soft, silent ghost minding my own business, unseen and unheard, no one to haunt.

'Why are you crying?' he asked. 'I didn't think you had much time for your dad. Is he really that important to you?' He put his hand on her hand and I thought my heart would crack.

'He's all I've got.'

'You've got me.'

'Have I?'

'Course,' he said. 'I love you.'

'Do you?'

'Yes, I do.' He nodded his head emphatically. 'But this isn't the best time. We'll talk later, yeah? I have to get ready. We're on soon.' He handed back the letter, dropped a kiss on her forehead. 'Wish me luck.'

'Good luck.'

Tommo turned to go, hesitated for a moment, turned back. 'Come with me, Bex,' he said. 'I've got something for you.' And he took her away, leaving me outside in the cold.

If only I smoked, I'd have something to do, though it would play havoc with my asthma, which was getting worse. I should see that doctor. Do yoga. Keep calm.

Then I saw it on the floor, the letter. I picked it up; Bex would be wanting that. I tried to fold it up, but I couldn't get it right. I couldn't help reading the words that crawled over the paper like ants in a nest.

Dear Rebecca

I trust this finds you well and that you are working hard at your studies.

I have some good news. Pauline Morris and I have become close. In fact, she has moved in with her son, Gary, who I believe you know from school. He's in your room for now but will sleep on the sofa when you next stay. He's only changed a few things in there, moved some of the stuff out to the attic.

Well, I look forward to hearing your news soon.

Yours, Dad

I made my way back to the dressing room, keeping an eye out for Bex. Tommo was there but no sign of her. I went to speak to him but he got in first.

'She's all right,' he said. 'Stop fussing. I'm getting this show on the road then I've promised to spend some time with her. She's upset cos her dad's moved in some tart and her spotty sprog, without even bothering to tell her.'

The letter burned in my pocket. 'Where is she?'

He was vague, waved his hand, said she'd gone for some fresh air.

'What did you give her?'

'Nothing.'

'But you said you had something for her.'

He gave me a look that told me I was a pillock.

'Oh,' I said. I left him then. I was the spare part. I'd go and wait in the van. But something stopped me. I had to see her. She was maybe wanting the letter. More upset than Tommo suggested. I went back down the corridor to head out into the open again when I heard this God Almighty crash. It came from the ladies' loo. I didn't even think, just reacted, the boy scout within always prepared and ready to help.

I put my head round the door. 'Everything okay?'

No answer. I made myself go in, I had this feeling, and that's when I saw her.

At first I thought she was playing a game. But then the shock of it hit me like a wet towel, taking the wind from me. She was lying on the floor, thrashing around like she was horizontally dancing. But she wasn't dancing. She was fitting. I wanted to collapse on the floor myself but I couldn't do that. I had to think. Think. The first-aid course I'd done on my Duke of Edinburgh. Make sure there was nothing she could bang herself on, no hard edges. Don't hold her. Wait for it to pass. Then the recovery position.

But it didn't pass.

Then thank God a woman came in, one of those trendy researchers with a clipboard and a walkie-talkie thing. She stopped dead, took in the scene, and shrieked at me: 'What the bloody hell are you doing?' As if I had done this thing to Bex.

'She's having a fit. She's my friend. Call an ambulance.' I heard the authority in my voice but didn't trust it. 'She's not coming out of it. She's not epileptic.'

'What's she taken?' The woman was calmer now but urgent.

'Taken?'

'What drugs has she taken?'

'She's not a druggie!'

'And she isn't an epileptic. So she must've taken something. I'll call the ambulance while you find out what she's on.' And she darted out and left me with Bex who was still fitting. Maybe it was subsiding, I couldn't really tell. She was getting nearer the pipes on the wall and so I put my hand on her head as if I was blessing her. There was a puddle by her jeans and I felt so sorry for her that she should be like this, here, on the floor of a toilet, helpless. I'd help her.

Then it was all a rush. The paramedics arrived, shooed me out once they'd got all the information I could give them, which wasn't much. Only then Tommo appeared, running his hands through his hair, muttering that it was cocaine. They did something to her, gave her oxygen, got her out of there and onto a stretcher waiting like a mortuary slab in the corridor.

Cocaine. She didn't do that sort of thing. But then I looked at Tommo and saw the horror on his face. *He'd* given it to her. The woman he was supposed to love. The bastard.

Only it got worse. When they asked who was coming to the hospital, Tommo went even paler than he already was. All these emotions passed over his face, his expression swerving and swaying. Just for a moment. But I saw. And I grabbed my chance.

'I'll go,' I said.

But then Tommo pulled it together. 'No, no, I'll go,' he said. And he reached out to hold Bex's hand.

'Are you crazy?' A voice hurled through the air. 'You're next up!' Christie was breathless, fearsome, glaring intensely into Tommo's panicked eyes, holding onto his arms like he was a child not wanting to go to school. 'This is your ticket to fame and if you louse it up, it's gone. For good. Let Cameron go. We'll follow on after the show.'

If ever a person needed to be in two places at once, it was now. There was that flicker again on Tommo's face. A momentary trip-up. But I saw it clear as day. Then it was gone.

'Sorry, Christie. I can't. Bex needs me. And I'm responsible for this.'

'We'll pretend we didn't hear that, mate,' the paramedic said.

And I stood with Christie, Dave, Hyper and Carl, watching the trolley being pushed down the corridor, Tommo trooping after it, away from the studio, away from the future they had dreamed about, away from me.

'I'll fricking kill that retard when I get my hands on him.' Christie stormed off to see the producer; she wasn't ready to give up yet but we knew it was over.

'Bollocks,' said Hyper.

Christie came back ten minutes later, found us in the van in the car park. 'We've been bumped. I hate to admit it but my dad was right. I should never have come to England. If I was that desperate for a year out, which I was, I should've picked California or some other place where the sun shines.' She released her hair from its pony tail, shook it out. 'I want to go home. I've failed.' She looked at us, shrugged, incomprehension in her eyes. 'I never fail. And all because I relied on other people to make it work. Other people like Tommo. I'm going to kill him. Slowly and with much pain.'

'What about Bex?'

'I don't want to kill her. She's just a dumbass for taking that stuff.'

'No, I meant, aren't you worried about her?'

'No, I'm not worried about her. She'll be okay. She's a

fighter. Though she should stick to fighting for her precious foxes instead of going out with Jerk-head.'

'Bex looked wrong, she was all wired up and puking and I did it to her, how was I to know she'd react like that, it was meant to be a one-off to give her a lift, I hardly ever do it myself but I scored some off a bloke.' Tommo was ranting, pacing up and down.

'How?'

'It's dead easy if you know where to look.' Tommo's voice was cracked, his eyes black and bleary. 'I wanted to help Bex, I didn't want to let the others down, I've messed up.'

'What happened?'

'Her temperature, her heart rate, she had an epi.' He stood still for a moment, his brain whirring so loud you could practically hear it. 'Maybe it was dodgy gear?'

'Maybe you're such a tosser you almost killed her.'

Tommo eyed me suspiciously, like he didn't know who I was.

It was me, Cameron Spark. He should be thanking me with all of his rotten heart. I saved 'his' Bex.

'Cool it, Scottie.'

'Cool it? You almost killed her.'

'She'll be okay. Come and see for yourself.' He grabbed me by the arm and hauled me along. 'She'll be okay.'

The hospital was a labyrinth of corridors. (Was I destined to spend my life searching aimlessly down corridors?) A bedlam of trolleys and swing doors and the shuffling half-dead. Blood on the walls, litter on the floors, the stench of illness and wrecked bodies. And more corridors.

When I finally got to see Bex, she was far worse than I'd been expecting; her face had a greenish pallor and her lips were pale and bloodless. She lay on a bed in a cubicle, quiet and still, a sleeping beauty waiting for her prince to kiss her awake. Only the prince of darkness beat me to it. Tommo had her delicate hand clasped in his dirty one, laying claim to her.

Bex didn't see me; she smiled at Tommo. Because Tommo had chosen her over the band.

She didn't know about his backwards glance. The hesitation. The big massive micro-second of a pause.

But I knew it. I saw it. And I didn't breathe a word.

'I'm so cold.'

Tommo pulled the blanket up to her chin and stroked her hair. I had to watch on, helpless, from a chair in this curtained-off hell.

'Bone-knocking cold... like you get on the moors... with the fog lurking... so you don't know which way to turn... you have to move fast... keep to the track... follow the landmarks before they're swallowed up... else you're done for.'

'Ssh now, Bex,' Tommo whispered, all concern, Florence Flipping Nightingale. 'You're safe in hospital. I'm taking care of you.'

'There was this girl at our school,' she blethered on, eyelids closed like she could see an image of this girl imprinted on the inside of them. 'Years ago. She went on this cross-country run. Never returned. They found her the next day... face down in the shallows of the Dart.' A tear ran down her cheek and I wanted to collect it, keep it safe in a jam jar. 'But our sadistic teacher still sent us out in all weathers. And you get all weathers up there. Snow in May. Bright sun in November.' She shuddered. 'I feel so sick. There's this smell. I think it might be me. I want to go home... I haven't got a home... I want my mum.'

Tommo looked at me, then back to her. 'Join the club.'

To be fair, he was doing a good job of playing the penitent lover, all meaningful smiles and soft body language, his spikey edges shaved off.

But then Bex asked this weird question and the dread of it was overwhelming.

'Am I dead?' she asked Tommo.

'No, you're not dead,' he said, shaking his head and grasping her hand ever tighter. 'Cameron got to you in time,'

140

he said. 'He saved you,' he said.

'Cameron?'

'Yes, Cameron,' he said.

Aye. It was me, Cameron. The superbloodyhero.

Edinburgh, December 2013
Boots

There's a God Almighty hammering on the front door, shattering the peaceful half hour that is *Countdown*. Myrtle, who has been blissfully conked out on the back of the sofa, launches herself against the window, gnashing her teeth against the glass, claws skating across the paintwork.

'You don't fool anyone, Myrtle. You're a big daft softie.'

'I'll get it then, shall I, Dad?'

'Don't worry yourself. I thought I had that conundrum then.'

The banging starts again. 'Is it Sheena?'

'No, Sheena always has a nap during *Countdown*. She hasn't been able to watch it since Richard Whiteley died.' A moment while we give silent thanks for St. Richard of Whiteley. 'She'll be over later for her tea.'

More banging.

'Can't be important.'

'Dad, are you hiding from someone?'

'Me, no. There was a time I had to be wary of the heavies but you sorted that out, didn't you.' He glances out the window, pulls back sharply.

'Who is it?'

'Your wife.'

'Amanda?'

'Unless you have another one tucked up your sleeve.'

'No, just the one. Just about.'

I'm out of my seat and on my reluctant yet expectant way to let Amanda in, when I see that she has already done that herself, standing on the doormat, in the shadows, handbag swinging from her arm like Margaret Thatcher.*

'Cameron,' she says.

'Amanda.' I'm going to make her work for whatever it is she is after.

'I'd like to talk to you. Can I come in?'

I think about pushing her out the door and onto the street but that would be cruel and disrespectful and whatever my feelings now, I should remember that I loved† this woman very much. I married her. I was committed and faithful to her. But, as Jeremy says, I didn't let myself be happy. But he hasn't yet explained to me how it is exactly that one can make oneself happy.

'Come in the kitchen,' I say. 'I'll make you a cup of tea.'

'You might want to put a drop of something strong in it.'

While I'm pondering this, Myrtle has extricated herself from the front room and is skidding after Amanda down the hallway to the kitchen.

'Sit down,' I say politely.

Amanda sits at the table. Myrtle sits at Amanda's feet, feet that are shod in fancy boots that wouldn't be suited to hiking up Arthur's Seat.

She reaches down to stroke the dog's ear. Myrtle licks her hand in return, the fickle traitor.

I remember my manners and make my wife a cup of tea. I am about to ask her what she wants to talk about when Myrtle launches on a new attack of barking as she scoots back down

---

*Did I say Amanda's English? From the posh bit of Birmingham. Rich parents, only child, spoilt. But kind and funny and passionate.
†Seeing that word in the past tense is wrong. I love her. I love her. I still love her.

the hallway, crashing into Sheena who has also let herself in.

Myrtle herds her straight into the kitchen.

'Ah, Cameron. Good afternoon.'

'Afternoon.'

'Good afternoon, Amanda.'

'Afternoon, Mrs Paterson.'

'Is your father about, Cameron?'

'He's in the front room.'

'I'll take him a cup of tea, shall I?'

'Okay.'

She clangs about, sorting a cup for her and a cup for my dad while Amanda and I discuss the merits of an electric collar because Myrtle is at it again, yelping with passion at a shadow. Maybe my mother has come to shoo away Sheena.

When Sheena has been shooed, Amanda coughs, clearing her throat in the way she always does to get my attention.

'I just wanted to say that I'm sorry it has come to all this. I don't know how I feel about anything anymore. Mum asked me to go and stay at hers for a while so I'm going tomorrow.'

'I see.' I picture Amanda back in her childhood bedroom in Edgbaston, rosettes pinned to the picture rail, a clock in the shape of a pony's head, a window overlooking a stripy lawn, cuddly toys lined up on her frilly bed.

'How long for?'

'I don't know.' She shrugs. 'A week, a month. I don't know.'

'What about your job?'

'I don't like my job. I hate doing admin. All I ever wanted to be was an actor.'

I remember her when we first met at Skeletours, dressed as a wench, acting a part of history, putting on a very fine Scottish accent. I remember the curry. Her hand on my leg. I remember her disappointment at her career. Her realisation that she needed what she called a 'proper job'.

'What about the flat?'

'That's what we need to discuss.' Amanda fiddles with

her bracelet. 'You could stay there if you want. Or we could consider other options?'

'That makes it sound like you're going for a long time. Are you going for a long time?'

'I told you, Cameron. I don't know.'

There's an irritating noise working its way through the following silence and I realise it's my foot tapping.

'I've got my disciplinary tomorrow.' I blurt this out, not intending to, but I have to tell someone and I realise how much I need that person to be Amanda.

'Oh, right. Where's that? I mean what is that?'

I show her the email on my phone. I've not shown Dad as there's no point. It will all be over tomorrow. One way or another.

She reads it quietly, hands my phone back.

Oh, she says. Tomorrow, she says. Good luck, she says.

She gets up then, washes her cup at the sink, splashing water all down her coat. A smart new coat I don't recognise, dark blue, bringing out the colour of her eyes. She wipes herself down and I am ashamed of the grubbiness of the tea towel. I follow her down the hallway, open the front door for her. She dips towards me and kisses my cheek.

'Let me know how you get on,' she says. 'Text me,' she says. And she's gone, leaving behind her familiar scent, something that hasn't changed.

London to Lancaster, 1986
Metal

It was a crappy morning. Rain and more rain. I went down to breakfast, a crappy buffet, but I only managed some crappy tea.

'How did you sleep?' Christie was there. 'You look totally wrecked. Like you've been in a fight.'

'I didn't sleep. The bed was lumpy, there was a team of gymnasts somersaulting in the room above and the whole cast of Cats was singing outside my window.'

'They were?'

'No, Christie. That's called irony.'

'I know irony, you patronising pig,' she said.

'I'm sorry. I'm exhausted.'

'You worried about Bex?'

'Of course. Aren't you?'

'Yes…'

'But?'

'Well, she'll be okay, right? She can put this down to experience. But Tommo and the band, well, you know it's over.'

'Not necessarily.'

'It is. It's over.' She swigged back her coffee, pulled a face. 'See you back down here in ten. We'll go see if she's ready to be discharged and get back to Lancaster. There's nothing for us in this city anymore. No streets paved with gold, that's for sure.'

The van was packed up and ready to go. Déjà vu. Hard to believe just two days had passed. Now, back to campus, back to life, as if this had all been a dream.

The wind bowled along the street, howling and cruel, and the rain lashed down on us. I'd always remember London like this. My first time and I never wanted to repeat it. My coat was heavy with rain and my legs were leaden, like one of those old-fashioned divers weighted to the seabed. Even the relief of Bex being alive didn't lighten my load.

Inside, the windows were misted over and there was a smell of wet dog. I was wedged in the back between the drum kit and an amp. Hyper and Carl had gone on ahead in the Cortina to collect Bex and Tommo. The registrar had agreed to discharge her as long as she got plenty of rest and consulted a doctor back in Lancaster. Which was just as well seeing as they didn't have a bed and she'd spent the night in a corridor.* Meanwhile, Christie would stay and organise the van, she said. She was going to ride with Dave and me, she said. She couldn't bear to breathe the same fetid air as Tommo, she said.

Mid-morning we pulled away, retracing our journey, through the hectic, blurry London streets, the northern suburbs, the greenbelt, the M1.

I took off my duffle coat, made a pillow out of it. The damp crept into my skull and I got a stomping headache but somehow that was a pleasant sensation. As if pain was a good thing. I stared at the back of the skuzzy seat in front where Christie sat, listened to her moaning to Dave, slagging off Tommo. I counted the words they were saying. Ten of

*This was 1986, remember. Thatcher loomed large. London hospitals were third-rate. Mines were shut. Docks were shut. Council houses were sold. Utilities and railways were privatised.

147

Christie's to every one of Dave's. I thought about my brothers, wondered what they were doing right now. Remembered the giddiness of the rusty roundabout and wanted to get off. I wanted the van to stop. I wanted to leap out and run. Along the hard shoulder, across the lanes, ducking and diving the cars and trucks and lorries, hurdling the crash barrier in the central reservation and doing it all over again on the other side, and on beyond into the wet endless fields. But the van kept moving northwards.

We were in a convoy, had somehow met up with the others; Dave was keeping an eye on Hyper's Cortina in his wing mirror. Tommo was in that car, no doubt nestled in the back with Bex, playing the caring lover. It should've been me with Bex, her leg in my lap, like the other day. But I was too tired to move my head, too tired to think about anyone else right now, even Bex. I wanted it all to go away.

Rain bombarded the tinny roof, like mini bullets fired from rooftop snipers. The windscreen washers squeaked every few seconds as they battled unsuccessfully with what was quite clearly a storm. Dave swore and lit up his four hundredth fag of the day. I gave in to the moment, the pain in my head, the squeak in my ears, fag smoke curling up and settling in my lungs. My breathing slowed and I twitched my way into sleep.

When I woke later, the rain was still lashing. Dave wasn't going his usual speed, and Hyper didn't seem bothered. They were dragging their heels, reluctant to put more miles between them and their broken dreams.

What was going through Tommo's mind? Was he wondering if he had made the right choice? Bex instead of the band… Whatever his choice, he'd ruined it for everyone: Dave, Hyper, Carl, Christie and most of all Bex.

When we stopped for a break at Knutsford, Tommo queued up to buy some soup for Bex who was waiting in the van. 'Stop staring at me, Cameron. I didn't mean to hurt her. She's fine. And yes, I know, it's the end of my beautiful career. All my fault, okay, you don't have to tell me.'

I said nothing.

'All I can see is my father's face, disappointment fixed upon it and I'm relieved he never bothered coming to see us at the studio.'

'You asked him to the BBC?'

'For some unknown reason.'

'And?'

'I got his secretary. He was unavailable. A meeting in Manchester.' He let out a huge sigh, a punctured balloon. 'You know what the worst of it is?' he asked. 'All this is my fault but, for some reason… I blame Bex.'

I blame Bex.

I left him then, slumped in the queue, and went out to check on her.

She was blotchy-faced and weary, leaning against the window, her breath fogging it up. I wanted to put my arms around her but I couldn't manage it.

'Leave me alone, Cameron,' she said. 'I'm tired.'

So I left her.

Hours later, the rain had cleared, miraculously for Lancashire, and we finally crawled off the M6 and onto the A6, through countryside and villages, past dark fields and bare trees. We were just minutes away from campus when we lurched to a sudden stop outside a pub. Tommo's last minute idea, his insistence more powerful than our protests.

Inside, we found a table by the fire. Someone got the drinks in. The mood was quiet, surly, sour. Christie went to the loo and as she made her way back, fresh lip gloss and brushed hair, she halted for a moment. She'd seen someone. I followed her gaze and spotted him, her tutor, over in the corner, on his own with a newspaper and a pint of bitter. And a pipe. He hadn't noticed her, too engrossed in his middle-class, middle-aged world. She sidled her way to our table, sat down next to me, her back to him.

'Has he seen me?' she whispered, not wanting the others to hear about her sordid little secret.

'Don't think so.'

'Good,' she said. 'He looks so old.'

I raised my eyebrows.

'Let him get on with his little life in his little town with his little wife and little kids and little pub and his great big pint of watery poop.'

I shook my head. The world and everything in it had gone very mad, mad, mad.

Bex slumped in her chair, morose by the fireside, the fierce heat from the logs pounding her cheeks. She looked feverish, as if she were going down with flu. I didn't feel so great myself, shivery and light-headed, not that she was paying me any attention whatsoever, far more interested in the old collie sprawled at her feet. She was stroking his tufty ears and I wished I were that dog, lying down next to her. I wished I could curl up in a tight ball and sleep forever.

She shouldn't be sitting in a pub. She should be recovering in her room, tucked up in bed, in the dark, safe, and away from Tommo.

The glum atmosphere was oppressive. A miasma of fag smoke hung over us. The fire crackled and hissed. Life would carry on but this was the end of the band. Maybe the end of Bex and Tommo. He was already cut loose, drifting, drinking too quickly, in a needy, desperate way.

And I remembered the letter in my pocket, folded carefully and kept safe. Now wasn't the right moment to remind Bex of it. She had to make sense of everything in her own time. Her dad was moving on, leaving her in the lurch, without a place to call home. She couldn't rely on him and she couldn't rely on Tommo.

I was only going to drink orange juice but Tommo stuck a vodka in it and I wasn't bothered to argue. I couldn't even taste it, was feeling more and more sick as the evening progressed. So I drank it and then another one that Christie got for me. Even she was drinking more than I'd ever seen. But I left it there at two. I knew my limits. I needed a Lemsip and my bed.

But Tommo insisted on another round. I asked for an orange juice, no vodka. I could do with the vitamin C, this cold I was getting.

'Sometimes you can be such a poof,' Tommo snarled. 'Orange juice? Call yourself a Jock?' He laughed as he said it, matey, jokey, ironic, but it wasn't funny. Not at all.

I went to the loo to blow my nose.

What felt like hours later, Christie told Tommo we had to leave as Bex looked exhausted. She did look exhausted.

'Let's get outta here.' Christie stood and, as we shuffled on our coats and gathered our stuff together, she nodded discreetly at her lecturer who was as startled as a rabbit caught in the headlights. With a pipe.

Bex gave the mangy dog a final pet and heaved herself up. I had to hang onto her arm to steady her. She stumbled a wee bit and her arm came free of my grip. So I held on again, more tightly, as I could see she needed my support.

Moments later, we stood outside, in the street, breathing in the cold air. Tommo was clearly under the influence and then, for a reason no one quite knew,* he took a swing at Hyper. Hyper ducked like a cartoon character and then responded with a left hook that caught Tommo smack on the cheek with a sickening crunch and had him off his feet and onto the pavement where he lay with his eyes closed.

No one moved.

Then Hyper, rubbing his precious piano fingers, abandoned his Cortina there on the street and got in the van with Dave and Carl. They skidded off and left us behind.

Christie, Bex, Tommo and me.

Christie was the one to go to Tommo, to reach down and

_____
*Later, in the statements, the witnesses were all vague about this.

help him to his feet. He rubbed his cheek, grimaced, wiped the grit off his jeans and staggered towards the Cortina. He didn't have the keys but the door was unlocked. Of course it was unlocked. The lock didn't work. And of course the keys were waiting helpfully in the ignition. Tommo half fell into the driver's seat and revved up the engine.

Christie was right behind him, furious, yanking open the door, trying to pull him out. 'You hoser!' she screamed.

'I'm fine. I'm dandy,' he said, resisting her, stronger than he looked. 'I've only had a couple of pints.'

'Get out the car. You're drunk and probably concussed. We can get a cab back to campus.'

'We'll be waiting all night. It's only a mile. We'll be fine. Come on, get in.'

'Go ahead. Kill yourself but you are not gonna kill me. I'm gonna walk.' And she stormed off.

Bex meanwhile got in the passenger seat, on automatic, out of herself, floating somewhere else, not caring, not thinking. Tommo pulled away, spectacularly stalled, giving me the chance to leap in the car, a stupid thing to do, I know. Such a stupid, stupid thing to do. I should've followed Christie. We could've walked back to campus together, let the others go. But I could not, would not, leave Bex alone with Tommo.

No sooner had I got in the back seat, shuffling over so I sat behind Bex, as close as I could be, Tommo kangarooed off. After a hundred yards or so he had the hang of it and I actually thought he might be okay, not totally blasted. He was driving very carefully, purposefully like he was doing his driving test. I put on my seatbelt all the same and just as it clicked, there was Christie up ahead, under the spotlight of a streetlamp, arguing with her lecturer, her arms wind-milling, her hair flicking. She was shouting, shouting at him, and he furiously grabbed her by the shoulder, quite violently.

Tommo slowed, pulled over, wound down the window. 'Get in!'

In a flash Christie kicked the Marketing philanderer, dived

into the back seat next to me and slammed the door, shutting in a waft of perfume and bitter air, her blonde hair shining like pearls in the moonlight.

'Who the hell was that?' Tommo asked. Then he swore as the engine cut out again.

'Just some dude,' she snapped. 'He totally has a crush on me but I put him straight.' She elbowed me to keep me quiet. Then there was this rap on the window and a mad face appeared. The dude. 'Let's go, Tommo,' Christie urged.

He'd got the engine turning over again, put his foot down and we shot off through the village and within moments were out on the open space of the A6, a short stretch then we'd take a right turn and head up the windy hill to campus.

Tommo seemed okay, cruised in the slow lane. Maybe he hadn't drunk all that much after all. He seemed in control. Maybe he was in control of the car. Maybe it wasn't his fault.

I might have been woozy, my instincts warped and out of sorts, but I knew something was wrong. The moon shone brightly, lit up Tommo's musician's hands gripped on the steering wheel with deliberation. He was forcing himself to concentrate. Concentrate? Knowing what he'd lost? With the drama back in the village? With booze in his bloodstream? What the hell were we doing?

Then, a light from nowhere. In the moment before I shut my eyes, I saw a dazzling white monster coming towards us. The wrong side of the road. Our side. It vanished as quick as it had come, but the car, the old Cortina, it swerved, spun, left the ground and flew up, squealing and wailing into the waiting night.

There was a rush of wind and noise. After, came a quiet so intense it hurt my ears. There was nothing. Only a space where our old lives used to be. I thought this must be the end of the world.

But it was only just beginning.

Bright Star

A creaking sound. The smell of smoke. A darkness so thick you could touch it. Shallow breath. Pain. Groaning. A ghost's sigh.

I lifted my head but it was too heavy for my neck. The world had slipped and tilted.

I reached out my hand in front of me, stretching my arm, as far as I could manage, to the space where Bex was supposed to be. But she wasn't there. Panic forced me to move, sit up, grapple with my seat belt, ease myself forward, bit by bit, inch by inch, fighting the hurt in my chest, forcing the air from my lungs.

I saw her shadow. But it wasn't her shadow. It was her. Deathly quiet. Slivers of glass glittered on her coat.

'Bex?'

'We have to get out. I can smell petrol.' Her voice, far off, husky, urgent.

Thank God.

I listened to her unclip her seat belt. The rustle of her coat as she scrambled to open her door and clamber out.

The wail of wind, the whoosh of cold air.

Fumbling for the door handle, but Bex already there, opening it, grabbing me by my jacket, heaving me out.

A field. Soft, soggy grass. The road had disappeared. We were in a field.

I struggled to my feet, dizzy and breathless, searched for her in the dark, but she was gone. I could hear her panting, shrieking like a vixen, banging, banging what must be Tommo's door. 'Get help, Cameron! Quick! Get help!'

I did as she said. I had to get help. So I hobbled towards the light, the university beaming like a spaceship on the hillside, out of reach, on the other side of the road we had left behind. I staggered across the field, towards that road, the A6, each step sickening, each breath useless, back to the verge, clutching my side, shards of glass scattering like stars in the moonlight.

The road was quiet. Then footsteps, running, a man from another car. *Someone's gone to phone for an ambulance.* The splatter of vomit. The smell of it, sharp and bitter. Cold, deathly cold wind.

Then a siren. Flashing lights.

Bex?

I looked round, couldn't see her, everything was moving when it shouldn't be.

I staggered back down the bank, weak legs, scorched lungs, but my body not mine.

She was kicking the car door, a woman possessed. Tommo was out, hopelessly pulling her, crying, urging her to get away. 'Leave her!'

'I can't leave her. She's stuck in there.'

Christie.

Bex banging, yanking the handle of what was no longer a door. I tried to help Tommo get her away from the car, grabbing one of her arms, but she wrenched it away; she was too strong, adrenaline whizzing, eyes glistening, shouting words I couldn't hear because of the buzzing in my ears, the panic in my head.

And then men, big men, stiff jackets, helmets, torch beams bouncing, clambering down the bank, shepherding us into a huddle away from the very place we wanted to be, big men wielding workers' tools, like they were going to dig the field, like they could be archaeologists, house builders, quarrymen.

Bex banged and kicked and banged that car until her knuckles bled and she would have carried on, she felt no pain, but she wasn't strong enough to tug herself away from those men. Only when she realised who they were, did she finally let go. And then she started to sob, a small, frightened lassie, and Tommo had to guide her from the wreck, helped along by a burly policeman.

The moon, the street lights. I could see it all now, back here on the road. The four of us should be up there, up on campus, in the JCR playing pool, working on essays, reading, dancing, laughing, but we were far away from there, in an upside-down world.

Fire engines. Ambulances. Police cars. An army of uniforms rushing round, on walkie-talkies, on a mission. Tyre marks veering off the road, muddy tracks through the field. Hyper's mashed-up mess of a car. Fire officers surrounding it. The head-cracking buzz of a saw, metal fighting metal, and Christie trapped and hidden away inside.

They had the door off. They were doing something to her. Two men stood to one side, heads down, shoulders hunched, their bodies saying what I couldn't hear.

And that's when my own body failed, when the ground came up to meet me and I saw the moon floating above, smiling grimly, and the stars all around merged and melted into one mass of light before swallowing me into a massive black hole.

I was on my knees now, chucking up my guts again, ribs taut with the strain, brain crushed in my head, blood in my mouth and my eye blurry, like the day of the hunt, a day from another lifetime, one I couldn't recognise as belonging to me. I was here now, in this nightmare, wet, cold, confused.

Then a blanket wrapped around me, warm and heavy, a voice asking for my name, and I wondered if it was my mum come back for me.

'Cameron,' I said. 'My name is Cameron.'

This person, I don't remember if it was a man or a woman, but they felt like an angel who just might make everything better if I did as I was told, this person bundled me towards an ambulance, lay me down inside it, a mini hospital, a mini heaven, all bright lights and technical contraptions.

I'd cracked my head open, they said. It would need stitching, they said. I might have concussion, they said.

My lungs were wheezing like Granny Spark's creaky old bellows and they gave me something to help me breathe. My head cleared a little and I remembered.

'Where are the others? Are they okay? Did they get Christie out?'

'Stop talking,' the voice said. 'Stay calm. Lie still. They'll be news later. Not to worry.'

But that's what they'd said about my mum. Not to worry.

Worry doesn't stop the bad things happening.

A fuzzy face loomed over me. Man or woman or angel, I didn't know, it didn't matter. I watched their lips move but it was all gibberish. They could've been reading the last rites for all I cared. The last rights and wrongs. The wrong, wrong, wrongs.

The song played on an endless loop, but it was mixed-up, in a fankle. 'Bright Star'. My eyes shut tight so I did not have to see. *Eternal lids apart.* I made myself remember the poem that Tommo had desecrated. I wanted to think of that and that alone. *In lone splendour.* There was nothing else for me to do except recite it, word by word, every word in the right order, till I had it word perfect. Then everything would be okay. This would just be a bad night, one to put down to experience. *Hung aloft the night.* Not a catastrophic one. *Sleepless Eremite.* Would someone call my dad, my next-of-kin, or would they not bother, I was only a wee bit battered after all. Not like Christie. *Her tender-taken breath.* I spoke the words, spoke them aloud to block out the vision of Christie entombed in the shattered car. *And so live ever.* But however hard I tried, I could not get the words in the right order. *Or else swoon to death.*

Then the hospital. Stark lights. Being pushed on a trolley. The old pram, round the garden, the streets, dressed up like a girl in Mum's clothes. I wanted to go back, hold Mum's hand one last time. But she was always out of reach and all I could do was grab the empty space where she used to be.

Edinburgh, December 2013

Yes

Jeremy says I must write this all down. All these words. The incident. The episode. The underground shenanigans. Whatever you want to call it. Words are important. They tell the reader or the listener your point of view. Words are who you are. Bex would've disagreed. She'd say actions are what count. But words come first, otherwise you are flailing around in the dark. In the beginning was the Word.

I'm not writing from a Christian perspective. I'm not sure if I have a faith. If I do, then it has been tested many times and it will, no doubt, be tested many more times to come. At school we were told that only the Elect would go to heaven. Now some people say that Heaven is here on earth, sitting cheek by jowl with Hell.

Hell is being a Scotsman stuck underground with a stag party of beer-swilling, rugby-playing Englishmen, much how a comprehensive teacher might feel doing supply work with privately educated, unruly, uncouth children.

There's always a ringleader. A frontman. On this day, down in the vaults, it was the one with the black hair, the irritating drawl, the smart-arsed, scrawny-arsed scrote of a Tory boy.

He reminded me of someone, of course he did. Jeremy spotted the likeness straightaway. (I don't pay him £55 per hour for nothing.) He gave me the creeps in a way our ghosts have never done. He had menace in his eyes. An attitude that had been formed and nurtured through genes, birth, upbringing, boarding school, university, jobs for the boys. Rugby balls. Cricket teas. Golf clubs. Everything I hated.

Believe me when I say I only did what I did out of the best of intentions. I was responsible for the whole group, remember. When this ringleader stepped over the line, I had to be there for the majority and get them to safety. There was nothing else I could have done, I felt, at that moment, other than do what I did.

And of course there were the two lassies. Did I mention the two lassies? They'd joined the tour at the last minute. Students, they were. Nineteen, twenty years of age perhaps. I had to look after them. They were my responsibility. That needs to be taken into account.

Lancaster, 1986

Money

A strange man was in the cubicle with me. He told the nurse he was my father and though it was hard to see with my blurry vision, I knew it wasn't my father. Wrong accent. Wrong smell. It was someone else pretending to be Dad.

'You were driving,' the man whispered in a sharp voice, just him and me in the curtained cubicle, shadows and muffled sounds beyond, out of reach. 'You were driving when the vehicle veered towards you and you swerved to avoid it and went off the road.'

'Tommo was driving.'

'I want you to say you were driving or Ptolemy will be kicked out of university. He's on his last warning. He was drinking, the stupid idiot. Four pints and two shorts. He might go to prison. But you have a clean slate. You only had two drinks. You'll be fine. Do this and you will be looked after.'

Looked after? I tried to work out who on earth this man was and then it all became clear. The voice. The dark hair. The handsome face. This was Tommo's father. And Tommo's father wanted me, Cameron Spark, to say I was driving.

I wasn't driving.

Tommo was driving.

'You know your father is struggling for money,' he said.

'One of your brothers – Edward is it? – he has run up some very large debts, and they need to be paid off very soon, or some very dangerous men will do him some very bad harm.'

'No,' I said. 'Edward wouldn't do that.'

'We all do things out of character. Except maybe for my son who always acts as one would expect. With supreme recklessness and no thought as to the consequences.

So you might wonder how will he learn from this? If you take his place? My answer to that is I will make sure of it. I will cut off his allowance. He will have to work for his keep.'

Tommo was driving.

But Tommo was over the limit.

And I, Cameron Spark, was fine, the man said. It was in my power to save Ptolemy's skin, he said. I could save my brother from some very bad men, he said. My brain filled my head. My lungs filled my chest. My gullet filled with sick.

And your father, he said. You can help him, he said.

But Edward…?

'Not Edward,' I said.

'My mistake.' He waved his hand like he was flicking away some dirt. 'Your brother, Andrew.' As though it didn't matter which of my brothers was going to get their head kicked in.

It felt like somebody had already kicked my head in, never mind my brothers. A piston pumping. The Edinburgh tattoo going full throttle.

'I want to puke.'

The man passed me one of those cardboard bowls that are never up to the job. I gagged and a spew of vomit spattered into the bowl and down my chin. The man gave me a tissue and I wiped myself clean. Laid back against the bed. Shut my eyes. Prayed he'd go away, leave me alone. I wanted sleep.

Go away.

When I opened my eyes, the man was still there, sitting on a chair, head in his hands, his expensive-looking coat nothing like my dad's tatty anorak. This was Tommo's dad. He had money.

And my family had a lack of it. And if these debts weren't paid, Andy could have a lack of working kneecaps.

'Tommo has told me about the three of you. This Bex, who has been taking drugs. This Canadian girl, who has no licence, no insurance, to be driving over here. And you.'

'Me?'

'He told me you are solid.'

'He did?'

'He said you are trustworthy and reliable.' Tommo's father waited for these words to sink in.

Solid.

Trustworthy.

Reliable.

Words. They floated on my muddled, sick brain. But not muddled and sick enough that I couldn't ask the question: 'How did you get here so fast?'

He smiled this dazzling smile. 'Ptolemy called me. Car phones are a wonderful invention.'

A meeting in Manchester.

'How do you know about my family?'

'I make it my business to find out who my son spends time with.'

I remembered that feeling of being watched. If I was paranoid, then I had every right to be.

'I know about the hunt. I know about Fylde bar. I even know about heavy metal fans from Hull. I don't know what Ptolemy has said about me. I assume nothing too glowing. But I care very much for his future. He is a loose cannon and he needs some restraint.' And then his closing gambit: 'Bex will be forever in your debt,' he said.

I took a deep breath and let it back out.

This man knew his son all right, but Tommo was wrong about his father. His father loved him. But Tommo wouldn't know love if Aphrodite herself gave him a snog while chubby cherubs flitted all around. But Bex loved him. And I loved Bex. I could do this act of love for her.

'Here's what's going to happen,' the man began. And he spoke in a way that both calmed me and turned my heart to a fistful of ice.

Later, the man was gone and Bex was sitting in his place. She smiled at me and even with her blood-pocked face and the swelling on her cheek, she had never looked so beautiful. Right now she could be dead in a silk-lined coffin with her hands arranged Ophelia-like around her tangle of pond-weed hair. But she was here, with me, living and breathing and needing my help.

'You don't have to do it,' she said. 'It's perjury. We could go to prison.'

'Not if we stick together,' I said. 'We'll be okay. We can do this. I know what Tommo means to you. If I can help sort out this mess, then I will. And Christie's strong. She'll be right as rain. All this will be a bad memory.'

I tried to believe those words. I really tried. If you loved someone, then you put them first. Whatever the cost.

And after all, this was my chance to be a superhero. To shine like a bright star.

'They're clamping down on drunk drivers. Attitudes are changing. Dad thinks you should be banged up for life if you kill someone.'

'Tommo hasn't killed anyone.'

'Christie could be dead for all we know. She could be lying in the morgue, waiting for her parents to come and identify her.'

'She'll be okay,' I said but she wasn't listening.

She was more concerned with her boyfriend. 'They'll kill Tommo in prison,' she said. 'I can't live without him.'

I drifted off.

People came. People went.

I think Tommo was there at one point, but I don't really remember. But I do remember I had this terrible picture in my head: Christie, being carried up the field, oxygen mask covering her face, her neck in a brace thing, surrounded by uniforms, a cluster of them around her, like a funeral procession, undertakers and pallbearers and mourners.

A nurse fiddled with my arm. Bathed my eye. Stitched my forehead.

Another nurse took my temperature, my blood pressure.

A doctor peered deep into my eyes with some metal instrument.

I slept.

When I woke later there was a different man by my bed. He looked familiar and my head throbbed trying to remember who he was and how I knew him. Then it came to me. The log fire, the collie dog with the soft ears. The man in the corner with his newspaper and pipe. Someone Christie knew. Her tutor.

'Don't move, stay there.' His voice was nice, smooth and reassuring. 'You're Christie's friend, aren't you?'

'Is she dead?'

'Dead?' He said the word like it was an ordinary, everyday word, which it was. Somewhere, at some time everyday, someone died. He was simply considering whether it was Christie's turn today. 'No, I don't think so,' he said. 'She's in theatre. They wouldn't tell me much until I explained the situation, that she's an overseas student. I just wanted to let you know that I've called Christie's parents and they're on their way to the airport. Toronto, I think they said. It was all a bit rushed and hasty.'

He gave me a weak smile and his words corkscrewed until they lay curled up tight in my skull. 'Is there someone I can call for you?'

I thought of my dad at home, listening to Barbara Dickson, doing his union work, his day job at the brewery, surrounded by the smell of malt and hops. I thought of Bex and her letter. I didn't know where the letter was. It could have fluttered away on the smoky night breeze. It could be trampled in the bloody mud of the field.

'No,' I said. 'There's no one to call. I'm fine.'

But by then I had another visitor. A burly policeman.

For the hand that rocks the cradle is the hand that
rules the world.
William Ross Wallace*

---

*Not the William Wallace of 'Braveheart' fame, but a poet.

Edinburgh, December 2013
Baby

The sky is clear and pale blue and casts shape-shifting shadows across the sodden grass. I'd forgotten how beautiful Rosslyn Chapel is, its stonework a testament to skill and hard labour and death-defying bravery.

I know all about death-defying bravery. I've had to endure the journey here, quaking in the passenger seat with Dad taking on the A720 and A701. Now he's wedged the Peugeot so close to the neighbouring Honda in the car park that I have to squeeze out, shape-shifting myself to ease through the gap without scratching the paintwork.

'Why are we here exactly, Dad?'

'Mum used to bring you.'

'I know. She loved it.'

'She did, aye.'

'You haven't been reading Dan Brown again, have you?'

'I've never read that *Da Vinci Code*. But I've seen the DVD. Sheena gave it me. She likes all that mystery stuff.'

'It's nonsense.'

'I know that.'

'Mum could've told Dan Brown a thing or two.'

Dad laughs and I guide him into the gift shop to pay for our tickets. There's building work been going on. Restoration.

Nearing its completion. I think about my gift shop with its skeleton key rings and ghost books. I think about my job. I stop thinking about my job because if I lose it, then what will this all have been for?

It's calm inside the chapel, despite the tangled knots of visitors. The candles are lit and some sort of Christmas thing is going on for the kids. Storytelling (I know all about that). It takes me back to school nativity plays. Tea towels on your head if you were a shepherd. Tinsel if you were an angel. I was always an angel on account of my curls but I hankered after the innkeeper's role. He was a problem solver. A thinker-outside-the-box. A superhero. 'You can have the stable out the back. There's a manger will do for a cradle. And the ox and ass will keep you warm. And the straw will soak up the blood. Amen.'

Dad and I wander around, together, on our own. I'm waiting for him to say something 'significant' to me. Why else would he bring me here?

Eventually, he sits me down on a pew in the south aisle.

'Look around you, son. The carvings tell a story. A knight on horseback. An angel playing bagpipes. The nativity. The fallen Lucifer. The dance of death. The star of Jerusalem. And all those green men. I know where they all are because your mum, she used to bring me here too. She was an historian. But she was also a romantic. She mixed things up, like her beloved Scott and Burns used to make stuff up.'

'They sound like they should have a TV cop show.'

'Quite the comedian in your middle-age.'

'I'm not middle-aged.'

'Forty-six is middle-aged.'

'Maybe.'

'At least you're not as old as me.'

'That's something.'

'You're the age your mum was when she died.'

'Oh.'

'Don't be downhearted. Whatever's going on with you and Amanda, you can sort it. And if you can't, well you just have to carry on. I had to carry on.'

'You had us boys. You had no choice.'

'There's always a choice. I could've laid down in the middle of George Street and let the traffic roll over me. I could've flung myself off the Forth Bridge or Arthur's Seat. I could've stuck my head in the oven.'

'It was an electric oven.'

'Well, you get my drift.'

'Aye, Dad.'

'But I carried on. I made your tea, I made you have baths. I made sure you were up for your paper rounds and that you had clean uniform for school. I nagged and fussed and fended off the wolves and somehow got you through to adulthood. Through that difficult time back in 1986. But you being forty-seven doesn't mean I stop worrying.'

'I'm forty-six.'

'Whatever.' He takes out a handkerchief and gives his nose a blow so loud it reverberates off the rafters. He inspects the contents briefly before stuffing it back in his pocket. 'Are you going to tell me what's going on with work?'

'It's fine. Something and nothing. I have to go in for a meeting tomorrow.'

'A meeting?'

'Just to talk through health and safety procedures. You know what a minefield that can be.'

'A good reason if ever there was for Independence.'

'Dad, if you had your way, you'd be back in the People's Republic of Orkney.'

'Sounds fine to me.'

A young mother walks past us, babe in arms. For a moment her hair is lit up by the candlelight so it looks like her golden hair is a halo, like a Madonna. But she is wearing Ugg boots and a parka and the baby smells of sick. I suppose even the baby Jesus smelled of sick. And poo. How did they clean the nappies back then? It must have been one long hard slog having a baby. If you survived the birth. If you survived the Romans and the stoning and the Jewish Law.

'You can talk to me anytime you like, you know that.' He rests his hand on my leg. I feel this pressure and I realise Dad is trying to stop my leg from jigging so much.

'I'm seeing a counsellor.'

'A councillor or a counsellor?'

'A counsellor.'

'What type is that? The political one or the shrink one?'

'The shrink one.'

'So you're saying you have someone to talk to.'

'I have someone to talk to.'

'Okay. Well, can I just ask you one thing?'

'I suppose.'

'Are you gay?'

'Where did that come from?'

'I thought I'd ask. You might want to unburden yourself.'

'No, Dad. I'm not gay.'

'Because it's fine if you are.'

'I'm actually not.'

'Okay, well, if you're sure, let's get on our way. It's cold in here and my bones are aching. Time for a whisky.'

'I've got a bottle of Macallan at home.'

'Have you now? Well, we'd better be heading back then.'

It's at times like this, squeezing into the Peugeot, juddering out of the car park and taking on the A701 and A720, that I wish I could still drive. Or that I had a dram of that Macallan in a hip flask.

Maybe I am finally a *bona fide* Scot.

And by came an angel who had a bright key,
And he opened the coffins and set them all free;
William Blake, *Songs of Innocence*

Lancaster University, 1986

Limit

I hadn't counted on the breathalyser.

'Breathe into that, lad,' the copper said. And I looked at his whiskery face, wondering why the burly man in uniform was holding out a breathalyser. 'We ask everyone who's been driving and got in an accident. Especially one as serious as this. Your friend's injuries are life-threatening.'

'I had two drinks. That's all. Just two. That's the limit, isn't it?'

'This'll tell us if you're over it, lad.'

I breathed into the bag, watched with rising horror, panic; the policeman's face grew more hostile, his over-sized body stiffening.

'I'm arresting you…'

But I heard no more. I looked around for Tommo's dad but couldn't see him. And then I was sick again. Sick until there was nothing left inside me except an overwhelming confusion that made me unable to see or hear or think.

Scotching the Myths

For years the hidden closes of Old Town Edinburgh have been shrouded in myths and mysteries, with blood-curdling tales of ghosts and murders, and of plague victims being walled up and left to die. Now new research and archaeological evidence have revealed a truer story, rooted in fact and – as if so often the case – more fascinating than any amount of fiction.

The Real Mary King's Close Official Souvenir Guide

Edinburgh, December 2013
Stag

I put on a suit for the occasion. It's a good suit, dark blue with a pin stripe. Dad irons me a shirt. Then Sheena irons it again so I can actually wear it without embarrassment.*

'Do you want me to come with you, son?'

'No, Dad. I'll be okay. It's just a meeting.'

'Well, let me know how you get on.'

'I will. Don't worry.'

I leave him with Sheena at the sink and Barbara belting out Tell Me it's not True.

An hour to kill before my meeting. I take a wander in the Old Town, up the Royal Mile, the High Street, Castle Hill, past the dark narrow closes, Advocate's, Fleshmarket, Mary King's. Mum used to bring me here too when I was a kid. Back then it was all joss sticks and hippy stuff. Now it's kilts, T-shirts and tat. Tartan, tartan, tartan everywhere you look. The tourists love it, in and out the shops, trying on cashmere gloves and comedy hats, bathing in the history, treading the cobbles, criss-crossing the Heart of Midlothian. Paving

---

*There are obvious links with the trial of '86, I know that. Being a historian I make connections, I see parallels. I had a suit then. I have a suit now.

stones worn with years of treading feet, towering tenements of darkened granite. Ghosts, underground horrors and hidden streets. St Giles', the Mercat, the pubs, the jewellers, the tobacconists. And then up towards the castle, looming out of the volcanic rock of ages past, the seat of such history and turmoil. Blood, torture, imprisonment.

There's Braveheart with his blue face and the Wallace sword, entertaining the crowds for charity, a Japanese lassie wielding his weapon, posing for a photo. Where else can you go and be surrounded by such theatre? Here, in Edinburgh, you can step back in time and shake the hands of those who went before. The living and the dead have never been so close.

Edinburgh, city of contrasts. Jekyll and Hyde. *The Prime of Miss Jean Brodie* and *Trainspotting*. Old Town, New Town. Twenty-five year Speyside single malt fashioned from the crushed horns of unicorns. And Buckie tonic.

Up above the ground, and beneath it. Heaven and hell. But let's not forget everything in between.

'Take a seat, Cameron.' This is a woman I have never met. Human Resources Manager for Skeletours Inc. For we in Edinburgh are not the only keepers of ghosties and ghoulies. There are other tours, down in England: York, Bath, London, Winchester. Skeletours Inc. is big business. Ghosts are big business.

She shakes my hand, Fiona McCabe. She is Edinburgh. Posh. And then there's the other one, the Assistant Director, monkey to the organ grinder by any other name, (an organ grinder conspicuous by his lily-livered* absence).

The Assistant Director, Daniel Cooper, also shakes my hand, briefly, as if bad luck is contagious. He's a southerner with a voice like Ken Livingstone's, 'Estuary English', I believe they call it.

'Take a seat, Cameron,' he says. 'Can I get you a glass of water?'

---

*I'm not sure where I grappled this phrase from. But you get my drift.

I shake my head. I don't mean to appear rude, I just don't trust my voice to come out in a manly fashion. And for some reason, I want to at least sound manly while I am being unmanned.

'Right, well, thank you for coming.'

We take our seats, a table between us, them on one side, me on the other.

'This is how the meeting is going to be structured,' Fiona McCabe says. 'First I will read the letter from Mr Sanderson that states his version of events. Then you will be given the opportunity to give your version. Then we will discuss a way forward which may, if necessary, involve me outlining the range of possible sanctions available to us.'

I wait.

'Is that clear, Cameron?'

'Clear as day.'

Clear as the day when the haar creeps in from the North Sea and spreads through the town like the plague.

Fiona McCabe reads out the letter. The letter is peppered with priggish language, accusatory in tone. I latch on to the words but can't make sense of them. Words like 'imprisoned', 'asthma', 'traumatic', 'claustrophobia'. Phrases like 'I thought I was going to die', 'I thought I would go mad'. 'I think I must be an English poof.' (Not that last one. That is me reading between the lines.)

It was only ten minutes for goodness sake.

'Only ten minutes maybe, Cameron…' (*Did I say that out loud?*) '…but when you are in total darkness, in the cold, in a place associated with paranormal activity, it seems like much, much longer. Ten seconds could be a minute. Ten minutes could be an hour. Especially if you have asthma. Can you see his point of view, Cameron?' Daniel Cooper's voice has taken on a belligerent tone.

'Maybe now's the time to hear Cameron's statement,' Fiona McCabe says.

'Right, well…' I cough.

177

'Would you like that glass of water now, Cameron?'

'Thank you, Fiona. That would be lovely.'

Lovely, lovely, lovely.

I picture both of them without their clothes. Daniel Cooper has a six pack and a hairy back. Fiona McCabe has pale skin like moonlight and breasts that need a sports bra, even when not doing any kind of sport.

It doesn't help.

Fiona McCabe passes me the glass of water – Scotland's finest – and I take a gulp that goes down the wrong way. I start wheezing and have to produce my inhaler and have two puffs.

Asthma.

'You have asthma, Cameron. Then you'll know all about it,' Daniel Cooper says, a sly smile twitching his lips.

'Take your time, Cameron,' Fiona McCabe says.

I'd like to take my time elsewhere to be fair, but I take a deep breath instead, ignore the crackles, and plunge back into the darkness.

Preston, March 1986
Trial

I woke up that morning in the B&B, in a single bed, Edward an arm's reach away in another. A twin room with a kettle and teabags and mugs. Dad with Gavin next door, Andy down the corridor. If this were a holiday it would have been exciting. But this was no holiday.

I never really believed this day would actually come. I thought Tommo's megalomaniac of a father would pull it out of the bag, Paul Daniels and a fluffy bunny.

But no.

Back when I was first charged, when I was given bail, I still trusted Tommo's father. And when I'd returned to the family home in Edinburgh, seeing it once more with fresh eyes – the leaking roof, the rotten windows, the damp in my press, behind my bed, the whole place riddled with it; I felt it in my lungs, relied on my inhaler more than ever – I knew it would take a potful of money to put it right but the pot was empty. Then there were Andy's debts. He'd got in with a bad lot. They were clamouring, making threats. We were out of our depth.

But I could make it all right. I could save my family. I just had to get through this and then we'd be back to normal. I'd transfer my degree, go to a poly somewhere. And, as Tommo's father reminded me, as if I needed reminding, I was of course doing this for Bex. To make her happy.

(Love is patient. Love is kind. Love is not selfish.)

I had to believe that. I had to stick to the plan. I had to save the day.

It was too late to save Christie. She was never going to be the same. But that was not my fault. That fault belonged to Tommo.

Edward was first to get up, made us both a brew and we sat in our beds like bairns in our pyjamas, supping and slurping and blethering about nothing, everything except what we should be blethering about, waiting for Dad to call for us so we could go down together to a greasy breakfast that I knew my stomach would never manage.

And now this day had come. And here I was in court. Preston Crown Court with my family who'd never come en masse to see me in anything before; no school concerts; no sports days; that was my mother's job.

They were all here now in their Sunday best, a rogues' gallery. But it wasn't the son that you would expect to see standing in the dock. It was the quiet one. The studious one. The university one. The guilty one.

Be proud of who you are.

'You look nice,' I'd said earlier when I caught her briefly on the steps outside.

'Me? Oh, I got this in Oxfam,' Bex said.

'This' was a dark suit. She'd be able to use it in court for her clients in the future. She'd have to attend hearings and trials over her career as a social worker. She'd already transferred course, to Manchester, taking Tommo with her, a one-bedroom flat in Salford. He was odd-jobbing, aimless, in limbo till this was over.

We were all in limbo till this was over.

'You look nice too,' she said.

'Tommo's dad bought the suit.'

'Oh,' she said. 'Right.' And then she went on to tell me how she'd come with Tommo, in the back of his father's car. His father sat up front in the passenger seat, she said. He had a driver, which was frankly ridiculous when there was so much poverty around, she said. At least the driver had a job, she said.

She made her excuses soon after and I watched her walk away wondering if this might be the last time I saw her.

As for Tommo, where was he? It wasn't him in the dock, waiting for sentencing. It was me, Cameron Spark, who'd admitted to being the bad boy, to driving under the influence. Not my illustrious companion, Ptolemy Dulac.

It was a terrible thing we were doing. Perjury. We could all get sent to prison for that. But we'd agreed; there was no going back. It would work out. I'd get away with a driving ban, a suspended sentence at the very most. I'd been given the best barrister there was. A QC. I was pleading guilty. I had a clean slate. I was a good lad from a good home. I was very sorry for what I had done.

Only this wasn't the straightforward swap of identity we thought it was going to be. In the hospital after Tommo's father left, the policeman came in with his size elevens. And I, in my confusion, in my horror, in my bid to do something heroic, I knew I had to see this through, even though I knew the odds had changed.

It was over all too quickly. The QC did his bit, said that Christie was recovering well in Canada, that she was adjusting to her new life. The Judge retired to read through the statements and the reports. Tommo and Bex had both written to say that without 'my' quick reactions, we could all have died. It was 'me' swerving in the nick of time that got us out of the path of the white van. But unfortunately the white van was never found. Unfortunately I was over the limit and driving a car without insurance. Unfortunately the Judge wanted to make an example of me. The drink drive campaign was being

181

enforced by the mighty hand of the Law. They were clamping down. Justice would be done.

Think you can drink and drive? Think again.

I had to wait down below in the court cell. I had to wait to be called back up. And I had to wait and listen to this old man in red inform me that I had a six-month custodial sentence. I had to go back down to that cell and hear my QC tell me that I'd only have to serve three months if I kept my head down. I had to answer the questions of a probation officer who looked more scared than me. Her one piece of advice: *If they offer you food, take it – you might have a long wait else.*

Then I was on my own, no idea what was happening, until they took me away in a windowless van to a hell I had no idea existed.

There was nothing anyone could have done to avoid an accident. The van was driving right at us. We could have ploughed into it, or we could have swerved. Tommo swerved. Maybe if he'd been sober he would have controlled the swerve. Maybe if Christie had been driving she'd have done better. But it's highly unlikely. Tommo probably saved our lives.

Thanks to 'my' driving it was a miracle we had all walked away. With the exception of Christie of course. Who was carried away from that dark, wet field, the bottom half of her leg left in Hyper's crushed Cortina where they'd had to amputate it in order to save her life.

What had they done with it? What happens to a limb? I still feel sick at the thought of this. Don't know how Christie could cope. Always wished I could go and see her but I wasn't allowed. I'd accepted the money from Tommo's father. I'd given it to Dad to pay off the debts, to stop the bad people from cutting off Andy's legs. I had to roll with it.

One act of recklessness, one ill-formed decision, can echo down the years. *Boom. Boom. Boom.* But how are you to know if that really was the wrong decision? Do you know at the time? Do you know with hindsight? Do you ever know?

The oven is hot but you touch it anyway. And you get burnt.

Oh what a tangled web we weave,
When first we practise to deceive!
Sir Walter Scott, *Marmion*

C/o HM Prison Preston, March 1986
Time

I was taken to a holding prison.* I hoped I would be moved on to Scotland, but I wasn't. It was a different system. I thought I might get taken to a Young Offenders, but I didn't. There were no spaces. I had to work it out as I went along, watching carefully, listening discreetly, biding my time. I had to act like I knew what I was doing. This was one of the hardest parts to play, being a dyspraxic, nineteen-year-old in a big man's world.

I was put into a cell with Stephen, who used to be a vicar till he was unfrocked for robbing a bishop of his silver. He spent most of his time reading the Bible. He wasn't interested in talking. He would stare at me with blank eyes so I wondered if I was really there or if this was all a nightmare I would wake up from.

Jeremy says that going to prison is a traumatic ordeal that needs to be dealt with. He says I should write down my memories but believe me when I say I have suppressed most of them. What I do know is that I tried to treat prison like it was a school residential. There were good kids and bad kids. Victims and bullies. Dark and sometimes a glimmer of light.

---

*Not Lancaster prison like the Jacobites in 1715, but down the road at Preston.

But within that structure and rhythm there was an unpredictability. Nothing was quite as you would expect.

I didn't expect there to be female officers. I didn't expect there to be someone like Rose. She was Irish and buxom but you wouldn't mess with her, the same way you wouldn't mess with your mum. She worked nights and always made five minutes to check up on me, said I reminded her of her son and I wished I could swap places with him. But I had swapped places with Tommo.

Rose encouraged me to read. She said I needed to spend my time learning something and you can always learn from books, be it biographies, history, fiction.

'Have you read this, Cameron?'

She handed me a book. *The Diary of a Nobody*. I wasn't sure if she was being funny.

'You remind me a bit of Pooter,' she said.

I read the book. Pooter is a prat. He has little self-awareness. Was I really like him?

'Am I really like him?' I asked her.

'Don't be offended,' she said. 'He's the sort of bloke you want to gun for.'

'A victim?'

'No, just your average bloke, trying his best but somehow making a cock-up.'

'Is that me?'

'Partly, yes. You're also part Adrian Mole.'

'Oh.'

'You have a good heart. Love goes a long way to making things better.'

I wanted her to hug me to her bosom but of course she didn't. But she gave me a smile and I felt I could do this, one book at a time.

Don't get me wrong, prison is *not* a holiday camp. It is *not* the army. It is *not* a school residential. But there are elements the same. The structure, the routine, the sense of having no control over the course of the day. The rules. The rule-breaking. The good kids. The bad kids. Victims and bullies. Dark and sometimes a glimmer of light.

Years later, I read that Rose had been stabbed by a prisoner. She survived but had to retire early. What sort of man would stab a woman in the back? I wanted to hunt him down. Hunt him down and rip out his heart with my bare hands and feed it to the neighbourhood dogs.

My first visit was from my dad. He put on that big man brave smile of his and talked nine to the dozen about the outside, which might just as well have been the moon. It was very hard to imagine life going on out there without me but it obviously was.

'You didn't have to go through with this, son,' he said. 'I'll make sure Andy makes it up to you.'

Sure enough, a couple of weeks later, I got a letter from Andy.

```
Dear Cameron
I hope you are doing okay. I feel awful bad
for putting you through this. I'm pretty
sure you've saved my life. Literally.
There are some bad people out there. Which
is stupid of me to say because there will
be bad people where you are.
Keep your head down, little brother.
You'll soon be back and I will show you
how my life is on track now.
I have a new job at the brewery. Dad is
keeping an eye on me. Tougher than any
prison guard!
Keep smiling. Don't let the bastards grind
you down.
Your favourite brother
Andy
```

He wasn't my favourite brother. That title goes to Edward despite having to put up with his bad habits in our shared bedroom over the years. I knew Edward the best. I told Dad I didn't want Edward visiting because I couldn't bear to see him go away again without me. I couldn't bear to think that I had to spend night after night with the unfrocked vicar while Edward had to stare at my empty bed.*

Then it was Tommo's turn. He looked sheepish as he walked in, treading carefully past the other tables, the tattoos and the vests, the growling voices, the officers standing close by, rigid and vigilant.

They'll kill him in prison, Bex had said. And yes, they would certainly have given him a harder time than they gave me. I have the ability to disappear. I have an invisibility cloak as my disguise. I can slip between the cracks, walk through walls. Though I have a tendency to fall over and sprain my ankle, to bash my head against door frames. Half-man-half-ghost. Nurd-boy-turd-boy Cameron Spark.

As he sat opposite me, a wretched look on his face, a depleted quiff, mascara-less, I felt sorry for him. I felt power course through me. This time I had won.

And then Bex. She looked less scared than Tommo. More sad than anything else.

'I'm so sorry, Cameron,' she said.

I wanted to hold her hand. I wanted to talk to her. But I sat there, arms folded, a man of few words. I made her do all the work, only giving her the odd glib comment. She asked me about a bruise. I said I fell over in the showers. I actually did fall over in the showers. I'm dyspraxic. It's what I do. I fall over, I trip over, I walk into walls.

I'm not sure she believed me. She knew a thing or two

---

*They were all still living at home, my brothers. Edward was just fourteen months older than me. Gavin two years older, and Andy another two. We all left eventually, only now I'm back.

about prisons. But I assured her I was fine. I'd be out in no time. I told her to get on with her new course, to concentrate on her new life, and not worry about me.

She smiled, relieved. She'd been let off the hook. She left quietly, without fuss, without looking back at me.

And later, when I poured my heart out to Rose, she hugged me to her bosom.

Edinburgh, December 2013
Incident

I was late for work on the day concerned. I'd had an argument with Amanda. The worst we'd ever had. To be fair, we didn't usually argue. I'd keep quiet, Amanda would sulk and normally by the time we went to bed, we would have made up. Never go to sleep on an argument is what all the relationship advice says. Well, the night before the incident, we turned our backs on each other. Amanda was soon asleep. Either that or she was making a good pretence of being asleep. I lay there in the dark, wide awake, as if I'd had ten espressos with Red Bull chasers. By the time morning came we'd slept through the alarm clock and were grouchy with each other from the off.

She stamped around the kitchen, banging cupboard doors and clashing plates. I hovered on the edge not sure whether to say anything or keep my silence.

Finally she shouted at me: 'WHY ARE YOU ALWAYS SO BLOODY QUIET! SPEAK TO ME!'

'What do you want me to say?'

'It's not about what I want, is it Cameron. It's about what you want. And you don't want a baby, that much is clear.'

'There's still plenty of time for a baby.'

'You're forty-seven.'

'I'm forty-six.'

'Whatever. I'm thirty-eight so we need to do this now.'

'I don't like being pushed into a corner.'

And then she said it.

'You would do this if you loved me.'

'I do love you.'

'Love's not just about words. It's about actions.'

'I fail to see how this will show you I love you. This has nothing to do with my love for you.'

'What are you frightened of, Cameron?'

'I'm frightened of a lot of things.'

'Are you frightened of being happy? Is that it?'

'Don't be ridiculous.'

I was empty, she said. I had nothing to give her, she said. Not even a baby, she said.

And then she left, slamming the front door and heading off to work in a fury of Amanda-ness. I almost felt like calling in sick but I knew I couldn't because there were already two of the tour guides off with impetigo.*

So I got myself ready and went to work.

It was a busy day. A group of school kids. A group of Americans. Various families. Courting couples who used the dark vaults for the odd grope and stolen touch. Charlene, our Kiwi, was busy. She loved it. The groups loved her. She is pretty with a huge sense of fun. But tiny-boned like a bird. When it came to the last tour of the day, I had a bad feeling. I suspect I should have listened to my feelings but then what could I have done? *That's all folks! The tour's off!* That wouldn't have gone down too well. I thought it best to get on with it. They weren't drunk, just loud and excitable. I gave the health and safety drill.

No wandering off. No lagging behind. You do *not* want to be lost in the vaults.

---

*A nasty contagious skin infection that made them look too much like pustule-inflicted plague victims.

Mind your heids. Mind your step. The ceilings are low, the floor uneven.

Inform me if you get panicky at any point and I'll radio up for assistance.

Et cetera.

I didn't tell Fiona McCabe and Daniel Cooper this version of events, which is the full, uncut version. It is none of their business what goes on in my home life. This is a work matter. And yes, I was tired and annoyed and wound up and that might have impacted on my decision-making that day underground. But believe me when I say I still don't know what else I could have done.

Edinburgh to London, Friday
Train

Waverley station. The 10.30 to London Kings Cross. A window seat next to some fat English suit with *The Times*. I will ignore him and read my *Scotsman*. I will ignore him and be normal, a normal passenger going on a normal trip to London. I will suspend myself in time, for a while, leaving the past in the past. Because that's where the past is supposed to be. In the past. Only it's not, is it? It's always with you, like a persistent terrier. Like a barking, fat dachshund. But sometimes I want to take that barking, fat dachshund by the scruff of the neck and throttle it. Or put the electric collar up on full blast.

```
The fat man reads The Times.
I read The Scotsman.
```

I am on the perilous journey to the buffet car when my phone starts to ring. I make it to the end of the carriage and answer outside the toilet.

'Cameron?' A woman's voice.

I was hoping for Amanda.

I was hoping for Bex.

I get Fiona McCabe and the news that I no longer have a job.

'It was only ten minutes,' I say. But it makes no difference.

```
I have lost my home.
I have lost my wife.
I have lost my job.
```

And why have I lost my job? Ten seconds can seem like ten minutes, Fiona McCabe said. Ten minutes can feel endless, Fiona McCabe said. When you are shut away in the dark, the cold, frightened, abandoned and, for all you know, left for dead, Fiona McCabe said.

I dash in the toilet. Sit down on the seat. Think back. Was it so wrong, what I did?

When we got to the underground room where the most paranormal activity goes on, I told them the story of a little boy called Samuel Macbeth. A little orphan boy who was all alone when he was left to die of the plague. I got the group to imagine what it must have been like and the man, Mr Sanderson, made a stupid comment. He said he'd like to shut his wife in there when she's in one of her moods. Stop her going out and spending on his Platinum credit card.

'It's not a joking matter,' I said. I know I sounded school-teachery, but he shouldn't have been making light of such a tragedy. He had no idea what it was like to be shut away. And then there were the two girls who'd joined the group at the last minute. The students. Mr Sanderson said he'd like to be locked away with the two of them.

It was at this point that I had to intervene. The atmosphere was menacing, threatening, and I was worried for the safety of the group, particularly the two young women who suddenly seemed vulnerable. I maybe should've radioed up for help but there was only Charlene available and Mr Sanderson could have caused all kinds of trouble. So I pretended to carry on as normal, shepherding them out to the next vault, where there was a slideshow projected onto a wall. I turned the soundtrack up high. As they assembled themselves onto benches to watch it, I beckoned him. I thought he'd ignore me, but he came over and I whispered to him. Not one of his friends saw, I made sure of that. Then I walked back the few steps we had just come. He followed me, expectantly, a little unsteady on his feet. And then I took my chance. I pushed him inside Samuel Macbeth's room. I shut the door and I locked him in. I locked him up. The arrogant, preening, sexist, racist and most probably homophobic prick of an Englishman.

And you know the most gratifying thing? Not one of his friends noticed.

Back in my seat, a can and a packet of crisps, living up to my Scottish heritage, wedged up against the window, I have to put up with the fat suit and his phone calls. Ten minutes can feel endless when you are imprisoned. I have another three hours to go. Back in the day, I had to endure three months. But I was shaped more and learnt more in those three months inside than I would've been and done during three years of university.

How were you shaped? What did you learn? Questions Jeremy has asked me. Questions I have asked myself.

Answer: It toughened me. It made me focus. It made me think.

Think you can drink and drive? Think again. This was the advertising campaign that was targeting students, that was partly responsible for landing me in jail.

But you can't always blame other people, Jeremy says. *You made a choice. And it could have been far worse. Christie was badly injured. She lost a leg. Her family could've got involved, tried for compensation.*

As if I had never considered this.

Her family kept right out of it. They took Christie back to Canada never to be heard of again. Until now.

And now I'm going to see her again. And Bex. And Tommo.

Are you sure this is a good idea? Jeremy asks.

I watch the spectre of my reflection in the window. Can't

believe I'm that same boy who went to Lancaster and made such friends. The boy in the kilt. The young man who went to prison and came out the other side with money. Saw his dad all right. Helped out his brothers. Paid off that bad debt. Paid the price for love.

But I don't know what happened to that leg.

Still an hour and a half to go. I could get off and catch the return train, the sleeper. I have lost my job and my wife and I need to do something about it. Not be going to a stupid, self-destructing reunion with people I am never supposed to see again. Why did they agree to this? Why did I agree to this? Why the hell did Christie invite us?

An hour and a half and I'll have to do battle with the Underground and find my way to the Ritz. Christie's paying for the room. I graciously accepted. A good night's sleep will help me face my past. I don't know what to expect. I might have paid for that accident with my freedom but Christie doesn't know that, does she? She doesn't know that I took Tommo's place. I've read the interview in the *Observer*, she says she can't remember. She says she was surprised it was me driving. She says she was surprised that I was over the limit as I wasn't much of a drinker.

I only agreed to say I was driving because Tommo's father said it would be fine. His calm authority, his voice, his words that sounded so different to my own father's. I was reassured on a night when everything was unsure. I wanted it all to go away. I had a cold. I felt rough, bewildered, shaken up. My head ached, my ribs hurt, my lungs burned and I wanted it all over. So I said, Yes, aye, I'd do it. And in return I'd save the day for everyone I loved.

I was compensated, fobbed off with even more money once I was breathalysed, because obviously they didn't want me changing my statement. But it was me, Cameron Spark, who took the blame, who went to court, who bore the brunt of a guilty verdict that should have gone to another man. It was me who went to prison and did the time that belonged to someone else. And Ptolemy Dulac walked away, out of my life, taking the woman I loved with him and injuring the other one, leaving a trail of hurt, deception and blood money.

Time in prison wasn't what I had in mind when I agreed to the plan. I really believed I'd only had two drinks, that I was fine to drive. But it turned out I'd had more. I can't remember it. What I can remember is Tommo calling me a poof. Tommo up and down to the bar. Bex morose with the old collie by the fire. Dave and Hyper and Carl quiet and sullen. Christie impatient and snappy, looking over her shoulder at that lecturer.

What I remember is Tommo going up yet again to the bar and ordering a round. I remember going to the loo, coming back and drinking my orange juice. I remember smarting at its bitterness, though I had a cold and everything tasted bad so I drank it all, thinking the vitamin C would do me good. But most clearly of all, I remember Tommo watching me and winking, his dark eyes mischievous. I wondered briefly what Tommo was up to but was too tired to really care. I just wanted the whole sorry day to be over and done with.

But I didn't know then that it would never be over and done with. The night would go on and on. It continues now, away through Scotland, across the border, southwards, southwards, through cities and fields, all the way down to London.

All I have left is my past. That is mine alone and no one can take that away from me. No court, no judge or jury, no Tory government, no assistant directors, no HR managers. No Tommo.

But they can take away my job. They can take away my wife. They can take away my freedom.

One Step Forward for Womankind.
Christie Armstrong is CEO of one of Canada's biggest wine producers, the Armstrong King Estates in the fertile Niagara region of Ontario. She is also the Founder and Honorary President of Happy Walk, a charity for children who have lost limbs – a cause that she knows about first hand after an accident led to her losing a leg nearly 30 years ago. Here, in this exclusive first interview, she talks about her life as one of Canada's most promising business-women, and the accident that nearly stopped all that from happening.
Interview by Hattie Woodman
Photographs by Nestor Williams
The Guardian

Christie Armstrong is on the phone. It's clamped to her ear as she beckons me into her suite at the Ritz and points towards a sofa opposite where she's sitting. She finishes the call and immediately apologises profusely, telling me that it was a 'really important call with a buyer from a UK supermarket whose demographic perfectly fits the market I'm trying to reach for with our Icewine. Man, it would be great if we can get it on their shelves.'

When she starts to explain to this non-connoisseur what

Icewine is, she quickly realises that talk of optimum harvest temperature, sugars and vine management is falling on deaf ears and laughs, saying, 'I'll quit the hard sell, just taste it.' The secret to Icewine is apparently the few seconds when the drinker moves the liquid around their mouth before swallowing, allowing waves of flavour. And she's right, the taste is absolutely exquisite. I can see why it's known as 'Niagara liquid gold'.

'Why have I never tasted anything like this before?' I ask her. She laughs even louder. 'Because until now, it's been Canada's little secret. We keep it for ourselves! But that's all going to change after our product launch the day after tomorrow and with luck, the British market will like it as much as you.'

I suggest it must all seem a long way from the last time she was in the UK, some 28 years ago as a 'Junior Year Abroad' student at Lancaster University studying for a Marketing degree.

'Yeah, I was really keen to travel and though I looked at California and New York, I wound up in rainy Lancashire as a JYA and until the accident, I loved every single minute of it.'

She tells me that she doesn't think about the car crash very often. Her memories are still extremely hazy from that time. Amnesia from the trauma. She's never been able to piece together the events of that night back in 1986 when she lost a leg. All she can clutch at are flashes of scenes. A trip back from London with her student friends. A convoy. A van and a car. A stop-off at a village. A log fire in the pub. Her friend stroking a dog's ears. Another friend buying drinks at the bar. A cold, dark night.

She can't even remember getting in the car that she was later cut out of.

She returned home, just two weeks later to recover and convalesce and was shocked when she heard which of her student friends was the driver. Blown away when she later found out about the drink-drive conviction that landed him in prison. Stunned that she'd lost half a leg and broken half her bones. And knowing that her friend – who she'd thought of as the solid and dependable member of their group – was responsible, did not help at all.

'The whole thing sucked. My life was ruined – at least I thought so at the time – and his was too.'

But time passed.

Her dad never totally got her decision to come to Britain as a student – or now for that matter – but he let her do it. He remained positive all along. Got her straight home to Canada. Found the best doctors, the best hospital, the best of everything to put her back together.

'My Dad was a rock and never, even after the accident, blamed me for getting in a beat-up car with a guy who'd been drinking. I've been through therapy, heaps of expensive therapy, to train my brain, to keep positive. I've been through my quota of doctors and nurses and chiropractors and pretty much all of the medical profession. I've also been through many, many legs, from the ugly ones back in the day to the most recent commissions, crafted by artists rather than engineers, with matched skin tone, hair follicles, perfect nails. One for heels, one for flats, one for skiing, one for sports. I can do whatever a two-legged woman can do.'

Her ex-husband Pete was cool with it from the outset, she says. 'I told him about the accident on our second date, even hitched up my skirt to show off the prosthetic. He said it was awesome, asked to touch it. So I let him and things progressed quickly from there.' She lets out one of those trademark laughs at the memory.

They got married and had a daughter, Mallory in 2006. But the marriage failed in 2011. 'Pete couldn't handle me working such long hours, being away from home so much. He got bored. Found someone else to keep him company.' She shrugs and you wonder what kind of man would want to leave a woman this sparky and clever.

'And how are you now, after the accident?' I ask her.

'Sometimes, even after all these years, I can still feel it, my lost leg. It's like I'm still whole, still complete. In my mind, I can run across prairies, climb up mountains, swim the great lakes, skate like a pro, quick step like Ginger Rogers. All with my own two legs. No pain, no wound, no scar. No stump.

'Sometimes it aches. It itches so I want to scratch it. It gets pins and needles. When I wake up, stiff and tingling, I have to remind myself what happened. And those same flashes of scenes replay themselves, jumbled up and reordered so I can never hold onto what happened that night.

'But, hey, I've done pretty well. I live a full life. Career, husband, child, home. Okay, so the husband thing didn't work out so good but hell, I tried. I guess I was so grateful that someone wanted me. That someone could look beyond my face and hair and boobs. Someone wanted all of me, even the ghost of my leg. I felt desirable and loved and wanted.'

When she discovered she was pregnant she was overjoyed, couldn't believe her luck. She worried all the way through those long months of waiting. She got large. The baby kicked. She told herself again and again, it will be okay. And then her mother got ill. Breast cancer. Spread to her bones. And she was gone just days before Mallory arrived.

'I thought someone had taken an ice pick to my heart, hacking out the part my mom filled. But when I held Mallory in my arms and saw that squished, flaky-skinned face, I knew I had something to fight for that was really worth it.

'Besides, when you've been lying under a heap of mangled metal, blood leaking from your crushed body, barely able to take a breath in or to push a breath out, when you've lain all alone on a cold, frosty night, in a field in the middle of nowhere, in a country far from home, thinking your time has come, when you lay there and no longer care what happens except that this pain of living is too much and you want it taken away... when you survive that, you know you can survive anything. But I miss my mom everyday.'

As for the husband, he faded, blurred into the background. She didn't even overly care when she discovered the affair 'with a freaking cheerleader'. With two perfect legs.

'I don't want people feeling sorry for me, thinking, Poor Christie, she'll never get another man. I don't need another man. I have my daughter. I have my dear old dad. I have the winery, signed over to me on my fortieth birthday. And I am damn well going to make it the best winery in Canada, up there with the estates of Bordeaux, Champagne, Napa Valley, Marlborough Bay and Stellenbosch.'

And she has the jewel. The Icewine.

'The wine choice in England sucked back in the 80s. And though it's much improved now, they don't have Canadian wine. I'm going to change all that.'

Equally important to her is her charity 'Happy Feet', which she set up three years ago.

'I'd been so busy with the winery – learning everything I possibly could from Dad and totally immersing myself in the business – that when Pete left, I realised that I had to do something more than just be Christie the obsessive business-woman. I was watching a news report about child soldiers in Africa and how so many of them had lost limbs as a result of war and the next day I set about creating Happy Feet. We work with kids in both Canada and the developing world to provide prosthetics for children who otherwise might not be able to have the kind of high-quality support that I rely on. I love my winery but I get a special kick out of seeing the difference the charity makes to so many young lives.'

At this point, a maid asks if she can get us tea or coffee.

'I'll take a coffee, please. And would you mind getting my leg for me. It's over on that chair. I have to go to the washroom.'

I wonder if the poor woman is about to freak, but to give her credit, she quickly recovers, fixes her smile and picks up the prosthetic.

'And don't drop it,' Christie says. 'It's worth 25,000 bucks.'

As I leave, I try once more to squeeze out of Christie

which supermarket she was talking to and she laughs that huge laugh and says 'Not even off the record, but trust me, you'll hear me shouting about it from Niagara when I sign that deal.'

And I've no doubt that I will.

Puttin' on the Ritz
Irving Berlin, 1927

London, Friday Evening
Cocktail

I put on the pinstripe suit, straighten my silk tie in the plush en-suite. I'm hoping the mirror will reflect back Sean Connery. But I look more like John Craven. With a perm. Tommo never did manage to trendy me up.

Amanda tried. I was her special project. I'm not entirely sure why she chose me as her special project. Maybe she had the end in sight, could visualise the finished article: husband, home, baby. Security. After all, ghosts are more permanent than actors. She said she'd had her fair share of actors.

Amanda was an actor herself, a 'resting' actor with a few years too many out of drama school and a need to do something off her own back, rather than sponging off her parents for ever. She became a tour guide. I became her manager. She did all the chasing. I was flattered. I let her.

We all went out for our usual monthly curry. She sat next to me and ordered chicken korma and a Cobra beer and before the night was out I'd had both my thigh and shoulder squeezed. If I hadn't restrained her she'd have played my bagpipe. The next time we went out – just the two of us to the Italian – she was more persistent. I was well on the way to being her special project.

But here I am on my own, my double-bed-in-a-suite-at-the-Ritz completely wasted, the project spectacularly dismantled. I should be running to catch a northern-bound train. I should be hunting down Amanda in her mother's frilly house. I should be rescuing her from that fossilised pony bedroom. I shouldn't be here, on the verge of walking into my past. I shouldn't.

I brush my teeth. Floss. Listerine. I need a drink. A glass of white wine. I have no valuables to hide away in the safe so I just leave the room with the Do Not Disturb sign on the door handle. Down in the lift. Into the huge hallway of chandeliers, palms and gilt. The high tea is over, the touristy queues diminished. It is hushed and orderly, all neo-classical bling and Louis XVI opulence.

In the bar, I order a large Pinot Grigio and find a table. The wine has that weird taste you get after brushing your teeth but it's a welcome feeling, the alcohol slipping down my throat. I'm a wee bit calmer, more stoical. Tomorrow might be a risk but what do I have to lose?

Another gulp because now I've spotted her.

Bex?

No, not Bex, far too young, but she's the spit.

And there she is, Bex herself, tall and slim still, hair shorter, lighter, caught back in a thick pony tail, the colour of a fox brush.

Bex.

I feel queasy, drinking on an empty stomach, caught unawares. But I should've known she'd be here tonight, which is maybe why I put on a suit, to impress her. As if that would impress her. And why would I want to impress her?

More wine. A deep breath. I shut my eyes and count to ten.

… seven… eight…

'Cameron Spark.'

I open my eyes.

Tight black trousers and a leather jacket. Skinny as ever.

'Tommo.' I stand up, try to put on my happy face but my

mouth is too full of teeth and tongue.

He shakes my hand. His nails are short and jagged, his grip tight. Tommo points towards a table on the far side of the room. 'There's Rebecca. With our twins, Ethan and Loulou. Come over, bring your drink.'

'Okay then. For a wee bit. I've got to meet someone soon.'

'Oh right, well, you've got time for another drink, haven't you?'

'Just the one.'

'Don't go getting all gloomy and nostalgic, now, will you. We've got all weekend to do that.'

'We have, aye.'

I follow Tommo to the table, with each step my chest constricting, my stomach contracting. I am teetering on the edge of passing out or vomiting. Teetering on the edge of the world.

But now I'm pecking Bex – Rebecca – on the cheek, breathing in her fresh smell, wisps of hair stroking my cheek and I am eighteen years old again, my future ahead of me, instead of behind. What twenty-plus years can do to a man.

I sit down, can't look her in the eye, try to concentrate as I'm introduced to their kids, my heart working overtime.

The boy's sort of like his father, the girl completely like her mother, (though with far too much make-up and a very short skirt).*

'What are you drinking?' Tommo's on his feet, reaching for my glass.

'Pinot.'

'Right, I'll get this round in.'

'No, let me. I insist.' I'm on my feet too, no idea why this need to insist but it's somehow important. I take the orders and go to the barman. At these shocking prices he can bring our drinks over. A Coke is £6 and a glass of Pinot £15. Tommo, Bex and the lassie – who easily passes for eighteen

---

*Why does Bex let her dress like that? What do I know about parenting? I want a baby, Cameron. With or without you.

– have requested Manhattans at nearly £20 a knock. But I do my best to make this seem normal, I'm used to such prices, such places. Life is good.

The next ten minutes pass by excruciatingly slowly. (Ten minutes can seem endless.) While I want to be here, with Bex, I want to ask questions, to delve into their lives, but I can't ask. All I can do is pick over the scraps. All these years and I can't say the words that have followed me round since that night in 1986. Words that have pestered and bullied and harassed me however hard I have tried to flatten and squash them.

I'm not ready for this.

I make my excuses, I have to meet this (imaginary) friend, not sure they believe me, but I need to get away.

'Have a good evening.' Bex stands up, kisses me on the check again. 'We'll see you tomorrow.' She smiles and a stab of misery cuts into me, shreds my heart all over again. I miss her. I miss my friend.

Tommo holds out his hand and my arm is heavy as I reach to shake it, like I've been lying on it awkwardly. Tommo smiles, that familiar smile, a hint of jest in his eyes.

I won't play along. I won't.

'See you tomorrow.' I nod at the twins. The lad carries on drinking his Coke but the lassie, she stops mid-text, grins, gives one of those half-hearted half-waves. And I turn and walk away, aware that I am being watched with curiosity by this family, trying my very best not to crash into the tables or trip over the chairs.

I pace the streets, up and down Piccadilly, a blur of Christmas lights, tourists, posh people. Past a huge Waterstones, the Royal Academy, Fortnum and Mason's. Shopping, shopping. Money, money. Spatters of rain so I duck into an Italian where I order a pizza and a Peroni. I'm not the only person eating alone, not the only saddo in the room. And I have a copy of the *Evening Standard*, which assures me that I live in the better of the two capitals.

I'm halfway through my tiramisu when I spot them walking past. (How could I not spot them? A double vision of Bexness, a double whammy of Tommo.) Fortunately I am not seated in the window, so they don't see me. Or at least I don't think so. Maybe just the lassie, lagging behind in her killer heels. She might've recognised me but I think I ducked behind the menu in time. She might've waved at me. In which case I probably should've waved back. But I'm hideously aware of being alone. If she saw me then she'd know I lied about having to meet someone. I don't want to come across as a saddo, or worse, a liar. Why didn't I wave back, embrace the situation? My dining companion could've been in the loo. He or she could've left to catch a train home. They could've blown me out. But instead, I pretend not to see her, like when you play hide and seek as a child and you close your eyes believing it will make you invisible.

I see Peter. I see Jane.
I see Loulou standing in the rain.

Rain, rain, go away. Come again another day. I hurry back to the hotel as fast as I can, waddling like one of those long-distance racewalkers, no umbrella, my soggy *Evening Standard* offering meagre protection.

Back in my room, I strip off, and get in the shower, embracing the hot, powerful water. I shut my eyes tight to squeeze out the memories brewing in my brain. Sometimes I could cry. Sometimes I actually do cry. Over stupid things, small things, trivial, tiny, miniscule things.

I never cried in prison. Not once. I knew if I let that happen, I would never stop and I would never survive. So I took everything that was dear to me, my friendship, my family, my pride, my memories, and I locked them up in a secret, secure place until I was released. Only, when I was released, when I returned home to my brothers and my dad, I couldn't open that place. I didn't have the strength.

210

I didn't look back. I didn't hanker after the past (my personal past – history was still my bag. My tartan bag). I craved the ordinary, everyday things. A long, hot bath. A home-cooked meal. *Countdown*. The only excitement I craved was the whisper of a ghost in the underground world of Edinburgh.

Life, on the whole, is boring. And boring is under-rated. If the stove is hot, and you feel you must touch it, wear oven gloves, because once you lose your safety, you realise that is all you crave. A shame Amanda never got that. She's one for risks. A flutter on the Grand National. A trip to Mecca Bingo. A last-minute getaway that's not been tried and tested on Trip Advisor. *I want a baby, Cameron.*

I turn off the shower and step out onto the bathmat, rub myself down, thoroughly, carefully, between every toe and in every crevice. If Amanda were here, the walls and mirrors would be steamed up, the floor deluged with a sea of soapy water and leg shavings.

Into bed in my tartan PJs, a bathrobe, a cup of tea and a biscuit. Shortbread. I shuffle under the sheets, relish the clean crispness of them, and turn on the television to catch up with the day's news, check the weather, mute it and open the hefty biography (Ramsay MacDonald), leant to me by my father (Andrew Spark).

Clean sheets. There was a time when I envisaged my wife changing the sheets, but Amanda soon put me right. She divvied up the chores and even though I'd grown up in an all-male household and was used to doing my fair share, I harboured this hope that someone might do those things for me, like my mother used to.

I can barely remember her now. (My mother, not Amanda. I remember everything about Amanda from her shell-pink toenails to the flag of St George tattooed on one smooth arse-cheek.)

The book. The biog. The words are black blobs on a white page, my mind far too jittery to make sentences out of them, mainly jittering towards tomorrow night, seeing Bex and Tommo again. Seeing Christie.

I let Ramsay MacDonald rest on my chest, heavy as a tombstone.

I got into biographies in prison. Mainly sports personalities, stories of overcoming adversity and training hard in the early morning, blah blah blah, and even though I hated sport, was always one of the last to be picked at school for football, swimming, whatever, I enjoyed reading about these ordinary people achieving great things in their field. (Though I still identified myself with the fictional Pooter. Thank you, Rose.)

I didn't think I'd ever achieve anything. But I survived prison. I came out (of prison, not the closet, thank you, Dad) and I got a job. I stopped my brother losing his legs, which partly made up for Christie losing one of hers.

I open the book again. The same paragraph. But I am back in the university library with Christie, me huddled against the radiator, Canadian Christie bare-armed in a Lancaster University T-shirt. I can remember the actual conversation, word for word, a memory so vivid I can't believe how old it actually is.

'You're going to manage the band?' I asked, bewildered. 'Why would you agree to do that job?'

'*I* didn't agree. I told them and *they* agreed.'

I laughed, quietly, as we were in the reference library, a pile of unopened books spread out on the table between us.

'Now I'm injured, I thought I might as well try something new. Despite what Tommo says, we Canadians do know something about business. And this is a business, like any other. And don't forget, I'm having a year exchange from the University of Toronto' – pronounced 'Trono'. 'Toronto's a big city. Lots of bands and I've seen a few.'

Then she flipped open her Marketing book and I watched her annotate it with her sharpened pencil, wondering why an extraordinary woman like Christie would spend time with nurd-boy-turd-boy Cameron, when she could choose anyone.

And I will see her again tomorrow, a woman who has done so much with her life, despite what we did to her that night.

Jeremy says there is irony here. It is alcohol that tore us apart. And it is alcohol* that is bringing us back together. Back to what, I have no idea.

I force myself to read till my eyes blink shut and the book falls with a slap onto my face. My heart quickens and I think I call out in fright but then I realise what has happened, where I am. When I am calm, I place Ramsay MacDonald on the bedside cabinet and fumble for the light switch. Darkness swamps me and I am back in the prison cell, lying as still as I can so the ranting vicar will forget I am there, won't wind me up or pass on his unwanted words of wisdom.

I put the light back on. The telly back on. I lie there, in my big bed with the clean sheets, watching *Newsnight*, volume down, listening to the lullaby lilt of Kirsty Wark, wishing Amanda were here, whispering words of love into my ear.

Just as I am drifting into that elusive place of sleep, the phone rings. For a second I hope it will be her, my wife. But it isn't. It is Tommo.

'Allright, mate? Fancy a nightcap?'

Tommo is clutching a glut of miniature bottles of cheap blended whisky. Against my better judgement and the déjà-vu-ness of Tommo appearing when I am in my pyjamas, I let him in. He sheds his jacket and boots and plonks himself onto my bed with an expansive sigh.

'You're in your pyjamas.'

'That's never stopped you before.'

'What?'

'The first time we met.'

'The first time?'

'You climbed in my bedroom window.'

'I did? Oh yeah. I'd forgotten.' He finds us two glasses,

---

*And have I mentioned the fact that Dad was a brewer? Yes, I think I probably have.

213

pours us both a dram, shoves one in my hand. 'Cheers.'

'Slàinte.'

'God save the Queen.'

'Long live the King.'

He shakes his head. 'McCameron McSparkle. I might've known you'd be a Salmondite.'

'Only an Englishman could make that sound like an insult.'

'It is an insult. The Tories will walk all over us if you get your independence.'

'They'll walk all over *you. We*'ll have our freedom. The Tories will never bother us again.'

I've stumped him. I've actually stumped him but there's little comfort. Something he said. Something eating at me.

Oh, yeah. I'd forgotten.

'What else have you forgotten?'

'Sorry?'

'You forgot the first time we met. What else have you forgotten?'

'I've forgotten plenty, what with having an addled brain, but I remember the important stuff.'

A moment's pause. Then I have to ask. 'Do you remember the last time you saw me?'

'Of course,' he says. 'That would've been in a somewhat less salubrious environment than this.'

'That's one way of putting it.'

'Sorry, shouldn't joke.'

'No, you shouldn't.'

'You're more direct than you used to be, Cameron.'

'Amanda says I'm evasive.'

'Your wife?'

'Aye. Just.'

Tommo tips back his whisky. Pours himself another. I sip mine. I'm better at whisky than I used to be but still not that great and even though it burns, the smell of it is comforting. Peat and malt and the bonnie lochs of Scotland.

'The bonnie lochs of Scotland? Are you getting all Rabbie Burns on me?'

'Did I say that out loud?'

'Yes, you did McSparkle.'

'Can you stop calling me that?'

'It's a sign of affection.'

'It's a sign of cultural appropriation.'

'What?'

'It's patronising.'

'I stand corrected.' He actually stands up, sways a bit. 'Cameron.' He salutes me.

'Thank you, P-tolemy.' I salute him back. Two can play at this game. He's not going to stamp all over me ever again. No way, MacJosé.

He shoves his feet into his boots, leaving the laces undone, props his jacket over one arm, bids me farewell.

I watch him stumble towards the door. I watch him leave. I listen to the Scotophobic numpty's clod-hopping footsteps jackboot back to Bex. I listen to my past trampling all over me again.

I am who I am, a woman in a smart black outfit with a guitar slung around her neck who knows she can sing.
Take it or leave it.
Barbara Dickson OBE, from 'A Shirt Box Full of Songs'

Saturday
Walk

It's still dark when I get up. Seven o'clock. The view from my room is of Green Park, skeleton trees doing a deathly dance in the wind. My heart is heavy when I see the rain. *Welcome to England, Christie.* Does the damp get into her battered bones? Does she have arthritis? Does she hate us all?

My phone beeps. Amanda? Bex? Dad. Of course. Only an old person would ring at such a time.

'How are you, son?'

'I'm okay, Dad. Just waking up.'

'Having a lie in? All right for some.'

Myrtle interrupts, barking like a Rottweiler. Then there's a yelp followed by silence.

'You've got the zapper then.'

'It works a treat.'

'I'm not sure Myrtle sees it as a treat.'

'Then she'll soon learn.'

'You can't teach an old dog new tricks.'

'You can with one of these up your jacksy, son.'

'I thought you loved that dog.'

'I do. It's called tough love.'

Tough love. Love is patient. Love is kind. Love is bloody tough.

'Was there anything particular you wanted, Dad?'

'Just checking you're okay. Have you seen her yet?'

'I've seen Tommo and Bex but not Christie. That'll be tonight.'

'Hold your head up high. Face your demons, then get out of there and back home.'

'Aye, Dad. I will.'

Be proud of who you are.

Determined not to be a complete tosser, I go down to breakfast. I am not avoiding the others by having it in my room. I am going to man up.

As I enter the dining room, they're already there, the four of them, Bex, Tommo, the twins. The daughter is without make-up this morning, the image of her mother at university. She looks up from her phone and gives me that half-wave. I wave back this time and walk over, slowly, carefully, eager not to make each step like something from the Ministry of Funny Walks.

'Morning, Cameron.' Bex smiles and Tommo does this ridiculous salute thing. The twins mumble. They've left me a space and Bex hails down a waiter with great panache to take my order.

The table resembles the scene of a debauched Roman feast but that's kids for you. My childhood home was always spilling over with wet trainers, bulky backpacks, oily motorbike parts. Christie has a daughter too but I don't suppose she'll be bringing her into this Bermuda triangle.

'You look really well, Cameron. You've filled out a bit. It suits you.' Bex is always brutally honest.

'I was a weedy teenager.'

'Does your wife feed you well?' Tommo asks, ignoring Bex's feminist glower.

'Amanda and I are on a break.'

'I heard that,' Bex says. 'I'm sorry.'

'So Tommo told you.'

She looks at Tommo. He shrugs. She shakes her head.

'How did you hear then?'

'I saw it on Facebook.'

'I'm not even on Facebook.'

Loulou and Ethan gawp at me, an alien.

'Let's just say Facebook has made this world very small,' Bex says.

The waiter brings me some tea, finds a space to set down the pot.

The twins continue to gawp.

Tommo piles three sugars into a cup of black coffee that the waiter has refilled for him.

Bex sips her own tea, blinks at me with those spider leg lashes.

'Do you have a girlfriend?' Loulou enquires.

I actually splutter. I wasn't expecting such a personal question so early in the day, especially not from a girl I've only just met. They are all waiting expectantly for an answer.

'Och, no.' My face is heating up with a teenage flush. 'I want to put my marriage right.'

'You're pretty buff.' Loulou reaches out and squeezes my arm. A tingle travels all the way along it and I have to keep my stick on the ice, as Christie would say. This is Bex's daughter.

'You should try Internet dating,' Bex's daughter suggests. 'Or speed dating. You'll get loads of women after you. Young, hot women.'

'Right, Lou. Leave Cameron in peace,' Bex intervenes at last. 'Go and get ready or we'll be waiting all day for you.' She hands over the room key.

Loulou finishes her orange juice, noisily, and with much sass, before grabbing her brother. 'Come on, Ethan. Let the *grown-ups* talk about *grown-up* stuff like mortgages and divorces.' She flounces off, pulling Ethan along.

'Sorry about that, Cameron. Hormones. She oversteps the mark sometimes.' Bex shovels sugar into her tea and stirs voraciously.

219

I wonder briefly how much Fairtrade sugar they get through in their household and then try to think of something to say, to show I am fine about being quizzed, that I am *au fait* with teenagers when really I am clueless. I was clueless when I was a teenager myself so how can I possibly understand the twins, the product of the other two people at this table?

'What age did you say they were?'

'Sixteen,' Bex says.

'Sweet sixteen.'

An embarrassed pause. I sound like a perv.

Help comes, unexpectedly, from Tommo. 'There's nothing sweet about them when they're drinking illicit cider in the park or smoking my roll-ups out the bedroom window.'

Bex shoots Tommo a sharp look. I cannot fathom the layers that lay beneath it.

'Your son's very quiet.'

'He's always been the quiet one,' Bex says.

'You know what they say about the quiet ones,' I retort.

'What do they say, Cameron?' Tommo is alert now after his sugar-caffeine hit.

'They're the ones to watch.' Awkwardness hovers above the table like a bird waiting to poop. The waiter deposits my plate of food. 'I was the quiet one, remember.' I cram my mouth full of bacon to staunch the flow of dodgy comments, praying silently to a god I still want to believe in that I won't be afflicted with Tourette's or say something racist, sexist, homophobic or vaguely right-wing (though being a Scot the latter is unlikely). But most of all I pray that I won't let slip words like 'crash', 'prison', or 'leg'.

The other two shift in their seats. Tommo clears his throat as if he's about to say something but he just carries on coughing. A smoker's cough. Bex hands him her glass of orange juice, a fleeting gesture of concern, which he sips and eventually the coughing subsides.

Maybe they are also worried about what to say. I've never really considered the possibility: Bex and Tommo stumped for words.

'So.' Bex swipes her breakfast plate to one side. The waiter swoops. She leans forward, elbows on table, close enough for me to make out the faintest of lines on her skin, around the eyes, the lips. 'What are you doing today?'

'Oh?' Don't these two communicate? 'Tommo actually asked me if I wanted to go to the Tate with him.'

'Did he? Right. That's a good idea. I'm taking the twins to the London Eye. Tommo hates heights. And I need to get Lou a dress as well. Maybe we could meet up later this afternoon?'

'That would be good.'

The waiter whips away my breakfast plate and other detritus from the table, while Tommo lectures us on modern art, finally exhausting his spiel just as I finish my toast.

'Um, so,' I begin, hesitate, push on. 'Did you two ever get wed?'

'No.' Bex says this firmly.

Tommo says nothing.

'Why not?' Maybe I shouldn't ask this question in terms of politeness and etiquette but we're surely beyond that ruling.

'No need,' Bex says. She briefly twists a silver ring on a non-wedding finger.

'You should really consider the financial and legal implications.' I sound like a pillock but I can't help myself.

'It's sorted,' Bex says. 'We have wills.'

'Right well, then, that's good. I mean, I know it's not romantic, but you have to think in terms of practicalities. Amanda and I signed a prenup.'

'A prenup?' Tommo splutters. 'Michael MacDouglas or what?'

'There's property involved.'

'So you're a property magnate?'

'We have a flat in the New Town.'

'The crap bit of Edinburgh?'

'The posh bit.' I wait for some reaction but there is silence. They are waiting for me to say more so I please my audience.

'Things aren't so good between Amanda and I right now. In fact I'm living back with my dad for the time being. And there's a possibility I'll be out of work before Christmas.'

'God, Cameron, really?' Bex touches my hand, a squeeze almost painful in its exquisite tenderness, the silver ring digging into my skin.

'The recession's been hard for everyone, mate.' This from Tommo, his voice rough as a badger's arse. What does he sound like when he sings now? Barry White? Leonard Cohen? Bonnie Tyler?

I can still feel the ghost of Bex's hand on mine. The echo of Tommo's voice continues to grate. The two of them still together, after all this time, considering their beginnings, is remarkable.

'You two are all right though?' I switch the focus back to them.

'The squeezed middle,' Bex says. 'But we have more than enough. We have a roof over our heads, clothes on our back and food in our bellies.'

I don't correct her assumption that I am talking financially.

'So, Cameron,' she says. 'Which way will you be voting in the referendum? Do you want to stay with the rest of us?'

'I take it you're talking about Scottish Independence?'

'Yes, I am.'

'There is such a thing as the Secret Ballot Act,* you know.'

'You don't have to tell me but I'm interested. And surely if you have a strong opinion you should share it. It's about your self-determination. It's important.'

As if she needs to tell me that.

'Well, Bex, to satisfy your curiosity, I'll be voting Yes. It's time we had our freedom back.'

'Your freedom?' Tommo sounds surprised. 'Is that how

---

*The secret ballot mandated by the Act was first used on 15 August 1872 to re-elect Hugh Childers as MP for Pontefract in a ministerial by-election, following his appointment as Chancellor of the Duchy of Lancaster. (Yes, Lancaster. Who'd have thought?)

you see it?'

'Aye, that's exactly how I see it. My freedom.'

Bex stands up, touches Tommo on the shoulder. 'We need to get going. We'll have to continue this hot debate later.'

Tommo stands up too, does as he's told, flicks the crumbs from his skinny black trousers. Not a word about kilts or tartan or Briga-bloody-doon.*

I stand up too.

The three of us all stand up.

'I'll meet you in the lobby, shall I, Tommo?'

'Yep. Give me ten minutes.'

'Right.'

I leave them there, by the wreck of the table, and make my way out of the dining room, without goose-stepping or tripping or pirouetting. But the day stretches ahead of me and I wonder how I will survive to the end of it.

Ten minutes can seem endless.

---

*A quote made by Simon Callow in *Four Weddings and a Funeral*. Which had its fair share of kilts.

Conquered, she was unconquerable, nor could the dungeon detain her; slain, yet deathless, imprisoned, yet not a prisoner. Thus does the pruned vine groan with a greater abundance of grapes, and the cut jewel gleams with a brilliant splendour.

Extract from an inscription on Mary, Queen of Scots' tomb, translated from Latin, in Westminster Abbey.

Irises

Not surprisingly, I like it in the Underground. (Jubilee Line. Green Park to Southwark.) It is reassuring and safe, a home from home. The place must be teeming with ghosts. The lost souls of the jumpers, the Victorian tunnellers, the druggies and the drunks. They must have a wail of a time in this subterranean world. If you'll pardon the pun.

Did you feel a sense of power when you locked Sanderson in the room?

Did you want to be his jailer?

Psycho-babble from Jeremy. I wanted to take control of the situation, yes, that is why I locked him up. But it wasn't the locking-up *per se* that was important to me. It was the keeping-everyone-safe part that was my priority. Locking him up was a solution.

But he reminded you of Tommo.

Did he?

Yes, I put it to you that he did.

Shut up, Jeremy.

'Who's Jeremy?' Tommo asks.

'No one,' I snap.

Tommo and I emerge from the depths of south London into a reasonable bright sunlight for December. We make our way towards Bankside power station, his old stride nowhere to be seen, replaced with a shuffle like my dad's.

'Do you come here often?' I'm not trying to be witty, it's just that Tate Modern is such a Tommo kind of place.

He shakes his floppy hair, takes out a fag for a quick puff. 'I've never been.'

'Never?'

'Nope. I avoid London.'

'Really?'

'My teenage life is a dim, hazy memory, like it belongs to someone else.'

'What about your father?'

'He's still alive, semi-retired in Hampstead with his new wife who isn't so new anymore. We rarely see each other. We barely talk.'

He looks over his shoulder, like he's checking for someone. His father? Or his younger self, maybe? The young lad who dreamt of fame and money and glittering prizes, who chose the less worn road up to a provincial northern mill town. Who got so near and then had it snatched from him. Who ruined everything. And where is he now? Middle-aged, in a hippy town in Devon, in a mind-numbing job in refuse and recycling. With a cough like a death rattle.

'As for my mother, she's still with the aging, withered Knob.'

Inside the vast Turbine Hall there's a cathedral-hush, an escape from the crowds, a remission from the jostling and the rushing. Time slows down. I can feel each breath of mine. I can hear each breath of Tommo's.

There's a piece by Tacita Dean called *Film* – a silent 35mm looped film projected onto this whacking monolith.

Tommo's intrigued. 'The images are analogue not digital,' he says. 'Like vinyl over CD.'

'You're still in a band, then?'

'You make it sound like you're asking if I'm still in the boy scouts. Not that I've ever been or done anything that requires a uniform, apart from boarding school but that didn't last long. Not after the marijuana incident.'

'So are you still in a band?'

'Course.'

'And Bex is okay with that?'

'Why wouldn't she be?'

'Because you're forty-seven.'

'I'm forty-six.'

`I am forty-six.`

`Tommo is forty-six.`

'Maybe you should focus your energies on a different hobby.'

'You think my music's a hobby?'

'Well, it's not like a job, is it?'

'I make some money.'

You're not exactly Jarvis cocking Cocker.

'What did you say?'

'I spoke out loud again, didn't I?'

'Are you all there, mate?'

'I might not be all there but at least I'm not still trying to be famous.'

'Who said I want to be famous?'

'You always wanted to be famous.'

'If I'd wanted fame that much I wouldn't have screwed it up the first time round, would I?' He walks off, heads out the hall and into one of the galleries.

I follow him. A shadow. I am a ghost that will haunt him forever.

We're in the middle of the water irises when he starts to cough. And cough. Hacking away. It won't ease. It's like it will never stop. Like he's actually coughing up his guts. I'm embarrassed at first, his coughing disturbing the quiet peace of Monet's pond. Then embarrassment turns to concern as the cough goes on and on and on.

'You look terrible. Let's get you out of here.' And I grab

227

his arm and lead him back through the galleries as he gasps for breath and I feel a panic in my own chest, my peripheral vision a blur of white walls and ghoulish structures and bright lighting. In the Turbine Hall there is more air and although his cough calms a little, it reverberates and so I steer him outside, into the cold freshness where he bends over, trying to exhume the cough. Dirty phlegm splatters on the ground, like a Rothko.

His coughing settles, stops, and we both stare at the mess on the floor. 'Are you okay?'

'Bit woozy.' His voice is hardly there.

'You don't need me to tell you what it is.'

'Yeah, I know.' He takes a breath. I take a breath. 'The fags. I'll cut back.'

'Better quit altogether. And go to the doctors. You might have bronchitis.'

He swats me away.

I ignore him and push him down onto a bench.

'A cold, that's all,' he mumbles.

We sit there in silence for a while. The sun has gone, leaving a washed-out grey sky hovering above the city's rooftops. People walk past. Pigeons peck. The wind bowls up the river. We sit there in silence a bit longer.

'The night of the crash you complained about a cold,' he says, out the blue, completely off message. 'We were in the pub…' He coughs, briefly, gets going again. 'You were stubbornly refusing to have a drink. I'd had too much myself. Didn't make the best decisions that night.' He shrugs, takes another breath. 'I've felt guilty ever since. Every night, the guilt haunts me. I lie in bed playing over every other decision I could've made. Not only that night but over my entire lifetime.' He shifts, wipes his snot on the back of his precious jacket sleeve, like a toddler, like a tramp. 'That way madness lies. So I take sleeping pills.'

Didn't make the best decisions that night.

'Maybe you need to see someone.'

'I need sleep.'

'You need to give up the fags.'

'I know I need to give up the fags.'

I look at Tommo, sitting there next to me on the bench, see his stubble flecked with grey, his wan complexion, a scar above his eyebrow. For some reason Bex loves this man. 'Then do it,' I say. 'Stop arsing around and do it.'

'Steady on, MacSporran.' He laughs and I can hear spittle struggling to find a way out of him. 'You might have a point, I'll give you that. If I do this, then maybe Rebecca will see I'm trying hard at something cos quite frankly I'm fed up of being a failure in her eyes.'

'Things not so good at home?'

'Been better.'

'Have you been playing around?'

'Playing around? Is that what you think?' He sounds outraged. Genuinely outraged. 'I've *never* cheated on Rebecca. And it's not for lack of opportunities.'

'The groupies?'

'Ha! Not exactly, no.' He shakes his head wistfully. 'Have you any idea what she'd do to me?'

'I can imagine. Put a red hot poker up your arse. Hang, draw and quarter you. Wear your testicles for earrings. That sort of thing.'

'Indeed, that sort of thing.' A wry laugh. 'But seriously, why would I? She's my soul mate.'

'Soulmate?'

'Yep.

He coughs, mutters, hobo-like. 'I need to sleep. When I sleep I don't have to worry that Rebecca doesn't want me anymore. But you always have to wake up. Sometimes I don't want to wake up.'

Tommo is poorly.

Tommo must go to the doctors.

Tommo is not right in the heid.

I coax him into a cab and we shudder our way back to the hotel. He's morose, staring blankly out of the window, past the Palace of Westminster where the Englishmen think they can rule over us Scots. Around Parliament Square, past Westminster Abbey* where Mary Stuart is buried, where Burns and Scott are commemorated, and past Churchill's statue lording it over the plebs. Down Whitehall, past the Cenotaph where the fallen are honoured, flags and poppy wreaths, Downing Street where that Eton boy who shares my name ponces about, then onto Trafalgar Square, Nelson's column, Canada House with the maple leaf flying, Cockspur Street and onto Pall Mall. St James Street. Piccadilly.

Bex and the twins are still out so I stay with him awhile in his room. I make him a coffee and he empties another dram into it.

'You look feverish. Do you have any paracetamol?'

'Try Rebecca's wash bag thing.'

'Where?'

'The bathroom. And I don't want any of her hippy crap.'

I go in the bathroom and – I don't know why – I lock the door. There's an array of wash bags but I know which one will be hers. Indian cotton with elephants. Inside, is of course the 'hippy crap'. Arnica cream, homoeopathic pills, Rescue Remedy. Body Shop make-up and Lush creams. And a packet of paracetamol which I nab. But for a moment, before I put back the bag, I clutch it to me, breathe in the distant, familiar scent of Bex that I now know is vetivert. Myrrh and violets. Earthy woodlands.

Back in their bedroom, I administer the pills and make myself a cup of tea. I could go back to my own room for a rest but I can't bring myself to leave Tommo's side. He really does look ill.

'So, Lou says she saw you last night?'

*Above the statue to Shakespeare in Poets' Corner is a small oval mural tablet with a lyre to John Keats.

'Last night?'

'At some restaurant. On your own.'

'Oh, well, yeah. My friend cancelled at the last moment. Some work thing. I ate on my own. Which was fine. The food was good.'

'You might be needing a passport soon to come down here and eat our English food.'

'It was an Italian restaurant. I ate a pizza and I drank a Peroni.'

'You Scots have got a chip on your shoulder. In fact, you've got chips everywhere.'

'Aye, and deep fried Mars bars, I know, I know.'

He coughs then. Serves him right.

Once he's recovered, he switches on the TV, channel surfs. Rude. Then the BBC News. And who would have thought it? Alex Salmond, the Saltire waving brightly in the background.

Tommo looks at me and we actually share a smile.

'So,' he says. ' Tell me about Amanda.'

I get on the bed next to him – Eric and Ernie – and I tell him about her latest job at the Festival, admin instead of acting. I tell him how we met at Skeletours (without the lascivious details). I tell him how beautiful and talented she is (*A Brummy? Has she thought of elocution lessons to give her a chance at a proper acting role?*). I tell him that she wants a baby but I feel the time has passed.

'You're only forty-seven,' he says.

'I'm forty-six,' I correct him.

'Think on, my man,' he says. 'You're as young as the woman who loves you. How old is Amanda by the way?'

'Thirty-eight.'

'Time's running out then,' he says. 'Women want babies. Simple as.'

Sexist nonsense.

'Do you love her?'

'Sorry?'

'No need to blush, Cameron. Man up.'

'I love her, all right. I love her.'

Tommo shrugs, ramming home his point that it's simple, which maybe it is. Or maybe it's just the hardest thing in the world, to love someone.

'I swore I'd spend the rest of my life looking after Rebecca,' he carries on, clutching his coffee to him like a talisman. 'I couldn't do any more for you, Cameron. I couldn't do any more for Christie. But I could love Rebecca with all my heart and all my soul. She was my bright star, my guiding light, my beginning and my end.'

'What are you saying? You're sounding like a song.'

'I don't know what I'm saying. I always sound like a song.' He squeezes his eyes shut. Opens them again, realises I'm still here. 'It should've been me serving that sentence,' he says, quiet as anything. 'I let you take the rap.'

I don't correct him on that one.

'And I know it must've been some kind of hell in there but it was all over after a few months. Whereas I'll have to live with the guilt for the rest of my life.'

'You have your freedom, Tommo. You have it in your reach. Why make life so hard for yourself?'

'I wish I knew the answer to that.' He sounds miserable, takes a slug of whisky. 'Thanks for looking after me, mate. I appreciate it. I feel rotten. Have done for weeks. I should see a doctor but you know what us middle-aged men are like when it comes to doctors.

'Have you talked to Bex?'

'Rebecca isn't the best of nurses. You have to be dying, preferably in an underdeveloped country, to get any sympathy out of her. She's never let the kids miss school. She's always worked, couldn't get time off. Always blamed successive governments for insufficient family-friendly working conditions.'

'Maybe there's more to it than that. A sense that you both escaped death and that your twins should thank their lucky stars they have the gift of life.'

'I don't know if it's anything as philosophical as that. You know her, always one for actions, not thinking.'

I'm remembering teenage Bex with her red paint and her placards. Then her son comes in, smelling of the cold and French fries, and I wonder what his passions are. Other than grunting and eating.

'All right, Ethan?' Tommo asks. 'Where are the women?'

'Shopping. Said they won't be long.' When he takes his eyes off his phone he notices his father sitting in bed with another man. 'What you doing in bed, Dad?'

'Feeling rough. Got this cough.'

'You've always got this cough.' Ethan slumps onto the end of the bed, the three of us sprawled like we're on a boat all at sea. He checks his phone again as it's been at least thirty seconds. 'Should give up the fags.'

'Good advice from your son there, Tommo.'

'Reckons it goes with his rock-and-roll image. Dad still wants to be David Hasselhoff.'

Tommo struggles to a sitting up position. 'David Hasselhoff?'

'No wait, sorry. I meant David Bowie.'

'You had me worried there for a sec, mate. No, wait. I am worried. That you should confuse David Hasselhoff for David Bowie?'

'Who's David Bowie again?'

Tommo is horrified, as if Ethan had announced he was thinking of joining UKIP. 'We should do one of those DNA tests.'

'Why?'

'Cos sometimes I wonder if you're my son. I mean you like Dizzy Whotsit and Diddy Doodah.'

Ethan shakes his head.

'Oh, never mind.' Tommo sighs. 'Let's get a drink. This cough of mine needs more whisky. Text your sister and tell them to meet us down in the bar.' He slaps Ethan on the arm, in a fatherly way, to show he's joking about the DNA thing.

His whole life, a bloody joke.

I'll have to live with the guilt for the rest of my life.

Well, Tommo, one act of recklessness, one ill-formed decision can have repercussions. Just take a long good look at me. What's that you say? You'd rather look at yourself? Of course you'd rather look at yourself. You're Ptolemy Dulac. Indestructible as Mick Jagger. As craggy and scrawny as a Rolling Stone.

And whoops, no. I didn't say that out loud.

As we go down in the lift, Ethan watches his father's reflection in the mirror. 'I was like joking, you know.'

'Yeah, what about?'

'David Bowie. Do you really think I've learnt nothing from you? I've got *Hunky Dory* and *Scary Monsters* on my iPod.

Tommo gives him a hug, which Ethan grudgingly accepts. And Tommo doesn't even mention that downloading Bowie is a sacrilege. That vinyl is the only way to listen to the master. Because that's what he is most likely thinking.

As we come out the lift, Bex and Lou are standing there with bags of shopping.

'Where are you off to?'

'The bar?'

'I don't think so. We've got sandwiches. Thought we could have them in the room. Cheaper than eating out. Want to join us, Cameron? There's plenty here.' She practically pushes us back in the lift.

There's not much room. I can smell her vetivert. Memories of a fox's brush and a vicious man in red. A red they call pink.

'You okay, Dad?' Loulou asks. 'You look like crap.'

'Thanks, love. I feel like it.'

'You can have a rest this afternoon, Tommo,' Bex concedes. 'But there's no way you're backing out of tonight.'

'Wouldn't dream of it, Rebecca.'

I've dreamt of nothing else. I want to get out of this lift, out of this hotel, out of this city, this country, and back to my home. Only that would mean leaving Bex and I've only just found her again.

Shop

3.30pm and the pavements of Oxford Street are buzzing with shoppers and hordes of what UKIP* would call 'foreigners'. Traffic is nose to tail; stuttering red buses, black cabs, cyclists. The Christmas lights are almost overwhelming. I want to look up all the time. Bex and Loulou – who've dragged me out with them while the other two nap – are doing the same, staring in awe at the shop windows, the skinny mannequins, the shoppers.

'We must seem like yokels,' Bex says.

'We are yokels,' Loulou quips back.

'Speak for yourself,' I say. 'I come from a capital city, remember.'

'Where's that, Cameron?' Loulou asks.

'Edinburgh born and bred.'

'Cool. I want to go to the festival there.'

'Which one?'

'The comedy one. It looks well good.'

'I try to avoid it, to be honest. The town gets even more touristy than ever. But you should go. Definitely. I can show you around.'

'Thanks, Cameron. That's awesome.'

'Come on, Lou,' Bex says, a wee bit briskly. 'Let's get you this dress.'

---

*UKIP: another reason to vote Yes.

Loulou gives her mother a smile of pure joy and strides ahead with the confidence of youth. Not that I ever had confidence in my youth. I have a smattering now but only in my own world. The one underground with the ghosties and ghoulies.

'If only the prospect of a new dress would do the same for me,' Bex says. 'My daughter might be exasperating but she knows how to be happy. That's quite a gift.'

'It is.'

Are you frightened of being happy?

We find ourselves, kettled by the crowd, outside Topshop. Loulou grabs Bex by the arm and steers her in. I can do nothing but follow, my first time in Topshop, through the throng, into banging music, horrifying mirrors, the smell of sickly-sweet perfume with a base note of dirty feet – only partially better than the traffic fumes swirling about in the cold air outside. I pat my coat pocket to check my inhaler is there. Maybe I should've offered it to Tommo.

The teenager lunges straight for the tiniest, flimsiest dresses and I watch Bex struggling not to pass judgement.

'She should be able to wear what she wants,' she says to me, 'but with my job, I know the worst that can happen.'

'You're still a social worker then?'

'Yep.'

Standing adrift in the massive store, while Loulou snatches up dresses, piling them over one arm, I feel very, very middle-aged. And launched out of my comfort zone.

Bex sighs. She must feel it too. 'I used to love Topshop,' she says.

'Did you?'

'Mmm. And Chelsea Girl. There was a massive one in Exeter.'

'I thought you got your stuff from the army surplus store.'

'Well, yeah, I did. I loved those monkey boots. Lou would shudder.'

'I've progressed from Burton's to M&S.'

'I wish Tommo would progress.'

We share a laugh.

'He'll still be in skinny jeans in his nursing home. In fact he'd rather go on an all-inclusive one-way trip to Switzerland than relinquish them.' She looks around, hands on her hips, hips as slim as I remember them. 'How old are you when you have to stop buying clothes from Topshop? I have a positive body image – but I don't want to compete with my daughter.'

We shuffle round the store after said daughter, thankfully bypassing the lingerie – though I notice Lou's appraising glance of the frilly push-up bras.

'I'm just grateful for the return of big pants,' Bex says. 'The vintage-style ones that hold you in. So much nicer than those cheese-cutter thongs and all that Brazilian nonsense.'

She sighs again.

I feel light-headed.

'Why don't you get a dress, Mum?'

'From here? You are joking, right?'

'Well, no, I wasn't thinking from here. You don't want to look like a slapper.'

'No, we wouldn't want that.'

The irony floats right over Lou's head. 'I was thinking like from a department store or something? Maybe Marks and Spencer's?'

'Has it come to that?' Bex throws me an embarrassed smile. 'Whoops.'

M&S. Solid. Reliable. Trustworthy.

The girl's expression alters, a hint of self-awareness. She hazards a more positive comment. 'You've got a great body for someone your age?'

'Gee, thanks.'

'All right, don't give me evils.' She pouts. 'Five minutes and I bet I can find something in here that won't embarrass either of us.'

Bex checks her watch.

'Five minutes, Mother.' Loulou hands over the dresses,

heads off into the unknown.

We retreat to the shoes, find a perch on a footstool.

'The sight of those tortuous heels makes my bunions throb.' Bex takes off her trainer – a trendy leather trainer rather than a naff running one – and rubs her foot. Does she have the same line of thought as me? *Christie. What type of shoes does she wear?* 'Maybe I could treat myself to a pair of wedges or some ankle boots,' she blethers. 'Then I won't need to get a dress. I mean, it's nice to see Loulou so enthused but I really can't be bothered to try stuff on. I want a cup of tea. Maybe a glass of wine. Definitely a glass of wine.'

'I guess there'll be plenty of wine tonight.'

'Of course,' she says. 'Whatever Icewine might be.'

We are quiet for a bit, thoughts jumbling about, spinning and spinning.

'So what's it like having twins?' I ask to break the silence.

She turns to look at me and my heart pinches. 'One's gobby, one's quiet,' she says. 'But both of them are untidy, filthy pigs. The hotel room is already drowning under a tide of discarded clothes and aerosol cans.'

'What's it like being a parent?'

'I make it up as I go along. I'm pleased Lou's gobby. I just wish she would embrace the political. Not the cosmetic.' She pauses a moment and I want to kiss her so much it hurts because I know I never will. 'Maybe she's in charge of her destiny in a way I could never hope to be.'

'Maybe,' I say. 'If any of us are.'

'I think we are. We can make things happen. It's whether we make the right things happen. I want to pass on my gobbiness to Loulou because I want her to change the world. And you need to be gobby, not just in what you say, but in what you do. Gobby is a lifestyle choice.'

'Did your mum pass this gobbiness onto you?'

'I can barely remember my own mother. But I suspect she had to keep her opinions to herself, with my overbearing dad. I have no one to keep the memories alive. My grandmother

239

could never talk about Mum without crying and I didn't want Granny to cry. I knew that would make me cry too. And I couldn't cry, I wouldn't cry, I can't cry, because if I did, if I do, I might never stop.'

She shrugs, picks up a black suede ankle boot. 'These would be okay. They look wearable. Comfy. Lou would be cross with me for using 'comfy' as an adjective to describe shoes...'

'No, Mum. Put that down.' Loulou appears, like a store detective. 'Stand away from the boots. Look at these beauties.' She's weighed down under another alarming heap of clothes.

Bex eyes the dress on top of the pile, a pink lacy thing that would be more at home on a glamour model. 'Who do you think I am? Samantha Fox?'

'Who's Samantha Fox?'

Bex holds in a sigh. 'Never mind. For now. Just discard that prawn-pink one. Have you got anything a little more... classy?'

'In Topshop?'

'I know it's a long shot.'

'Aha! You shouldn't judge.' Loulou's clearly relishing every moment of bossing her mother. 'What about this one?' She dumps the dresses onto her mother's lap, selects a little back number. Zips, cobweb sleeves, a reference to punk that makes Bex reach out to hold it. More Siouxsie Sioux than Samantha Fox.

'I'll try this on.'

'Yay, go Mum.'

'Yes, all right, enough of the cheerleading. Let's find the fitting room. I'm not going in there alone. And please, God, don't tell me it's a communal one.'

'Mum, you worry too much about the physical.'

'You will one day too. When you're old like me.'

'You're not old, Mother. You're like knocking on a bit but you're okay. You just need to make more of an effort.'

But to me, Bex is beautiful. Still beautiful. The beautiful

girl (woman) I remember. I sit and wait for them, wondering if this is what it is like to be Tommo. How I wish I could trade places with him. I did that once. But could I ever do it again?

Ten minutes later – *ten minutes can seem endless* – they appear back in front of me.

'Well?' I ask.

'A pair of Spanx and she'll be a MILF.'

'I have no idea what you're talking about.'

'Good,' Bex says. 'Ignore her.' She turns to her daughter. 'I presume there's a compliment in there somewhere but we need to have a serious chat sometime very soon about feminism.'

'Yeah, whatever. Can I get a pair of shoes to go with this dress?' Lou's all sweetness and light. 'Please.'

'Okay. Just be quick about it.'

Loulou rummages around the shoes with the highest heels and the pointiest toes.

'She used to brandish that little word to maximum effect in the sweetshop on a Friday after school, asking for another strawberry shoelace,' Bex says.

'Which word?'

'Please.'

'Ah. That word.'

'Demands were much smaller back then. A lot cheaper. But I'm so chuffed to spend time with her – no arguing or moaning or sulking. You've helped. Tommo would never dream of coming in Topshop. It's like having my little girl back. I'd quite possibly promise her breast implants for Christmas if she asked. Thankfully she hasn't.' She looks at me and I see a spark of the old Bex.

'I miss it. The small shoes, the lullabies, the nappies flapping on the washing line. I miss spending time with my daughter. But I can't tell her that. If you name something, teenagers react. You have to go with it, not verbalise feelings. Feelings are bad unless discussed with friends or announced to the world via Facebook. You certainly don't share them with your parents.' She sighs that old Bex sigh. 'Teenagers are bloody hard work.'

'I certainly found it hard work being a teenager.'

Bex has tears in her eyes. 'You had to go to prison when you were just a bit older than Ethan. I can't imagine it. Well, I can. I knew enough about prison what with Dad working at Princetown. But when I visited you, it was a surprise.'

'In what way?'

'You actually seemed to be coping. You coped a whole lot better than Tommo ever would've done which made me think it was the right decision, despite the lies, despite the perjury, but now, I don't know. I don't think Tommo has learned anything.'

'Trouble in the garden of Eden?'

'It was never that. At best it was a half-hearted garden, where we struggled to keep the grass cut and the shrubs pruned. Now it's overgrown with Japanese knotweed.'

'You always had a way with words.'

'Actions are better than words. I don't want to be a moany woman. I want to be that woman back at university, in Fem Soc, in the anti-apartheid movement, a hunt sab.'

'You can be,' I tell her. 'But first, time for that glass of wine.'

And she takes me by the hand. She actually takes me by the hand.

Kilt

Definitely an occasion for the kilt. I wasn't sure when I packed it but after my conversation with Tommo, I know I need to wear it. It is my heritage. My armour and protection. You're never too old to be a superhero.

God save the King.

I have a bottle of Champagne clutched to my breast like a bairn. I walk the corridors to their room. (I am indeed forever doomed to walk corridors.)

I knock loudly and wait.

Ethan lets me in, says something that sounds like 'all right'.

'Ah, it's the old man of Hoy,' says Tommo. He's gaunt, tired, still in bed. His sandwiches from earlier unopened. Several empty miniatures.

'You look like shite.'

'You look like Bonnie Prince Charlie.'

'The prince would've looked nothing like this. That's a Romanticised view of us Scots you like to portray. But seriously, you really do look rough.'

Lou comes out the bathroom. 'Wow, Cameron. You look awesome. And Champagne! Swag or what?' She relieves me of the bottle. 'Dad, Cameron's brought fizz. Can I have a glass?'

'Thanks, Cameron.' Bex is here now – where did she appear from? – in the Topshop dress that could be Vivienne Westwood for all I know about fashion. But I know she looks beautiful. 'Take a seat.'

I make my way to one of the armchairs by the window, dodging phone chargers, odd socks, ransacked suitcases, Bex right behind me, gathering up a clump of clothes so I can sit down.

There is a small pop. We look round and see Loulou licking the neck of the bottle.

'Lou! What are you doing?'

'I'm getting our guest a drink. He could be like dead of thirst by the time you or Dad sort him one out.' Then she pours a glass, tipping it in a worryingly expert way.

'*What?*' So much teenage angst and issues and rites of passage are contained in that word. In that expression.

'We need to have a chat later, Loulou.'

Loulou rolls her eyes and pouts.

'You can open a bottle of Champagne?' I ask, chirpy as David Tennant on a manic day. 'Very sophisticated.'

'Teenagers in a small town have to do something.' She glances sideways at her mother, challenging her, knowing full well that Bex will hold back, desperate to unearth information on her daughter's secret life.

'Teenagers with too much money and time on their hands,' Tommo says.

'We had to make do with Irn-Bru.'

'Gross.' Lou pulls a face, changes the direction of the conversation in that way only teenagers and politicians can. 'Dad's got a gross cough. Mum's always banging on at him to give up smoking. He won't eat. Keeps moaning about needing a fag but won't go out in the rain.' She pauses for a breath. 'So he's dead grumpy.'

'You really should eat, Tommo,' Bex says. 'There'll only be canapés tonight. You'll be starving when we get back and there's no way you're ordering room service.'

'Stop nagging, the pair of you. I'll be fine.' Tommo wafts us away, shuts his eyes, his face a death mask, a ghost of its former self. He is disappearing before our eyes.

'Where's Ethan?' I ask.

Bex points to an interconnecting door. 'The twins are sleeping through there. I'd better see if he's up.'

Lou joins me, sits in the other armchair. 'Cheers,' she says.

'Bottoms up.' We chink glasses.

Loulou crosses her legs, one long limb over the other, and a ghoulish sound buzzes in my head. Scraping metal. Shattering glass. Shrieking sirens. The crash is always there, swimming in my skull, tugging me under. The echo of voices, the concentrated breaths, the quickening heartbeat.

'Is that like a Scottish phrase?' Loulou asks.

'Sorry?'

'Bottoms up.'

'I think it's one of yours.'

'Mine?'

'You English.' I gulp back my drink. I take my eyes away from her legs. And I certainly don't let myself think about bottoms.

I am not a perv.

Bex is back, followed by a shaggy-haired son. She pours herself a glass of bubbly, while he lies down on the bed. (His other passion is obviously sleeping.) She takes a sip and then busies herself hunting down earrings, shoes, bag, faffing about, not able to keep still.

'I saw you in that restaurant last night,' Loulou says to me in a quiet voice. 'On your own.' She places a tendril of her hair behind an ear mutilated by a battalion of earrings. 'Didn't you want to eat with us? Is this a nightmare, being back with old student friends?'

Bex throws a warning look at me and I realise they've never told their children the story of our time in Lancaster. Which I can understand. I mean, why would they? But then, why are they here? A solution for their relationship? Peace with their past? 'Are you ready to go, Lou?'

'Almost.' She gets up slowly, reluctantly, from the chair, her dress somehow shorter than it was in Topshop. She totters away and disappears through the connecting door.

'You look great,' I tell Bex.

'Not quite up to the standards of the Ritz but it'll do.'

'You look gorgeous.'

'The old Cameron would never have said that. You've changed.' She shakes her head. 'Of course you have. We all have.'

'Don't look so worried.'

'Do I look worried?'

'Yes, you do.' And I wonder if she thinks I've spent all these years planning to get back at them through their children. Maybe she thinks I'm mad. A loose cannon.

'Mum says it's not Dad she should be worried about.' Loulou's back, bottle in hand. She tops up my glass. 'It should be you,' she says.

'Me?'

'Mum says you're clearly depressed, a prime candidate for suicide, a male in his mid-forties, a failed marriage and the possible loss of your job and home.'

'Lou!' Bex glares at her daughter but it has no effect except for eliciting a shrug.

'Just sayin'.'

'Well, don't just say. Think.'

'She's right.' I lean back in my chair but misjudge its angle, bumping the back of my head and jarring my neck. I sit upright again. Hear a click. Old bones. 'I should be depressed. But I'm not. At least I don't think so.'

'You'd know if you were depressed,' Tommo says, a voice from the bed.

'That's not necessarily true,' Bex says.

'The social worker's always right.' Back to Tommo.

Bex slugs back her champagne and holds it out for Lou to refill.

When the glass is full-to-overflowing, Lou checks her mother for a moment. 'You haven't blended your make-up properly, Mum,' she says. 'You'll draw attention to yourself.'

'This from the girl with fake eyelashes and a Jaffa orange face?' Tommo quips.

Loulou pouts.

Bex downs her drink.

'Maybe we should go,' I suggest.

'Yep,' says Tommo. He rolls out of bed and I see that he already has his suit on, the crumpled look only Tommo can get away with. 'Let's hit the high road.'

I want to hit Tommo. I want to kiss Bex. I want to lie down on the floor and have a hissy fit of a tantrum. But I go with them, from the room, down the sodding corridor, into the lift, down to whatever the evening has in store for us.

The grapes for Icewine are harvested only when a sustained temperature of -8°C or lower is reached, between December and February. By this point, the grapes have dehydrated and the juices have concentrated. This makes for a unique, full, rich flavour.

Armstrong King Estates, Ontario, Canada

Glass

We're back in that lift, the five of us, all glammed up, the
smell of vetivert vying with cologne, perfume and Lynx.
I'm glad for my kilt, its comforting heaviness, its freedom.
Amanda would never let me wear it; thought it was all a big
joke. But then she was from Birmingham. Home of Ozzy
Osbourne and Duran Duran.

The lift stops and the doors open.

'Are we ready?' Bex doesn't wait. She's out, leading the
way to the Burlington Suite where the event is taking place,
six fifteen so we shouldn't be the first, shouldn't be late, but
any minute now we'll be seeing her. We'll be seeing Christie
Armstrong.

The Burlington is already heaving by the time we get there,
thanks to Lou's last minute eyelash crisis. We had to wait for
Bex to fix it. She couldn't. In the end it was me who helped
her stick it back on. I used to do this for Amanda.

A silver tray of white wine is proffered by a waiter in
black and white – like a snooker player – and we all swipe
a glass. A clear head is needed but one of these will calm
the nerves a wee bit. Nerves that make me want to fetch up
and we don't want puke all over the fancy carpet. Not a nice
photo for the society pages.

The room is braw. Swanky. Oil paintings of toffs in wigs

and gowns, fat powdered faces and fancy clothes. A million miles from the plastic pint glasses of Fylde JCR. A million miles from my granny's croft in Orkney. English accents all around. Surround sound. Suits and ties. What money can buy. My eye. I've lost the others already. Billy-no-mates. A student again, not the man who stepped into someone else's shoes and ended up inside a prison cell.

And there she is, Christie. I see her unmistakeable blonde head through the swarm of guests. She is standing by a display of wine. Bottles and glasses, all shapes and sizes, gleaming like jewels. She's listening politely to some ruddy Hoorah Henry, that broad toothy smile of hers, that sleek easy manner.

Christie. She is standing. Standing. I half-expected a wheelchair but she appears unchanged. Still tall, athletic, graceful. I can only see her from the waist up so I don't know what... well, what she looks like... down there.

Only now she's walking towards me, people parting the waves as if for the queen. *Just call me the Ice Queen.* A smile on her face, her eyes bright, her hair golden. I concentrate on her clothes. A vibrant blue dress. Classic, silk, graceful. Mad Men style – fitted bodice, cinched waist, flared skirt with nets, falling just below the knee.* And stilettos. Two of them. I focus on her breasts instead of her shoes, which somehow, I don't know how, seems better. They are of course bonnie breasts but that's not the point. The point is not to look at the leg, or the absence of a leg, or whatever is or isn't there now, because she has two legs, two feet, a pair of heels, because here she is, in front of me, and I am kissing her on both cheeks and she is wrestling me into an awkward hug.

'It's been too long.'

'Aye.' What else am I supposed to say? I have no idea how I stand with her. Or how she stands with me. Or how she stands at all.

'You seen the others yet?'

---

*I clearly learned something from Amanda.

'They're here somewhere.' I make an exaggerated attempt to look for them, swivelling my head this way and that like an owl. Like that girl from *The Exorcist*.

'And the kids?' she asks. 'What are they like?'

'They're teenagers.'

She waits for me to elaborate.

'They're all right. The girl's friendly. The boy's quiet.'

'So the apples fell a long way from the tree then?'

'Don't they always?'

'Not in my case. I'm half-Mum/half-Dad.'

'Except it would be grapes from the vine, not apples from the tree.'

She laughs. 'That's pretty funny, Cameron.'

I laugh too but it comes out too loud and people standing nearby turn their heads to see what's so funny.

'What d'ya think of the wine?' She nods at my empty glass. 'You like it?'

'Very nice.'

'Can I get you another?'

'No, thank you. I'm okay for now.'

'Wait till you try the Icewine. You'll be blown away.'

'I'm sure I will.'

She smiles at me. Her lips are a little thinner, tighter, than I remember them. A slash of blood-red lipstick. 'You drink then?' she asks.

'I'm sorry?'

'You like a drink these days? You never used to be one for drinking.'

'I have the odd glass of wine.'

'None of the hard liquor?'

'You mean whisky?'

'Or vodka?'

'Why?'

'No reason,' she says.

But there's a reason. And the reason hits me like a blow to the stomach.

251

Christie doesn't know. She doesn't remember. She still believes it was me driving the car.

'To be truthful, I never felt comfortable blaming it all on you, Cameron.' She cuts through any sense of protocol, piercing the heart of the matter. 'Tommo and Bex were the ones to louse up that whole *Top of the Pops* thing. It was Tommo who insisted we stop off at the pub. I could've said no. I could've called a cab. I could've walked or even gotten a lift off Richard. But I was crazy, and a little freaked by Richard, and without thinking I jumped inside that wreck of a Ford and, just a few minutes later, it was totalled. And I was very nearly totalled. But I somehow got out of there alive and for that I'm thankful.'

I feel my tear ducts threaten to spurt. I must not cry. I will not cry. I will not touch the oven or I will get burnt.

'It wasn't intentional,' she says, gripping my arm, her fingers strong. 'It was a series of events that started when you cracked my rib. Or maybe further back when I decided to buy a bun with raisins. Or when I decided to study overseas. It's pointless blaming anyone for what happened that night.'

I have to rub my eye, sniff back some snot. She hands me a napkin.

It's pointless blaming anyone.

Is it? I do. I blame someone. I blame Tommo for what happened on that cold night in Lancashire, the wreck of our young lives strewn across a wet field, the lights of campus glowing in the distance, the stars bright above us.

Christie excuses herself, says we'll talk later, that she has a speech to give right now. I watch her walk away into the throng. With her $25,000 leg.

'I came here as a child, some function or other, dragged along by my father to keep a colleague's son company.' Tommo is beside me, yellow-tipped fingers clasping an empty glass. 'I must've been eleven, twelve, the other boy around the same age. The other boy liked football. Thought the Sex Pistols

252

was a swearword.' He takes a breath, lungs like a rain stick. 'I slunk off once I'd scoffed enough food and tippled enough of the grown-ups' booze. Explored the hotel, followed the sound of music, found a beast of a piano in the lobby, a smart man playing it. I stood up close to the smart man, mesmerised by his delicate girlish fingers flitting across the keys. The notes swarmed inside my head. Made me dizzy with a joy I couldn't name. In a quiet moment the man let me sit alongside. He played 'Bring me Sunshine'. A blissful few minutes when parts of my life connected and the world made some kind of sense.'

'You couldn't do that these days without a CRB check, a health and safety risk assessment and the parent or guardian's written permission.' I'm quite pleased with this retort, but Tommo fires me a dark look. He is on his way to being drunk, pilfers another glass from a passing tray, winking at a pretty red-haired waitress.

'Where's Bex?' I ask.

'She's disappeared somewhere, hunting down Christie no doubt. She's in a stonker of a mood, hates being late for anything. But we're here now and in a couple of hours it'll be over and I can crawl back to bed. All I can think about is sleep.'

'All you can think about is sleep? Are you joking? What about Christie?'

'Well, yeah, there is that. I do want to see her. But I don't know if I have the energy.'

'For God's sake, man. You have to deal with this.'

I leave him then, the sensitive soul, the middle-aged bairn, and seek out the pretty red-haired waitress with the wine. One more glass and I'll be ready to carry on.

Christie chinks a silver fork on a glass.* She waits till she has everyone's attention, introduces herself – though

---

*Riedel Vinum Extreme Icewine glasses are shaped to enhance the aroma and taste of Icewine.

everyone in the room must know who she is: the beautiful, clever Canadian businesswoman and philanthropist who also happens to have a prosthetic leg.

'Ladies and gentlemen, welcome and thank you for coming, especially on such a wet night. You Brits sure know how to welcome a girl.' She does a Marilyn Monroe pout.* The audience respond with an exhalation of laughter. 'I'm going to begin with a story, back in 1968, the year I was born. The year everyone was smoking pot.' Another rumble of laughter. 'And the year my mom and dad decided to go into the wine business.'

She asks for the lights to be dimmed, presses the button on the remote in her hand. There, on two large screens, is the landscape of her home. Wide open skies, like that bit at the end of every episode of *Little House on the Prairie* where the Ingalls girls run down the hill through the meadow grass. Only here, the landscape is flatter and vines stretch into the distance, as far as you can see. And there is her father, the man I never met, the big bear of a Canadian. He talks about the pioneering spirit of the Canadian wine industry back in the day, and I notice Christie dab at her eye with a napkin. A daddy's girl if ever there was one.

The video is holding the audience's attention. Reporters scribble notes in books, on iPhones and tablets. The video finishes. The lights are back on.

She shuts her eyes briefly, opens them again. 'This Icewine is going to be sold in Fortnum and Mason's. It is going to be served by white-gloved sommeliers in Claridge's, the Savoy, here in the Ritz. This is going to work.' She holds the gaze of her audience, the press, the wine critics, the vintners and buyers, us.

She opens a bottle of Icewine, a tall thin bottle, pours a glass, slowly, for dramatic effect, demonstrates how to drink it, how to hold it in your mouth for seven seconds, to savour

---

*Marilyn Monroe starred in the 1953 film noir *Niagara* with the tagline 'a raging torrent of emotion that even nature can't control'.

it, to let the flavours dance on your tongue, to let it roll all around, and then swallow.

'This is Niagara liquid gold. No spitting allowed.' Then she instructs the waiting staff to go ahead and serve. 'Bottoms up.'

There is a rousing round of applause and she beams a smile. But she is clutching her glass so tight, I worry it will smash into a thousand pieces in her hand.

I see the others and make my way through the throng to join them.

'What do you make of it?' I ask.

'Banging,' Tommo says.

'Lush,' Loulou says.

'All right,' Ethan says.

Bex says nothing. Her eyes are elsewhere.

I turn to follow the direction of her stare and there she is, Christie, approaching us, nearing us, standing, standing before us with that smile.

She kisses Bex on both cheeks, European for the moment.

'Congratulations, Christie,' Bex says. 'That was really excellent.' The words sound empty, hollow, as if she's making them up.

'Glad you could be a part of this special night.' Christie's words seem sincere, genuine, from the lips of a true Canadian. She turns to Tommo. They kiss awkwardly. 'What do ya think of the wine?'

'Bloody great,' he says. 'I'm sure it'll go down well over here.'

'That's good to hear.' Christie looks pleased, relieved even. 'So these are your kids, right?'

'Yep, Loulou and Ethan,' Bex introduces them.

They shake hands, are surprisingly charming.

'Listen you two I was given these tickets,' Christie says. 'Do ya wanna go to the movies up there in Leicester Square? I'm not exactly able to go tonight. This must be kind of boring for you guys.'

'I don't know,' Bex says. 'I mean that's very thoughtful. But they'll be fine here.'

'How about I give them to you anyways.' Christie reaches for her handbag and produces them, checks the time. 'The showing's in a half hour so you don't have long.'

'Can we, Mum? I really want to see this film. Don't you, Ethan?'

'Yeah, Mum. We'll be fine.'

'They'll be fine, Rebecca,' says Tommo, a grimness in his voice, a shiny shroud of sweat across his brow.

'Come back as soon as it's finished. We'll be in the suite but, if not, you know the number, don't you?'

'Stop fussing, Mother.' Loulou accepts the tickets and pulls her brother away before Bex changes her mind. 'Thanks, Christie,' she shouts over her shoulder.

Christie shakes her head. 'Geez, have I got this to look forward to?'

'How old's your daughter?' Bex asks.

'Mallory's six.'

'It's just round the corner, then. Though to be honest, Lou's always been spirited.'

'I guess there's nothing wrong with being spirited. We should know that.' A smile flutters between them, delicate as butterfly wings.

Christie offers us more wine, hails a waiter who tops up our glasses.

'So do you mind if I ask you a question?' Bex looks at Christie.

'Sure. Go ahead.'

'Why did you invite us? I mean, it's like one of those films when people are summoned and you're waiting for some big secret to be revealed.'

'A big secret? Do you know something I don't know?' Christie flicks her hair, whispers to her assistant who is hovering proprietorially nearby. With a minute gesture, something Christie does with her hand, the assistant leaves them alone.

'You look amazing,' Bex says. 'You'd never know.'

'Never know?'

'Your leg.'

This is awkward. Really awkward but Bex presses on, Tommo and I watching, listening, silent. An inappropriate expression comes to mind: a car crash. I have a sip of wine to make sure I don't say it out loud.

'I so wanted to see you that night at the hospital. But they wouldn't let me.' Bex's face is flushed, her voice wobbly with emotion. 'They wouldn't let any of us. And then Cameron was arrested and it all got muddled.' She shakes her head like there's something stuck in there she wants to shift. 'I'm sorry we never got to… say goodbye, I suppose.'

'Too bad it all had to end like that.'

'Too bad?' Bex's eyes widen, the spider-leg lashes flicker. 'That's an understatement.'

'I guess,' Christie says. 'To be honest I don't remember much at all from that night. There was the inn, the pub, in that country village. I remember I didn't want to be there. I wanted to get back to my room on campus, especially when I saw Richard.'

'Richard?'

'The professor.' Christie wipes a finger across her brow, to move a stray strand of hair. Perfect hair. Perfect brow. Botox? 'He's here tonight actually. You remember him, Cameron?' She turns to me. They all turn to me.

'I remember him. I think we all remember him, banging on the car window, scaring you witless.' Her tutor. Someone else's husband. 'He came to see me in the hospital room,' I go on. 'He was kind. He smelt of pipe smoke. Said he'd called your parents.'

'He did? That was him?'

'He wasn't the only visitor I had that evening.' I look at Bex. Everyone wanted a piece of me.

'Everyone wanted a piece of you?' Christie looks

257

confused. They all look confused.

'Did I speak out loud again?'

They nod.

'Ignore me.'

They ignore me.

'I lost a big piece of me that night. Back in that bright yellow crappy car.'

Christie has said it. The leg. It's out there, so to speak.

'I'm sorry,' I say. And I am sorry. Of course I'm bloody sorry. But there are others who should be more sorry, while I am maintaining this thirty year long charade.

'You get through it,' Christie says. 'My parents were amazing,' Christie says. 'I had the best care and I still do,' Christie says.' And she lifts the hem of her silk dress and we stare, the three of us stare.

I have to pull back, restrain myself from reaching out to touch it.

'It looks incredible,' Bex says. 'You'd never know.'

'It made me rely on myself, not my body.' She is wistful for a moment. 'It's still pretty awesome though, eh?' Then she laughs that raucous Christie laugh.

'Yeah, it's pretty awesome,' Tommo says.

We all nod in agreement. It's pretty awesome. Idiotic puppets.

I'm light-headed. The room is stuffy. The oil-painted bigwigs on the wall leer at me, the Hoorah Henries in their London finery swim around me.

Bex pulls at the fabric of her dress where it clings to her middle.

Tommo launches on a coughing spree.

I take my chance and go for it: 'Why didn't you pursue me? Through the courts? For money, for compensation? Why did you walk away – oh God, sorry.'

Christie smiles. 'No problem.' She looks towards the carpet, then back up at me. She might not have been expecting this honesty off us Brits, so soon in our re-acquaintance, but nothing fazes Christie. 'Why would I do that?' she asks. 'We knew you were going to be prosecuted. I knew you didn't do anything on purpose. I told my parents I wanted nothing to do with it. I wouldn't give evidence. I couldn't remember anything. And I knew you, Bex and Tommo would tell the truth.'

I feel nauseous. The rich, sweet, pungent wine. The knowledge I am here with Christie while a big secret stokes inside me like the worst heartburn, a malignant tumour.

I lied in court. I said I was driving. I said I was guilty. Tommo and Bex backed this up with their statements. We lied. We could tell Christie now, but we won't. And guilt? Guilt is far worse than perjury. Guilt is a life sentence. Tommo, Bex and I, we all know that. We've lived through that night every night. Over and over and over.

Tommo has knocked back another drink and his cough is a background phlegm-fest as he speaks, falters, tries again. 'It's going well tonight,' he manages. 'I had a brief chat with this guy from the *FT* and he was raving.'

'Oh right,' Christie says. 'I guess I better go find him. Where is he?'

Tommo points him out and Christie heads straight there, leaving us with an enigmatic glance over her shoulder. Tommo starts to cough again. The bright lights burn my eyes. I want to go home.

'Nice wine,' Tommo says. 'But I could do with a cold pint of Kronenbourg. Do excuse me.' And he bows and disappears into the crowd.

'What do you reckon to all that?' Bex says. 'Are you okay?'

'Am I okay? Why do you ask?'

'Because this must be a strain for you.'

'It's a strain for all of us.' I hear myself snap at her, the last thing I want to do, but I'm halfway to being drunk, my head woolly, like one of my gran's jumpers is stuffed inside it, the yarn unravelling and tangling and I know I should stop

259

drinking now. Concentrate. I have to get through this evening but I have this sensation, almost euphoria; I have this power in my hands but I don't know what to do with it because my knitted brain won't tell me.

'Cameron? You look pale.'

'I'm a Scot. A lack of sun and an absence of vitamins.'

'Don't make fun of yourself. Don't let Tommo get to you.'

'I can handle Tommo.'

'What do you mean?'

'Don't worry. I won't do anything stupid. It's you I worry about, still with him after all these years.'

'What's that got to do with you?

'Nothing. It's got nothing to do with me.'

'Exactly. Concentrate on your own failing relationship. Ask yourself why Amanda's walked out on you.'

With that, I walk away from Bex. I leave her stranded in the room because I cannot bear to be so near to her and for it not to be okay.

I felt it just then, the four of us together again. I felt this energy crawl inside me, twist around and threaten to rupture. But I must contain it for now. I've waited for this without knowing I've waited for this. So I can wait a wee bit longer.

I must watch Tommo. I don't want him walking away from me again. The last time I saw him was in that stinking visiting room, Tommo sitting opposite me, a table between us, the Berlin wall. He moaned about his crappy job in a crappy office as if he deserved sympathy. As if I'd just swapped shifts with him, not put my life on the line. There were hard men in that place. I could've had my throat slit, my head bashed in. But I scraped through, made it to the other side, avoided the cracks, the spiders, the bogeymen.

Apart from that first night, when I slipped in the shower. Bex saw the bruise on the side of my face when she came to visit a few days later. *What have they done to you?* Her eyes were filled with concern. I told her what they all said and she shook her head because she knew. Or she thought she knew. And maybe I didn't salve her conscience when I could've done. I might have done this for her, this whole going to prison business, but that didn't mean I didn't want her to worry about me.

'Cameron, isn't it?'

I stop, look round, see an old man sitting in a chair to the side of the room. A slightly worn suit, shiny cuffs and thin knees. A fine head of snow-white hair. Glasses. 'Do we know each other?'

'I wouldn't say "know", not in a deep sense. But our paths have crossed.'

'They have? I'm afraid I don't remember. Did we work together?'

'I was one of your lecturers.'

'Aye, of course. Dr Grey, is it?'

'Professor Grey now actually. Ms Armstrong thought I might like to see the fruits of her Marketing degree.'

The lecturer. The one with the wife and kids. The one who gave Christie more than good grades. The one who was sitting in the pub with a pipe and a paper. The face that stared like a mad man through the car window. An old man for real now.

Does he still have a wife? Do his children love him?

'I'm so very pleased it turned out rather well for her. After the tragedy of that night.'

'Aye, a tragic night.' I'm worried I sound like Fraser in *Dad's Army*. We're all doomed. Maybe we are all doomed. We can all be doomed together.

'I came to see you in the Infirmary.'

'Excuse me?'

'I came to see you in the hospital that night. I had to creep about because I didn't want the police asking me questions.'

'I don't remember much from that night.'

'The human brain is a remarkable thing.'

I wait for him to elaborate but he doesn't. In fact he goes off on a tangent, like a teenager, like a toddler.

261

'I'm sorry you went to prison but I assume that's all behind you now. I don't suppose you'd be here otherwise.'

'I don't suppose I would, no.' I want to make my excuses. I want to get away from this old man. But I can't do it.

'I also assume money changed hands?' he goes on. 'From Ptolemy's family, no doubt. I know they were well-to-do. I know yours wasn't.'

The room tips a little. I might just slide with it, slide and fall over. 'How do you know this?'

'I was first on the scene in my car. I raised the alarm.'

'That was you?'

'It was.' He takes a small sip of his Icewine, holds it in his mouth as Christie demonstrated, then swallows. 'As soon as the first ambulance arrived, I slipped away. You see I'd drunk rather a lot. Like your friend.'

'He was never my friend.'

He waits for me to elaborate. I don't.

'I also saw Ms Stone in the Infirmary. I told her I'd contacted Christie's parents. She was the saddest picture I have ever seen. I've never forgotten that.'

'Then I did the right thing?'

'You did the right thing,' he says.

I don't have a chance to delve further into this because my phone rings out. It's Dad.

'What is it, Dad? Why are you calling me?' I'm outside the Burlington room, pacing the corridor (surprise, surprise). All I can hear is Barbara. 'Farewell to the Whisky'. 'Switch her off, Dad. You're muffled.'

'Sorry, son.' He leaves me hanging on. Barbara continues to sing – *So sit down beside me and I'll soon gang hane* – then she's muted. Dad's heavy footsteps, coming back to me. A fumble, then: 'Are you putting on the Ritz?'

'As we speak, Dad.'

'Did you see what I did there?'

'How long have you been saving that one up?'

262

'Just since this morning, son. How are you doing?'

'I'm okay, Dad. Don't worry. I'll be home tomorrow.'

'And the lassie?'

'Which one?'

'The Canadian one.'

'She's okay. She's doing amazing. Much better than the rest of us.'

'She came from money. Money comes to money.'

'Tommo comes from money.'

'English blood money, son. English blood money. Your mother would have something to say about that.'

'But Mum can't talk, Dad. She cannae talk.'

A bark. Myrtle attacking the front door. A yelp. Silence. And then Sheila. *'I've got my magic knickers on, Andrew!'*

'Oh God, Dad, really? I have to go.'

'Aye, Cameron, sorry about that. I'll see you tomorrow.' And the line goes dead.

I wonder whether it might be best to go up to my bed and put my head under the pillow, smother myself now. The world is going mad and I am going mad with it. But something draws me back into the room, less crowded now, people drifting off home, to restaurants, the theatre, lap-dancing clubs.

And there's Tommo, slumped on a seat with an empty pint glass in his hand. I sit down next to him, weary now.

'Can we leave?' Still the posh boy, the spoilt brat.

'It's not all about you, Tommo.'

'I know it's not all about me.'

'Then why are you letting her go?'

'Letting her go?'

'After all I did for you. Your life would have been so different. You might not have Bex. Or the kids.'

'All right. Steady on, McTaggart.'

'What are you going to do when they've left home and you're old and lonely?'

'I'll have Bex.'

'But will you?'

'Has she said something?

'Not exactly. But I can tell she's not happy.'

'I'll do whatever it takes to make her happy. Why do you think I gave up my chance of success for her? Why do you think I'm still trying?'

Heat's coming off him, sweat's shining on his face. He starts to cough and a waitress is there beside him with a glass of water. He drinks it slowly, trying to hold it together. He coughs again. And again.

'I need some air.'

'I'll come with you.'

'I'll be fine. Really.'*

Tommo gets up and I follow him, man-mark him. I'm his shadow, his ghost. (Boo.) Nowhere to run, nowhere to hide. I am the kilted spectre. Superfirstaider.

Halfway across the room and I wonder what it feels like for Christie, treading this bouncy carpet with a fake leg. A ghost leg. Do you have to concentrate more? Do you forget how to walk? How would a dyspraxic like me manage it with my two left feet?

A flash from the photographer brings us up short. Blinded for a second. When I can see again, Bex and Christie are standing beside us like a double act. The dynamic duo.

Tommo shifts and fidgets and it is like Christie can see right through him, like she has X-ray specs. Like he is the incarnation of guilt. Guilt. She has to find out.

'You guys want to go do something? Get a drink? Something to eat? A walk?'

'I could do with some fresh air,' Bex says.

Tommo coughs. Shrugs in a noncommittal way.

---

*Never let a choking person leave the room. It's human nature to want to retreat. That's when you can fall down, stop breathing and die, no one there to step in and help. (Duke of Edinburgh. Health and Safety. Common sense.) And when you bang the choking person on the back, try not to crack a rib.

'Sounds like you could too, Tommo. That okay with you, Cameron?'

'A walk would be good.'

Christie smiles. She must enjoy seeing me squirm at the mention of the word 'walk'.

Don't mention the walk.

'You okay in that kilt, Cameron? It could be blowy out there.'

'I'll fetch my jacket.'

'Come with me,' she says. 'I have to change my leg. We'll meet you guys down here in ten.'

Ten minutes can seem endless.

I get my jacket then go with Christie to her suite: I sit on her bed. Her bed is bigger and grander than the bed in my suite. Her suite is a lot bigger and grander than my suite.

I am here, in the Ritz, watching Christie get ready. She reapplies her make-up, checks herself in the mirror, rearranges her breasts in the tight dress and puts on her coat so they are hidden from view. All for a walk in the dark with three quasi-strangers.

'I was never really a fan of dresses but I thought it would look better in the photos. I guess I could change into something more comfortable but I honestly can't be bothered right now. Some fresh air and I'll be ready to hit the sack.'

'You look amazing.'

'Thank you. So do you, of course. That kilt really does it for me.'

'Really?'

'In a wild, natural kind of way.'

'That's a compliment?'

'Sure it's a compliment.'

She goes to her suitcase and takes out a leg. A half leg. Changes it over. (A bit different to a false eyelash.) 'So you run ghost tours?'

'I did. I did run ghost tours.'

'Oh?'

'I lost my job.'

She picks up her iPhone from the bed, slips it in the pocket of her fur-lined Parka, sits down on the bed, next to me, the way we used to sit side by side in each other's rooms on campus. 'What happened?'

So I tell her what happened. The whole Sanderson thing. Jeremy. But I don't tell her why it happened. The significance.

'I'm sorry, Cameron. I'm sure something else will come along. A better offer.'

'I hope so. I mean, it's all I know. I've been there since, well, since I came out of prison.'

'Maybe it's time for a fresh start.'

I shrug. 'Maybe.'

'Are you married? Kids?'

'Separated. No kids.'

She waits for me to go on.

'Amanda wants some space.'

'She should try Canada if it's space she wants. We gotta a whole load of the stuff. I was telling Bex they should come out for a vacation. The kids would love it.'

'They probably would. I get the feeling they'd rather be anywhere but home right now.'

'Teenagers always want to be somewhere else, right? That's what got me into this trouble in the first place.' Christie knocks her leg, as if for luck.

I look at it again, look up at Christie's beautiful face, admire the brain inside that head, the courage inside her heart. 'Is that how you see it?'

'I've seen it in all sorts of ways.' She checks her nails, like she's having a manicure, not facing her demons. 'I thought I was okay with it but it's kind of playing around in my head, you know, being back, seeing you guys.'

'Don't you remember what happened at all?'

'Very little but I keep picturing the back of Tommo's head. Why would I do that? I was behind the driver. I can't see you

266

anywhere. I just hear this scream and I think it must be mine.'

'I remember the screaming,' I say. 'The tyres screeching. Being thrown forward like someone was kicking me in the chest and then everything stopped and there was this awful silence. Then my head was filled with buzzing, like there was a swarm of wasps in there, feeding off my brain. I heard Bex though. She was saying we had to get out the car. She could smell petrol. She and I both somehow scrambled out. We got Tommo's door open and dragged him from the wreck. But we couldn't open your door.' I turn to face her, next to me on the bed. 'We tried, Christie. We really tried, especially Bex. Then there were people moving us away and I couldn't see you anymore. I thought you were dead.'

'So did I. Maybe I did die and then decided what the heck, I might as well give this life a second chance, even one-legged.'

'How do you keep so positive?'

'It's the Canadian way. She takes out her compact, slashes some more red across her lips. 'This is turning schmaltzy, Cameron. I don't do schmaltzy.'

'I know that. I read the interview you did for the *Guardian*.'

'You read it?'

'Online. I googled you.'

'What did you think of it?'

'It was very honest.'

'No point in being anything other than honest.'

'Well,' I begin, hesitant but feeling a need to be schmaltzy. 'I'm sorry it didn't work out, your marriage.'

'Don't be. I'm over it.' She flicks her hair like she is flicking away the image of her ex-husband. She pulls me up with her, off the bed and out of the room.

As we wait for the lift, I know it's time for me to open up. (Jeremy would be proud. Job done.) 'I miss my wife,' I tell Christie. 'I want her back. I was never able to love Amanda as she wanted to be loved. Because, even after everything that happened, I was still in love with Bex.'

I'm not sure I know what 'love' means anymore. Even Myrtle only offers me cupboard love. Love wasn't a word bandied about in my childhood home. There were no 'I-love-yous'. No hugs or kisses. An all-male household, the members of which expressed their affection for each other in the medium of hair ruffling, back-slapping and Chinese burns.

But once I had known. And I made a choice. I made that choice out of love. For my family. For Bex.

'Too schmaltzy by far, Cameron,' she says and pushes me into the lift. 'But at least you're being honest.'

Lake

Off we set. Four go on an adventure. Up Piccadilly, down Piccadilly. Along streets and around squares. We end up on a vast busy road. Park Lane. Speaker's Corner. Marble Arch. Bayswater Road, Lancaster Gate. Hyde Park. In we go.

By now Tommo is struggling to keep up with the rest of us. I put him to shame, striding along with my kilt swaying, a woman on each side.

Christie turns round. 'So you're sounding a bit unfit there, Tommo.'

'Just a bug thing,' he wheezes. 'I'll shake it off in a few days.'

'The smokes don't exactly help.' She reaches for his roll-up and takes it from his hand. He is so surprised – not that he should really be surprised by anything Christie does – that he relinquishes it straightaway. She stubs it out with her shoe and I'm trying to remember which leg is missing, which foot she is using. The real or the fake, though there is nothing fake about Christie. That's his speciality, Tommo's speciality: fakedom.

'You okay, Tommo?' she asks. 'You look like a Lost Boy.'

'A lost boy?'

'Like in Peter Pan. Like you're motherless.'

'I am motherless,' he says.

'I'm sorry. I didn't know she'd passed.'

269

'She hasn't. She's still living in France with Le Knob.'

'Not exactly far. Why don't you just go see her?'

'Everything's always straightforward for you, isn't it?'

'You have to make things happen if you want to live fully.'

'You sound American.'

'Shut the hell up.'

We walk on, Bex and I bookends to Tommo and Christie, the park vast and shadowy.

'Come to think of it,' Christie says, 'you are a little like Peter Pan. You know, the kid that never grew up.'

'What do you mean? I'm all grown up and working in the refuse and recycling department of the local council, I'll have you know.' Tommo uses a mock officious voice and she gives him this smile tinged with something unnameable. Sympathy, maybe. Pity, perhaps.

We walk on, the four of us.

'There's a statue of Peter Pan not so far from here,' Tommo says.

'That's neat. Where?'

'Kensington Gardens.'

'Where the Diana memorial is?'

'Yep.'

'I'm not going to worship at the shrine of Diana,' I say.

'You leave our royals alone, John Brown. They made your Scotland what it is. All that tartan-mania and frolicking in the glens.'

'Your Royals are German. And you're half-French. You should be allied with us, not England.'

'I live in England.'

'You live in a backwater.'

'What's wrong with that?'

'Guys, cut it out,' Christie shouts at us. Really yells in a way I've never heard. Then she pulls herself together. 'Let's go see Peter Pan.'

'What time is it?' Bex asks. 'The kids will be back soon.'

Christie checks her watch. A Rolex. Platinum with

diamonds. (I've seen similar in the jewellers in Princes Street, staring in at the window displays with my nose pressed up against the glass like the little match girl.)

'A quarter after ten,' she says.

'Best keep that watch hidden,' Tommo says. 'Some bugger will have your hand off.'

'Geez. I don't want to lose a hand as well as a leg.'

I rub the back of my neck. A ghost's breath upon it. But Christie full on laughs and so does Tommo, and I remember the pair of them in the back of the car on the way to the Lakes, flirting and joking and wondering if they would get together and so leave Bex for me.

Then Tommo starts to pech again and has to stop walking. He is stooped. He is shrinking. He has to bend over, hands resting on his thighs like he's just finished a half-marathon, spitting on the ground.

'You sure you're up to this, buddy?'

'I'm up to it. We're headed that way.'

I see him glance at Bex but she is trailblazing ahead, her own pace, her own mind, her own woman that no one can touch.

Am I dreaming? Peter Pan? We are standing in the middle of a park in the middle of London by a statue of Peter Poncing Pan. Christie is taking pictures on her iPhone. Bex is watching her, hands in the pockets of her winter coat, a massive scarf wrapped round her voluminous hair. Tommo lurks in the shadows, like a mugger.

It is dark. It is cold. A siren moans in the distance.

'Let's walk round the lake,' Bex suggests.

'Call this a lake?' Christie says.

'It's called the Serpentine,' I say.

'Actually this end is called the Long Water,' Tommo corrects me.

Smart-Alec-Know-it-all-Show-off.

We lumber off in a weird group. A kilt, a false leg, a

cough, my beloved.

Déjà vu, snatches of memory. A hike up a hill through fog and snow and sleet. Bex limping with a twisted ankle, sitting with her leg in my lap.

It's spitting now, a soft drizzle that clings to our coats like dew as we walk along a path, skirting the lake, through shadows and dappled lamp light, bushes and shrubs on each side. No traffic and the smell of horse manure so we could be deep in the countryside.

When we get to the Serpentine proper, Christie seeks out a bench and sits down. Bex and Tommo sit down too, one on each side of her, Bill and Ben, George and Mildred. There is a space next to Bex so I take it, having to squeeze up a bit. She shuffles along but I can still feel her coat against mine.

'Do you mind, if I take off my prosthetic? My stump's sore.'

'Course we don't mind, Christie.' This from Bex, speaking on our behalf but making a mess of it as she sounds unsure. Tommo and I remain silent.

'Well, that's *stumped* ya!' Christie quips, a souped-up accent, overegging a bad joke but that's the point. The whole point.

We laugh, all four of us. Quietly at first but then the laugh gathers momentum and becomes a welcome release of emotion. I want to say something nice, something to commemorate this moment but Christie beats me to it. 'I'm kind of surprised that you two made it.' She pats a leg each, one of Bex's, one of Tommo's. 'How have you managed to stay together all these years? I only managed five with Pete. Probably only two of those were any good. I've had longer and more intimate relationships with my doctors.'

'We're not married,' says Bex. 'Maybe that helps.'

'Knowing you could just walk away if you wanted?'

'We have kids. A home. A life together. That's not easy to walk away from,' Bex says.

'So did you ever get to be that go-getter, change-the-world

272

social worker?'

'Not exactly,' Bex says. 'I mean, I *am* a social worker. I work with old people. But I'm never going to change the world.'

'But you're making it a whole lot nicer for those old guys. That's more than most.'

Then Christie goes on to tell us about her charity which helps out kids with missing limbs – land mines, wars, just your average sort of thing. And I feel like a school boy. My first day at school, sitting on the teacher's lap and weeping. Puking in the book corner over the Ladybird books.

I am Pat.

I am Susan.

I am nerd-boy-turd-boy Cameron MacJudas.

I have to do something.

'Last time we were sitting together was at the television centre, waiting for the band to go on.'

I throw it out there, a bone for the dogs to pick over.

No one speaks for a while. Christie is busying herself with her leg. Tommo is hunched over. Bex has turned to stare at me with those eyes I've never forgotten. Eyes that sustained me through my time in prison, knowing I was there for a reason.

'Who can forget?' Bex breaks the silence.

'I've forgotten a lot.' Christie's voice is soft; we can only just hear it above the rustle of the trees. She takes off her prosthetic and lies it on the ground in front of us like a macabre peace offering.

We all stare at it, the lifeless leg.

I shut my eyes, see a flash of white lights, hear my own voice urging *Swing over! Swing over!* A splash of vomit as it hits the road. Someone standing over me, asking if I'm all right. A man in the hospital, offering me money, telling me to say I was driving. I wasn't driving. Tommo was driving. I'm so confused now, I'm beginning to question my own memory. But I remember saying, Yes, I'd do it, I'd take the blame. They said it would work out. I'd get off. But it didn't work. I didn't get off. There was the breathalyser. The grim policeman hovering like Death. They said I'd have my licence taken away. A fine. So I pleaded guilty, did as I was told, knowing there would be a reward. But most of all, I knew I was doing it for Bex, who couldn't live without Tommo. And I could step in and take his place. Even after everything Tommo had done, after everything Bex had done, I loved her. I love her still, I think, though I'm not sure why love should make me feel this way. But I do know it is pointless. It has to stop.

'I'm going for a slash,' Tommo says, before disappearing into the bushes.

I wait for him to be out of sight, then I say: 'I haven't forgotten either. I remember finding Bex on the bathroom floor. I thought she was dying. Then there's this woman, she walks in and calls an ambulance. And soon they arrive and they're putting her on a stretcher thing and carrying her down the corridor. And I remember you, Christie, looking more annoyed than concerned. I remember you telling Tommo not to go with Bex, urging him to stay and do their act. To let me go instead. That she'd be fine with me.'

'You said what?' Bex sits upright, turns to Christie. 'You told Tommo to stay?'

'Easy, Bex,' Christie fires back. 'We knew you were going to be okay. I guessed you'd taken something, and you know what? That was your decision.'

'Yes, it was my decision,' Bex counters. 'But it was a stupid one. My boyfriend gave me the cocaine as I'd had some difficult news that day. I was really down. He wanted me to be all right.'

'He wanted you to be all right so he could go on stage,' I tell Bex.

'You know nothing about Tommo, Cameron. Nothing. You've always warned me off him, but he has a good side. He cares about stuff. About me.'

'I think I know him pretty well,' Christie says.

'What's that supposed to mean?' Bex is on her feet now, fuming.

I look at Christie, wondering what she's going to do.

'He was ambitious,' she says. 'He would have made it big time had he gone on that show.'

'We don't know that,' Bex says. 'No one knows that. You were the ambitious one, pushing him to let me go to hospital without him, right when I needed him most.'

'Sheesh, Bex. I thought you were a strong independent woman. Why the hell would you need him to come? Cameron would've been there for you. It didn't have to be *your* man.'

'Yes, Christie, *my* man. You were after him. You were a man-eater.'

'Thanks.' Christie runs a manicured finger over her sleek eyebrow, exaggerating the gesture for effect. Like she's Mae West. Someone strong and scary and brave. 'So much for the sisterhood.'

'Screw the sisterhood.' And with that Bex bends down and scoops up Christie's leg. She grips it in her hands like it's a cricket bat, a baseball bat, and I actually think she is going to whack Christie around the head. But she doesn't. She walks down the gentle slope towards the water and she hurls the dismembered fake limb into the air where it quivers for one beautiful, glorious nanosecond before falling with style into the lake with a resounding plop.

'Who's the man-eater?' Tommo has emerged from the bushes, struggling to do up his flies. 'And what was that splash?' He looks at each of us in turn, utterly confused.

Then Christie pushes herself up from the bench and hops to the edge of the water, watches helplessly as her $25,000 hand-crafted prosthetic disappears into the darkness of the water. Then, miraculously, it bobs up again, caught in a floating branch.

'My leg! I can see it! It's right there!' She swings from relief to anger in a flash, lurches towards Bex: 'What the hell

275

did you do that for?' As she says these words her remaining leg gives way but I am there, Superkiltman, at her side, supporting her, the fury boiling in her body. She lets me hold her as she shouts at Bex. 'Have you any idea how much that costs!'

'Claim it on your insurance.' Bex slumps back onto the bench, keeping her distance, arms crossed like a grumpy child.

'It's not a freaking accessory,' Christie shouts. 'It's a leg. It takes forever to get one of those made. You can't just go to Walmart and buy one. I need it for walking, seeing as I lost one of my actual legs in a car crash caused by you guys.'

Wow. She said it. All this time and we finally hear her say – well, shout – those words that have chased us down the years.

'What do you mean?' This is Bex. 'Don't you turn this around on me. If you weren't so pushy we would never have been in London.'

'So it's my fault for trying to make a success of that crappy band?'

'Hey,' says Tommo. 'We were not crappy.' Self-absorbed piece of jobbie.

'And what about you?' She turns her head to meet my gaze. 'What have you got to say?'

'I have plenty to say. In time.'

'I don't have time right now. I need my leg. One of you has to go get it.'

She waits. Another siren yowls in the distance. Then quiet.

Tommo is standing beside her now. 'I'll get it.' He takes hold of her left arm while she reclaims her right one from me, then he helps her hobble back to the bench where she sits down as far away from Bex as she can.

'You can swim, right?'

'Course I can swim,' Tommo says. 'They don't call me Johnny Weissmuller for nothing.'

'Johnny Weissmuller is dead.'

'Thanks for that.'

'You're welcome.'

Tommo coughs. Phlegm thrashes around inside his lungs. He wrestles off his leather jacket and chucks it over the back of the bench where it hangs like a corpse. He slowly heads down the slope, tentatively, into the water, his hair shining black in the dark.

But then I find myself wading in after him. 'I'll get it! You've got a cold Tommo, let me!' *Let me*, like I'm teacher's pet. Like I'm back in the JCR the night before the hunt. *Me! Me! Please choose me!*

'Hey, you two!' We stop, up to our thighs in icy water, Tommo's legs skinny as hell, my kilt floating like a girl's skirt. 'Whoever gets my leg, gets a reward. 25,000 bucks. That's Canadian bucks, if you're wondering. What d'ya say?'

She is not unaware that she sounds like a medieval princess. Throwing down her handkerchief. The gauntlet. Whatever it is she throws down, we launch ourselves into the water. The deathly cold water. Water that is far colder than I expected it to be and I had expected it to be cold. But I have a mighty warmth radiating inside me, lighting me up. It gives me strength. It gives me super powers. I strike out into the dark waters, towards the glow of the leg in the moonlight, or is it lamp light, we're in the centre of London, after all, in the Serpentine, Tommo and I fighting for a leg.

I'm so close now. Waist-deep. Inches away.

I lurch with all my might and the leg is in my grasp. I have it. I have won. I am the victor.

I should head back to the bank, hand it over to Christie, keep my eyes on the prize. But I don't. I whack Tommo with it, not as hard as I would like to, just a blow across his shoulders, but it's the sentiment that counts. 'This is for Culloden!' In a flash, Tommo makes a lunge and grapples it back. Whacks me harder than I whacked him. 'This is for the Krankies!' he grunts. Then he whacks me again. 'And the Bay City Rollers!' My strength explodes. I jump up, pushing down on Tommo's shoulders, dunking him under the water, his hair in my hands like seaweed. There is a tussle. Limbs splashing about in desperation. But I am determined. I grope for Christie's leg, find it, grab it, yank it, finally grip it in my hand, raising it aloft like it's Wallace's sword. I paddle towards the shore, kilt ballooning around me while Tommo coughs, behind me now, the enemy, sputtering and swearing but still coming after me. I have a foot on the bed of the lake, and another, and I'm stumbling towards the edge, the shore, dry land, when something rushes up to hit me in the face. *Smack!* I have been rugby tackled, thrown forward into the cold, hard-as-glass water, my breath snatched and swum away with. I have no sense of where I am or what I am doing. My body takes over, floats for what could be ten seconds, ten minutes. I have no sense of time. Then finally, I come up for air, my face stinging, eyes smarting, my mouth full of muck, my kilt weighing me down. It is only when I've struggled to get up, to stand up, that I realise I no longer have the leg. I am empty-handed. I am the runner-up. I am the loser. And yet again, Tommo is triumphant.

Bex and Christie stare with disbelief at the farcical sight of Tommo emerging from the freezing water looking nothing like Daniel Craig, especially with a prosthetic limb in his hand. He is breathing heavily, panting like a dog. Like Myrtle after her daily postman mania.

He hands over the leg to Christie who is sitting demurely on the bench like Diana herself. The vision in red outside the Taj Mahal. The vision in blue by the Peter Pan fountain. With a leg missing. He hands it over in an absurd, gallant style. She inclines her head, accepts it, holds it at arms' length as it drips filthy water onto the path. Tommo takes off his shirt, unbuttoning it with cold fingers, peeling it off his wet skin, a Nirvana tattoo inked across his chest – Nirvana, really – using the shirt like a handkerchief to wipe away at the slime that has gathered during the leg's brief adventure, shivering and shaking, muttering like a nutter to himself, to no one, coughing and barking and spitting gunge onto the path, centre stage again, and I think of him at the Sugarhouse in the dry ice, strumming his guitar, singing out loud with that voice that couldn't hold a long note but that had something special and I think of the trip to London, the BBC, that letter folded up in the pocket of Bex's old man cardigan, the letter I picked up and read, that could've blown away on that cold frosty night on the A6. I think of her convulsing on the floor of the toilets at the BBC, holding her head. I think of Tommo's face: the flutter of anguish, the anxiety of making a choice.

He chose Bex.

And Bex reaches out to him now, puts her hand on his bare, boyish chest. 'I think we'd better go back. You know, check on the kids. And get you dry and warm. Why the bloody hell did you take off your shirt? On a night like this? You'll catch your death.'

'I'm fine,' he says. 'I can't feel the cold.' He smiles at her and takes her hand. He is eighteen years old again, messing about and being cool, an irresistible force. I want to scream at her: *Did you know he blamed you? He blamed you for messing up his precious career as a pop star. Did you know?* But this chance is taken away from me. Tommo slumps to the ground and the skies open.

I'm the one who looks after him while we wait for the ambulance. I thought it was a joke at first, Tommo being an arse, but then Bex freaked out, saying his name over and over, her hair dripping, her clothes soaking.

She's calmed a wee bit, stroking his hand, whispering things I can't hear, not even sure if Tommo can hear them, his head in her lap.

They appear from nowhere, sorting Tommo out, lifting him onto a stretcher where he lies coughing and retching and it sounds pretty bad and Christie looks horrified and Bex is saying sorry again and again and again.

He's taken away, a mask over his face, Bex beside him, still clutching his hand. He lifts his other hand, the non-smoking one, like he is waving to Christie and me but I don't know if he is beckoning or saying goodbye.

Christie has attached her prosthetic.

'Does it hurt?'

'Not really. I'll be okay. We'll get a cab when we make it to the road.' She holds onto me as we follow behind the others, like mourners in a funeral procession.

'I feel awful,' she says.

'Don't.' I am firm. 'Don't feel bad. This is what you might call karma.'

'Do you believe in that stuff?'

'Aye. Your past comes back to haunt you.'

'Do you believe in ghosts?'

'I do. I do believe in ghosts. But look, Christie, there's something I need to tell you.'

'No.' She stops, stands still, closes her eyes, swaying a wee bit so I hold on to her gently. I am soaking wet, frozen through to the bones but I stand with her, mirroring her, except I keep my eyes open.

'A white flash of light,' she says. 'The screech of rubber tires.' Her breathing quickens and I hold her closer. I believe I can feel her heart beating against mine. Boom boom. 'I'm hurled upwards, banging my skull against metal, then I'm tumbling, my ribs breaking, my collar bone snapping, my spleen ruptured, my leg trapped, crushed, darkness.'

'Christie…'

'No,' she says again, firmly, eyes still closed. 'I dreamt of home. I saw my mom and dad. He was out on the estate, inspecting the vines, she was in the office, bossing people around. I felt the hot Ontario sun on my skin and heard the Niagara River as it fell over the rock. Then it was like I was in a barrel, like the old school teacher who went over the Falls. I was a leaf on the wind, a snowflake in a blizzard, plunged deep into the waters. I was beaten up and drowning. Then I seemed to get through it. I thought I'd take a nap. Sleep it off. Then I'd be okay. I'd make it home. That's when everything went quiet and I thought I was dead.'

'Christie…'

'I heard voices. Felt vibrations rumble through me. Someone held my hand and squeezed it. They said they'd get me out of there. I didn't know where "there" was. My mind was empty. I remembered nothing. But now I see black hair. I see a leather jacket. I see Tommo.' She opens her eyes, shudders like a ghost has walked over the grave she was very nearly lowered into all those years ago. 'I know what you're going to tell me,' she says. 'Tommo was driving, wasn't he?'

I nod, solemn as an undertaker.

A beat.

'You went to prison for God's sake? Why would you cover for Tommo?'

'He was drunk and I'd only had two drinks. His dad came to the hospital and asked me if I'd do it. If I'd swap places. And Bex was distraught. She knew Tommo would never survive prison. They said I'd get a suspended sentence.'

'Wait a minute. Tommo's dad. Tommo's rich dad with the sacks of gold. He gave you money if you'd take Tommo's place?'

'He was over the limit.'

'So were you.'

'I'd only had two drinks.'

'But the breathalyser said otherwise.'

'I know it did. But I truly believed I'd only had two drinks.'

She stops, takes this in, carries on walking, striding fast. I have to hurry to catch up with her so I don't get left behind. 'It seemed too late to go back and change my mind,' I tell her. 'And my family needed the money. And there was Bex. I did it for Bex.'

She stops again, stares at me intently so I can't look away as much as I want to because the shame is too much.

'Shut the hell up. I can't believe I never questioned this. I could never get a hold of it, that night. It was slippery, fluid, always changing but always the same black hair. I should've known.'

'We tried to make the best of a terrible, terrible situation.'

'And Bex went along with it?'

I nod.

'The weak, pathetic, love-struck bimbo.'

She was weak, pathetic and love-struck, but not a bimbo.

'And you took his place, over the limit?'

'They said it wouldn't be as big a deal for me as it would be for Tommo who was wrecked. Who'd already been hauled up on a drug's charge, remember.'

'The bastard,' she hisses. 'Sorry, I shouldn't say that when he's so sick, but what the hell?'

'We all willingly got in that car.'

'I wanted out of there. Richard was being creepy. The trip to London sucked. I don't remember thinking anything but that.' She pauses for a moment. 'But when I came round and they questioned me, explained to me what had happened, I told Dad I just wanted to go home. I persuaded him to drop any idea of pursuing you through the courts.'

'You did?'

'When I knew you'd been charged, I was shocked, but I didn't question it. And when I heard you'd gone to prison I knew that was retribution enough. You didn't need my dad chasing you to the gates of hell.'

'The gates of hell?'

'My dad's a dramatic person. It's the sort of thing he'd do.'

'I thought I'd only had two drinks,' I say, another of those Lost Boys.

We carry on walking along the path, one foot in front of the other.

282

Thatcher changed the political landscape of British politics, transforming even the Labour party. Her rise from a grocer's shop to death at the Ritz is a story that still divides opinion today.
June Purvis, *Emmeline Pankhurst: A Biography,* *(Routledge, 2002)*

St. Mary's Hospital, Sunday Morning Corridor

The last time I was in London I was in a hospital looking after Bex. This time she is looking after Tommo.

Christie and I got a cab back to the hotel to check on the twins. They were very quiet, even Loulou. They wanted to go straight to the hospital but Christie persuaded them to stay put, to get some sleep, they could see their dad in the morning.

I don't know if this was for the best. When my mum went to hospital she didn't come back. All my life I've been unable to shake off this feeling that had I gone with her she might have been okay, which I know is stupid.

I find Bex, wandering the corridor (yes, yes, I know) outside the high dependency unit, her face crumpled with worry, a hospital blanket wrapped around her. It's serious. I only have to see her eyes to know that.

'He has severe pneumonia,' she says. 'He needs oxygen to breathe,' she says. 'It's my fault,' she says.

'Your fault?'

'I was so angry with him I couldn't see that he was ill.'

'You're not his mother.' My words sound spiteful even to my own ears. I touch her arm, to show her I care.

'He never had a mother to speak of.' She is protective, moving away, siding with Tommo, as she always has, as she always will.

'You're still not his mother. He makes his own decisions.'

'Heavily influenced by me. Otherwise they're the wrong ones.'

'But he came with you that day. He stuck by you.'

'Yes, he did. But I've spent the last twenty-five-plus years feeling bad about that. And now I've been nagging him to give it all up, the playing in grotty bands in grotty pubs to grotty audiences, but it's what he loves, it's what he does and maybe he's going to die.'

'I'm sure it's not that bad?'

'He's very poorly. They're going to X-ray his chest. They looked concerned.'

She looks concerned too. Very concerned. Her forehead is wrinkled into a frown and she is fiddling with the silver ring on her non-wedding finger. She stops mid-twiddle. 'What about the kids? Are they okay?'

'They're with Christie. She said she'd stay with them.'

'Oh, that's good.' She sighs. 'I know they're old enough to look after themselves but they'll be worried sick.' She sighs again. 'That's nice of her.'

'She's a mother. She'll understand.'

We don't speak for a few moments, both lost in thoughts, then Bex says: 'There's a relatives' room. Let's go there.'

We go there, sit side by side on a sofa, listen to the tick of a clock.

Bex breaks the silence. 'The old people's friend.'

'The old people's friend?'

'Pneumonia.'

'But Tommo's not old. He's barely middle-aged. He's forty-seven.'

'He's forty-six.'

'People get over pneumonia all the time. They have antibiotics. He's not overweight.'

'He smokes.'

He certainly does. One fag after the other. Like my dad, smoking since he was a kid. He has to stop or it will kill him. 'Maybe this will make him give up?' I sound uncertain even to my own ears. I am actually uncertain.

'That's true.' She grasps my hand and I'm back in my room on campus, top to toe with Bex in my bed, with the clean sheets, wondering if I dare reach out and touch her.

I feel an overwhelming sadness. For my younger self. For Bex. But not for Tommo. I've nothing left for him.

A nurse comes in the room. 'We're taking him up in a moment if you want to see him briefly.'

'Taking him where?'

'His X-ray.'

Bex drops my hand, on her feet in a flash. Same old, same old. Tommo beckons, Bex goes without a backward peep. That's how it is. I accepted it long ago. I have loved Bex from afar. I did whatever I could to make her happy.

It was always Tommo that made her happy.

The heavy door clunks shut. I am alone on the IKEA sofa, clutching an IKEA cushion to my chest like a teddy bear. The clock on the wall says nearly midnight. Maybe I'll turn into a pumpkin. Maybe Tommo will turn into a cabbage. A vegetable. Maybe he'll die.

It is so clear now, sitting here alone in a room that must have witnessed so much grief. I know, as I have known deep down for many years, that I was well and truly conned by the father and son duo. I, Cameron, only had two drinks that night. I, Cameron, only willingly had two drinks.

Like Christie, there are things I now remember clearly. And like Christie, the things I now remember clearly are to do with Tommo.

Tommo calling me a poof. Tommo up and down to the bar. Tommo watching me and winking, his dark eyes mischievous.

And the orange juice. It tasted bitter. I thought it was

the cold I was getting, a sore throat and a runny nose. But it wasn't. It was the vodka that Tommo spiked it with.

Tommo is an English bastard. I am a Scottish fool.

I stand behind her, watching and waiting. Bex is holding Tommo's hand; their fingers are entwined. *Still, still to hear her tender-taken breath and so live ever – or else swoon to death.* His hand is safe in hers. It won't pluck a string again. It won't strike a chord. If he gets out of this place, he could take Bex and the kids around the world. He could hunt down his parents and make his peace with them. He could accept money from them to pay for his children to go to university, to travel, to do whatever they want to do, to make the most of their talents and passions and skills.

But for now.

'You need to rest,' she says. 'Take your hand in mine,' she says. 'Marry me,' she says.

It might be a dream, the strangeness of the night, but I am pretty sure that's what she says.

Anyhow, Tommo says yes. I hear him loud and clear. He says yes. Yes. Aye.

And this is my chance. I could say it. I could tell Bex that Tommo blamed her for the whole sorry *Top of the Pops* fiasco. I could tell Tommo that I know he spiked my drinks. I could.

But my phone goes again. Tommo and Bex both turn to look at me as I fumble with it, doing one of those comedy catch things that is part of my repertoire.

'Fracking hell, Cameron,' says Tommo. 'You pick your moments.'

'I'm sorry. I really should take this call.'

'Go ahead,' he says. 'Don't mind me,' he says. 'I'm only dying,' he says.

I'm back in the relatives' room with the clock and the sofa.

'You were supposed to text me about the meeting,'

Amanda says.

'Do you have any idea what time it is?'

It is nearly three in the morning.

'Yes, Cameron, I know what time it is, thank you very much. I have a pony clock on my bedroom wall that is driving me insane with its ticking. I couldn't sleep. Did I wake you?'

'No, I'm in the hospital.'

'Are you okay?'

'I'm okay. It's a long story.'

'Well, anyway, you were supposed to text me. I've been lying awake worrying and so I just thought I'd phone you and ask.'

'I'm sorry I forgot to text you.'

'Don't worry about that just tell me what happened.'

'Not good news, I'm afraid.'

'Oh?'

I sit on the sofa, the reality gnawing away at me now. I have no job. I blew it. 'They sacked me,' I confess.

'They sacked you? Really?'

'Really.'

'After all those years you put into that place.' She is outraged on my behalf and I am grateful for that.

'It seems Mr Sanderson wasn't too impressed about the whole being-locked-in-with-the-ghosties thing.' I try to make light of it though I know it was a stupid thing to do. 'He has asthma.'

'Everyone has asthma these days,' she says.

'Including me,' I say.

'You're a genuine case, Cameron. I've seen you at your worst, remember.'

'You have and I'm sorry.'

'Me too.'

'How long will you be at your mother's?'

'I'm not sure. She's fussing around me, bringing me breakfast in bed and taking me to lunch at the golf club.'

'Sounds good.'

'It's awful, Cameron. I feel like I'm twelve again.'

Amanda had an even worse teenage life than me. An all-girls' school that excelled at music and sport. She can't hold a tune in a bucket and she's almost as dyspraxic as me.

'At least you have a mother.'

'I'm sorry, Cameron. That was thoughtless.'

'No, I'm sorry. I shouldn't have said that, Amanda. You're entitled to your feelings.'

'You've been seeing Jeremy, then?'

'Is it that obvious?'

'It's good, Cameron. I'm proud of you.'

'You are?'

'I am.'

'Look, I'd better go. I'll speak to you tomorrow. I promise.'

'Do you mean today?'

'Yes, today.'

'Take care then.'

'I will. And try not to kill your mother.'

'I promise. As long as you tell me that long story tomorrow. I mean, today.'

I return briefly to Tommo's room. He looks up and gives me his half-salute. There is a cannula in the back of his hand hooking him up to fluids and drugs. Bex gets up wearily from her chair, where she has been keeping vigil, and comes towards me. Hugs me. Holds me in her arms.

'Thank you, Cameron,' she says. 'For everything you've done. You're a star.'

But I'm no star. I am a spark. Sparks will fly. Stars will spin. Planets will crash and collide. Time and matter will disappear into black holes.

London Euston. Another train. Another destination. First-class so I can think in some kind of peace, though maybe now is not the time for thinking. No more thoughts, no more words, just action.*

I said goodbye to Christie early this morning. She was napping in Bex and Tommo's bed, the twins next door. She heard me knock and hopped over to let me in.

'How is he?'

I told her. I told her what I could.

'How have things been here?'

'I told the kids about the race to save my leg. I told them their dad was a valiant hero and I've transferred $25,000 into Bex's bank account. Loulou knew her details. She's a canny one, as you Scots would say.'

'We're not all tartan and whisky, you know.'

'I know. You've got haggis and neeps as well.'

And I remembered her quip about the beavers and moose long, long ago. 'Touché.'

She laughed. She remembered too. 'It's been crazy, eh? Meeting up again. Bex throwing my leg. You two in the lake.'

'Crazy, indeed.'

'Look, Cameron. I have an offer for you.'

'Oh dear. I don't have a good track record of accepting offers.'

'Well, this is unlike any other offer you've ever had,' she said. And she laid it out straight and I must've looked unsure because she said, 'Go speak to your wife about it.'

'Okay,' I said. 'I will.'

Then I hugged her goodbye, a Canadian bear hug, and she said, 'Sheesh, Cameron. I think you just cracked a rib.'

I think of Christie now, as I sit on this train, London to Birmingham. I think of that smile, that laugh, that way she has of looking at the world, facing it full-on, and I know in my heart, in my mind, and in the very depths of my soul, that out of all of us, the four of us, she is the brightest star.

---

*Deeds, not words, as the suffragettes would say. 100 years on and us Scots could take a leaf from their book.

Those who have insight will shine brightly like the brightness of the expanse of heaven, and those who lead the many to righteousness, like the stars for ever and ever.
Daniel 12:3

Edgbaston, December 2013, Sunday

Cricket

The view from Amanda's bedroom is reassuring and calm. A long suburban lawn. Established shrubs and bushes. A herbaceous border. A rockery. A pond with a miniature Monet bridge. And at the bottom, a whacking great weeping willow.

When I phoned her from the train to say I was coming, she sounded surprised, reticent. But she was there, waiting for me at the station, waiting for me in her mother's 'run-around'.

That was two hours ago. Her mum and dad are out for the afternoon at some fundraising do or other. We've had some tea and Madeira cake, I've told Amanda about Christie's offer* and we've slunk upstairs to her bedroom with the rosettes and the pony clock to listen to the crappy music on her iPod (Elton John actually leaves me hankering after Barbara). Her parents will be back soon so I don't have much time. I'm about to suggest something when she beats me to it.

'Sit down, Cameron,' she says gently, patting the space next to her on the single bed with its flowery duvet cover and plethora of scatter cushions.

I remove the cushions and pile them up on her window seat, take one last look at that whacking great willow tree

_____
*I will get to this eventually.

swaying sadly at the end of the lawn and sit down on the bed, not in the space, but by her feet, so I can look at her.

'Why did you come?' she asks.

'Okay. Here's the thing.'

'What thing?'

'A big thing.'

She raises an eyebrow and I remember our monthly curry, her chicken korma and Cobra beer, just like Christie once upon a time when she still had two legs and I had a chance of happiness.

I still do. I still have a chance of happiness.

Take it, Jeremy says. *Take it.*

'I love you and I want our marriage to work. Let's go home.'

'That's good,' she says. 'Because I have some news.'

My phone rings. She says, 'Go ahead, answer it.'

I let it ring. 'Tell me,' I say. 'Tell me your news.'

'I'm pregnant,' she says.

'You are?'

'Yes, I am. Quite a bit pregnant.'

'How much pregnant?'

'Nearly half full. Nineteen weeks.'

'And are you okay? The baby? Is everything okay?' I start to cry.

'Yes, Cameron. we're fine. Now come here and hold me.'

I crawl up the bed and hold her. We lie down side by side. My tears make her mascara run and I wipe away the inky mess with the sleeve of my shirt, smudging it all over her face so it looks like she's been up a chimney.

Gradually, my crying subsides as relief and joy bubble up into some new chemical I have never experienced and as my body relaxes, I think I can feel a bump of a baby pressing against me.

'I have a scan next week, on Thursday,' she says. 'Back in Edinburgh. At Simpson's. Will you come with me?'

'Of course,' I say. 'I'm not going to let you down ever

again. Till death do us part and even then I will come back as a ghost to watch over you.'

'Unless I die first, of course.'

'No, women always live longer.'

The phone goes again and this time I answer it because I see who is calling. And I know what she is going to say.

Scatter my ashes, strew them in the air.
Lord, since Thou knowest where all these atoms are,
I'm hopeful Thou'lt recover once my dust,
And confident Thou'lt raise me with the Just.

James Graham, Marquis of Montrose, on the eve of his execution in 1650

Edinburgh, December 2013, Tuesday
Braveheart

I am waiting in the café, Myrtle at my feet, a half-drunk cappuccino delivered to me by Gina, the thesis-writing barista. It is five to ten. He will be here soon.

I have the window seat so I can see him walking up the road, still upright for a man of his age. Grey, groomed hair, a leather briefcase, an expensive-looking coat that is nothing like Dad's tatty anorak.

I stand up as the door opens, give Myrtle a gentle kick when she growls, though part of me would like to watch her sink her teeth into his Gieves and Hawkes tailor-made trouser leg.

'Cameron.' He proffers his hand.

I reach across the table and shake his manicured hand, and I make sure I have the firmest of grips. 'Monsieur Dulac.'

'Call me "Gerard",' he says, his French accent still clear after all the years of living in England.

He sits down, places his briefcase carefully by his feet, his hand-made loafers polished to a shine a soldier would be proud of. Polished by someone else's hands, no doubt.

Gina takes his order. Earl Grey. With a slice of lemon.

'You're probably wondering why I asked to meet you.'

'I'm curious.'

'Losing a child is something no one ever thinks will happen, except in their worst nightmare.'

Losing a child. As he says these words, I can see the ghost of his son in his intense, dark eyes. And that's what Tommo is now: a ghost.

'I wanted to see you in person,' he says, 'I owe it to you. And to my son.' He looks out the window, rolls his shoulders, turns back to me.

My foot is jittering. I make a conscious effort to plant my toes to the floor, feel the solid comfort of Myrtle against my leg. What does he owe me? What does he owe Tommo?

Gina brings his tea. A pot, a hot water jug, tea cup, two slices of lemon in one of those ramekin things.

'What happened, if you don't mind me asking?'

'No, I don't mind you asking.' He takes the lid off his teapot, leans forward a little to smell it, replaces the lid. Sits still for a moment so I wonder if Gina has brought him the right tea but I can smell bergamot, orangey and floral, so it must be Earl Grey.*

'As you know, he was very sick in London,' he begins. 'Pneumonia. He had no chance to fight it because his lungs were full of tumours, his body riddled with cancer. It's a wonder he didn't succumb sooner. He got weaker and died two days ago.' He says this like he can't believe it. Who *can* believe it? Tommo dead.

'I am very sorry for your loss, Gerard. Genuinely. I don't know what else to say.'

'Thank you.' He pours his tea. The cup rattles. 'I believe Rebecca phoned to tell you.'

'Yes, she did. It was a shock.'

'I thought nothing he could do would shock me but this was certainly unexpected.' As if Tommo planned it. As if Tommo was ever in charge of his destiny.

'When's the funeral?' I don't know why I ask because I

---

*I have a finely tuned sense of smell from working below ground, in the dark, listening out, always on the alert.

know exactly what Gerard will say.

'Next Thursday.'

Thursday.

Does the anguish of making a choice flash across my face? I hope not. Because in my mind I am quite, quite clear.

'I'm very sorry, Gerard. I won't be able to come. My wife is having a baby and it's her ultrasound scan that day, here in Edinburgh. It's important I go with her.'

'Of course. You must do what you think best.' He sips his tea, quite the English gent for a Frenchman. 'It is right for you to concentrate on your future rather than dwell on your past.' He sighs, puts sugar in his tea, three spoonfuls of it. He is on the verge of saying something, hesitates, then speaks.

'I have a letter from her,' he says. 'She knew I was coming here today so she quickly wrote it yesterday. She was adamant you had it.' He reaches into the breast pocket of his coat, which he is still wearing, pulls out a letter and I remember that other letter, folded over and over and shoved in a granddad cardigan.

I begin to open it but he says, no, not now, wait till he's gone. He has something else he must tell me first.

I arrange my facial features into an appropriate response, hopefully a mixture of anticipation and politeness.

'I am sorry,' he says.

'Excuse me?'

'I am sorry,' he repeats. 'For what both Ptolemy and I did. For our... arrangement. It was very wrong of me to put you through all that. And it was wrong of me to step in and help my son. He learnt nothing.'

Words I never thought I would hear. Words that are both soothing and disconcerting, for I know I am not without blame. And I know, just as my mother taught me all those years ago, reading me stories as she sat on the wicker chair with her Brooke Bond, me in bed in my tartan pyjamas, I know that the past makes us who we are, but that we must learn the lessons the past tries to teach us. And most of all, we must not be bitter because then we cannot be happy. And happiness is what we must strive for. (You're welcome, Jeremy.)

'Maybe Tommo – Ptolemy – didn't learn anything but you must know that I did. I learnt a lot. I learnt so very much.'

He nods, takes a sip of his tea, and then Myrtle chooses her moment to growl again. He reaches down and strokes her behind the ear. She falls at his feet. His well-shod feet.

'I must go now. I have much to arrange.'

'Are you going back to London?'

'Actually, I am going to Devon. Rebecca is meeting me at Exeter airport.'

'Give her my love,' I say. 'My very special love.'

As I watch him take his leave, I know I have made the right decision. Amanda, the baby, and me. We will be keeping the union and making it stronger. Happiness is there for the offering and I'm going to put a big fat tick in the Yes box.

I hold the letter tight as I walk up the Royal Mile, comforted by the tartan tat and the sound of skirling bagpipes, the Christmas lights and the rush of people. I stand near the Heart of Midlothian* and I open it. A man comes by and spits on the heart, so I move away to a safer distance, perch at the foot of the towering statue of the Duke of Buccleuch.

Totnes, Monday 16th December
Dear Cameron
Knowing that Gerard was coming to see you, I wanted to write you a letter. Forgive me if it seems rushed; it is rushed. My thoughts are all over the place so take what you will from this.

Tommo got worse soon after you left. The X-ray

---

*The Heart stands in the place of the old Tolbooth prison. It is meant to be in the exact place of the death cell where convicts awaited the gallows. Some people spit on it – for contempt, for good luck, tradition.

showed us what was wrong. All those years of smoking and angst were bound to take their toll. I wish there had been time to get married – I think you knew I asked him and he said yes – but it wasn't to be, and really it didn't matter. The thought was there. The possibility. And I have the twins, my boy and girl, to show that our relationship was worth something. It was worth something, wasn't it?

Finally, I want to say sorry for what happened. I should've been stronger. I'll never forgive myself for that. And I know Tommo was sorry too. He might not have said it but I know how heavily that guilt weighed on his shoulders all these years. At least he is clear of that now. And I want you to know that I in no way hold you responsible for his death. He might've got cold and wet and bashed about a bit in the park but he had cancer and he was going to die regardless of the pneumonia. I just wish we'd had more time. Then we could've got married and tied things up better. But it wasn't to be.

So, Cameron Spark, I hope you work things out with Amanda and I wish you happiness in your future and send love from us all.

Bex xx

I am not entirely sure how to take this letter. Does she actually hold me to account for Tommo's early demise? Does it mean the scales have been balanced? Check and mate?

Either way, I feel the cold rush in from the Forth and I slip like a ghost into St Giles.

The hush wraps around me like a hug from my Granny Spark, the Viking from the north, the storytelling knitter. She set alight the idea of legends, she sparked my imagination. She encouraged me to peel back the layers, to peek through the gaps. My Granny Brown was all about the history, the facts as she saw it: us Scots against our English oppressors. My own mum was bewitched enough by my father's Orcadian blood to weave the myths of her country into the cloth of history. And this union, she passed onto me. And I will pass it onto my child. Our child.

I go up to the Holy Blood Aisle and light a candle, say an awkward, silent prayer for Tommo, that his soul will be set free. That he will not be destined to wander the underground world. While the candle burns, I look around me. All is quiet. I take the letter and I hold it to the flame, watch it catch, and turn from a spark to a beautiful orange the colour of a fox's brush.

Unfortunately, being dyspraxic, I am not very adept at fire craft, despite my time doing the Duke of Edinburgh award (it's a miracle I ever completed that). I don't really know what to do with a burning letter. Have I learnt nothing from the touching-the-oven incident?

I let it go and it falls like an incendiary bomb to the floor so I stamp on it as quietly and quickly as I can with my foot, wishing for my old Clarks Commandoes which might not have felled women, but which would not have caught fire like this brogue of mine. I have to take it off and whack the floor with it, beating the flames like a maniac. By now there is a crowd of American tourists standing around. They are all agog, thinking I'm yet another bloke acting out a part. A heretic. A mad monk. A raving Plague victim.

When the fire is out, thankfully and mercifully, I take a bow. They clap and I hand round my scorched shoe for a collection before making a hasty exit as a guide marches towards me.

I give the charred shoe and its £11.55 gratuity to a drunk on the Cowgate on my way home. He asks me for my other shoe. So I give it to him and walk the rest of the way home in my socks.

I probably should've waited before burning the letter. I could've revived the idea of a bonfire in the back garden, set a match to everything and started over.

Believe me when I say that burning the letter was not an act of vandalism – it was to do with freeing myself from the past. Jeremy told me about it. You write a letter to someone – usually a dead person who you miss – in my case that would be my mother. (Maybe I will do that yet.) Then when you have written all you want to say, you let that letter go. You can throw it to the wind, you can scatter it across the waves, or you can set fire to it.

So I set fire to it – not that I'd written the letter; I'd received it. But the sentiment is the same. Letting go. Though I probably shouldn't have done it in a cathedral, the High Kirk of Scotland no less. But it's done now. It's gone.

I also read somewhere that Native American Indians believe that when you write to a deceased person and then burn the letter they can read it in the smoke and ashes. Most of the ashes of Bex's letter are stuck to the sole of my brogue, which is now on the foot of a drunk on the Cowgate. But I think I will write my mum a letter, nonetheless, and then she can read it, wherever she might be.

House

My feet are stone cold and filthy wet by the time I reach home. I stand on the doorstep, shivering, peeling off my socks and put them straight into the bin before letting myself in. The house is deathly quiet. No Barbara, no Myrtle. Dad must be next door or walking the dog. But there's a light on in the kitchen.

Fight or flight? Jeremy asks me.

It's a no-brainer. I pick up an umbrella from the stand in the hallway – it doesn't matter that it is flowery and pink – and I creep in my bare feet towards the light in the kitchen. I am all ready to pounce like a ninja with a brolly when I see that it is Andy, sleeves rolled up, lying on his back under the sink. Fixing the dodgy tap.

'Andy?'

He fair jumps out of his skin, bashing his head and swearing like the docker he could've been if we still had docks to speak of.

'Sorry,' I say. 'Thought we'd had a break-in.'

He wipes his hands on a tea towel and slings it on the draining board.

'Do you need to finish that?' I point to the cupboard under the sink.

'All done,' he says and I watch him put back the bleach and Jeyes and Kiwi shoe polish. 'Another sticking plaster on the wound.'

'The house?'

'Aye, it's getting tatty again. He needs to sell up.'

'I've told him.'

'The only one he'll listen to is Sheena. He thinks the world of her, you know.'

'I know.'

Andy stretches up to full height, which is a couple of inches more than me, though he has a much wider body. He has a belly on him. No wife to nag him. No wife to take care of him.

'Cup of tea then?'

'I'd prefer a can,' he says.

I go to the fridge. It's well-stocked, with proper food, vegetables and everything. Sheena is looking after Dad's heart. She just needs to tackle those lungs now. I take out two cans of Deuchars.

'Slàinte,' he says.

'Back at you.'

We clink cans. Brother to brother, oldest to youngest.

'So how you've been?' he asks me. 'Dad said you're having trouble at work. And with Amanda.'

I take a sip and remember why I usually drink wine. 'I've lost my job.'

'What happened?'

I tell him what happened. He laughs at me. 'Good on you, Cameron. I'm surprised you didn't do it sooner.'

'What, break up with Amanda?'

'No, you dobber. Your job. I'm surprised it took you this long to get wound up by those English tourists.'

Feeling more confident, I tell him about Amanda. And the baby. He goes all soppy, grabs me round the neck and mushes up my hair. 'Nice one, curly bonce.' Then he has a think, scratching his head like Stan Laurel. 'Why the hell are you living here if there's a bairn on the way?'

'I'm not actually sure.'

'And what are you going to do about work?'

'That's the other thing,' I say. And I tell him about Christie's offer.

'So maybe you'll be able to buy some shoes.' He looks at my feet, black and shrivelled. 'Go and get cleaned up. I'll make you something to eat.'

'Right, I will. I'll have a bath.'

'Good idea.' He finishes his can and picks up mine, which I have left un-drunk on the table.

'And Cameron.'

'What?

'Thank you. For what you did. Back in the day.'

'Forget it, Andy. Really. Forget it. Let's put it in the past.'

I leave the room quickly because I don't know what it is about Andy but he always makes me feel like crying. Like greeting my bloody heart out.

It's quite a party by the time I come downstairs, clean, dry, with a fresh pair of woolly socks (me, not the party).

Not only have Dad and Sheena returned but also my other two brothers, Gavin and Edward, have piled in. Despite us all living in Edinburgh, the four of us boys gathered here around the kitchen table doesn't happen that often.

And Myrtle. I can't forget Myrtle who is sprawled, calm and placid, in Andy's arms, no electric collar. The dog whisperer.

'I'm glad I've got you all here,' Dad says, firing up some classic Barbara, 'I know him so well' (from *Chess*, the musical by the Abba boys and Tim Rice, helped along by the wee Elaine.) 'We've been away up the town,' Dad says, breathless and peching so I have to suppress thoughts of Tommo. 'I bought a ring for Sheena.' He blushes the colour of a Heart's shirt. 'We're getting hitched.'

There's a pause all round. A moment. Then Andy, the oldest, steps in to offer congratulations, says the right thing and the rest of us follow suit. Dad looks relieved, but not as relieved as Sheena.

'I won't ever try and replace your mum,' she says. 'But I do promise to take care of your dad. Starting with the cigarettes. Now, who's for a whisky?'

'Let me,' I say. 'I have some Macallan's.' And the surprise that follows, that I, Cameron Spark, should be in possession of a fine single malt, is greater than the surprise over the engagement of two septuagenarians.

Check and mate.

Later, when everyone has gone and the house echoes with memories, Dad and I sit in the front room, the fire lit and a cup of tea each with a splash of whisky.

'So, I was thinking of downsizing?'

'That's great, Dad.'

'It's getting too big, the stairs are a struggle and Sheena would like a bungalow.'

'It's a great idea.'

'And, Cameron, I can pay you back the money you gave me.'

'No, Dad. I don't want the money. It's English gold.'

'English, Scottish, British, whatever it is, I want you to have it. Please. Sheena has her house to sell too. We don't need it. You need it though, son. You don't have a job.'

'There's something else, Dad. I've told Andy. I couldn't tell you all earlier, all together. I was overwhelmed.'

'What is it? Are you okay?'

'Amanda is pregnant,' I say, making the words real. 'And we're back together.'

Then I cry, bawling like a bairn myself and my father holds me in his arms, holds me still and close. The stink of fags is pretty overwhelming too, but worth it.

'And there's something else,' I say to him, once he has let me go and I can breathe again. He's dabbing at his own eyes.

'Oh?'

'I've been offered a new job so I don't need the money.'

'That's great, son.' He strikes up another cigarette. Sheena needs to marry him fast and get stuck right into the new regime.

'Where?' he asks. He shifts in his chair, something ticking over in his brain, like the sunburst clock above the fireplace.

'Canada.'

'Canada?'

'In Ontario. Head of tours at Christie's winery. A good salary, a car. And houses are cheaper there. I'll be fine, Dad. We'll be fine.'

'Christie offered you a job? How come?'

'Part luck, I suppose. The wine estate is expanding. The brand is growing. They've had this British launch. But back in Canada she wants to organise the tours better. They don't really have anyone with experience. Twenty years beneath Edinburgh has taught me all about tours.'

'You won't go locking anyone in the cellars.' He chuckles, the comedian.

'Ha ha, Dad. No, I won't,' I say and I don't know if I am flushing from the memory or from the fire's glow.

He finishes his fag, aims it with skill into the flames, sits back in his armchair and breathes out a big wheezy sigh.

'You and Sheena must keep the money, Dad. Use it to come out and visit us. It's only seven hours from Glasgow to Toronto. That's if you can last that long without a puff.'

'Don't you worry about me, son. I'll face my demons the way you've faced yours. Well, Sheena will sort it.' He chuckles again, has a think, scratches his bristly chin. 'I'll not visit in the winter if that's all the same. But I'm chuffed for you, son. I always knew you'd pull through this. I'm proud of you.'

Be proud of who you are.

He must see me looking up at the clock because he says: 'You can have that clock, Cameron. To remind you that it's your time in the sun.'

'There'll be a lot of snow too.'

'You have to trudge through the snow to appreciate the sun on your skin. And remember, you're a long-time deid.'

'Thanks, Dad. Cheery thought.'

'You're welcome,' he says.

Baby

The visit to the hospital brings me out in a sweat. I keep telling myself it will all be fine, it will all be good. We can put our pasts behind us. The box is opened and scattered to the four winds. To the depths of the sea. To the ends of the earth.

The sonographer calls us in. I help Amanda onto the bed and she lifts up her top so that the mound made by our baby can be clearly seen.

After she has had gunk splattered onto her belly, and the bloke has moved the thingy backwards and forwards, after we have seen that there is one tiny heart beating, one bonnie bairn, the right size, a good position and no bagpipe, we say aye, we want to know the gender, we want to hear that we are having a baby girl and I know Bex would say why do you need to know? Why define your baby by its gender before it's even born? But I ignore her whisperings and I clutch the knowledge of a daughter to me. And I squeeze Amanda's hand and she squeezes my hand back. And I don't cry. I smile and I hug her and I smile some more, clinging on tight to this most excellent piece of happiness that I will carry with me always, in my heart, across the ocean and away into the future.

'Let's call her Annie,' she says. 'After your mum.'

The past tugs at me. My mum. My lovely mum.

'Yes, I'd like that,' I say. Because the past is always with you.

'Either that,' she says. 'Or Myrtle.'

Work

I have a new job. Once upon a time alcohol broke my life, and now alcohol is putting it back together again. It is wine all the way. It's wine o'clock.

I lay the suitcase on my wee single bed, open it up, ignore the image of a trunk with my mother's name on the side. This one has my name written neatly on a leather luggage label.

Myrtle leaps into the suitcase and sprawls across it, end to end.

I leave her there for now, don't have the heart to move her, getting soft, head down to the living room, to the window. My old street. I never had that desire to travel, always wanted to be here in Edinburgh, but now I'm ready to go, knowing I will always be able to come back and that this amazing, awesome, dirty, beautiful town will be with me wherever I go.

Myrtle creeps up on me, sits by the fire and grooms her rear end. She must have the cleanest dog rear end in Scotland.

'Do you have to, Myrtle?'

Myrtle growls. Yes, she does. At least she's not barking.

The kirk bell rings out. Three o'clock.

Tommo will be buried by now, put away in a dark box, in the cold, hard winter ground of Devon.

A tear falls from my eye, splashes on my hand, as I think of her face, her children. But she is in my past. I have a future.

And Bex? The world is hers now. She can put it to rights. You can do quite a lot with $25,000, Tommo's legacy, amongst others.

We are both free.

Toronto

July 2014

'How much longer, Mommy?'

'Any minute now, Mallory. You're being such a good girl.'

There is a mumbled, incoherent message on the loudspeaker.

'What did he say?' I ask.

'I'm not actually sure,' Christie screws up her pretty nose. 'I figure it must be their flight.'

We wait together. Christie, Mallory, Amanda, Annie and I.

'Let's watch out for them, okay?' says Christie to her daughter. 'See if you can spot a lady with long, fire-coloured, curly hair, like thingy from *Brave*.'

'Merida,' Mallory says.

'That's the one.'

'And then there's her twins, a boy and a girl who are teenagers, nearly grown-up actually. The girl will most probably have lipstick on.'

'Like you, Mommy.'

'Like me.'

'When can I have lipstick, Mommy?'

'Not for a long time.'

'How long's a long time?'

'That's a great question, Mallory.'

Christie looks at me and I shrug. Annie is in my arms. I want to hold her always. Never let her go. But she will grow up, become a girl like Mallory, a teenager like Loulou, a woman like Bex or Christie, but hopefully just like her mother.

'There they are, Mommy,' says Mallory.

And there they are indeed. Ethan is pushing a trolley, Loulou is carrying duty-free bags. Bex has a sparky look in her eye, something of the girl (woman) I used to know.

Christie takes Mallory's hand and walks bright and breezily over to Bex and the twins.

'What do you have to say, Mallory?'

'I like your lipstick?'

'Not that, no. The other thing we practised in the car coming to the airport.'

'Oh, that thing.' Mallory takes a deep breath and puts a big smile on her face. 'Welcome to Canada,' she says.

And Christie puts her best foot forward and hugs her old friend so hard she might possibly have cracked another of those fragile ribs. The only fragile thing about Christie Armstrong. Though as the last few months have shown me, she has a softness for her daughter I could never have imagined back in the day.

Time can suddenly skid away from you like a car on black ice. You can be right back where you started. But you can also be right back here, in the future.

Later, after we check into a hotel in downtown Toronto, after we have a swim in the pool, and a cocktail in the bar, a day of sightseeing planned out for tomorrow, Amanda and I take Annie up to our room, the light on top of the CN Tower shining brightly like a star.

Annie is sparko in the crib and Amanda and I share a bath, one of those shallow Canadian ones that we have had to get used to. I wash her back, I kiss her neck. I hold her close and then later, much later, after our own act of union, as we lie in bed, I walk my fingers over her beautiful plump English bottom. On one cheek the flag of St George. On the other, a new one, the blue and white Saltire, the cross of St Andrew. I kiss them both. I wonder briefly if one day she will get a maple leaf. And I wonder where exactly she might put that one.

I lie down next to her and breathe in the laundry fresh smell of cotton sheets. And when we get home to our place in Niagara-on-the-Lake, I vow I will be the one to make sure the sheets are always clean.

Thank you, Jeremy. And goodnight.

Endnote

I think there's been one too many footnotes so here's an end one. I realise I never came back to Maid Lilliard. My mother used to tell me her story. It's a remarkable story. Henry VIII of England wanted to secure the alliance with Scotland and the marriage of the infant Mary Queen of Scots to his son, Edward, but in December 1543, the Scottish Parliament rejected Henry's offer and renewed their alliance with France instead. So Henry did what any right-minded, self-obsessed, onto-his-sixth-wife, fat, syphilitic, in pain, blood-thirsty monarch would do and declared war against Scotland. The war was later called the 'Rough Wooing'. In 1545 during the Rough Wooing –which was very rough and not much wooing going on at all – the Scots had a decisive victory over Henry VIII's army at the Battle of Ancrum in the Borders.

If legend is to be believed, Maid Lilliard was at this battle and, after her lover was killed by the English, she set about them with fury, slaying them left, right and centre. Despite being severely wounded she fought on until death.

And get this: The inscription on her grave states:

Fair maiden Lilliard lies under this stane.
Little was her stature, but muckle was her fame;
Upon the English loons she laid mony thumps.

And when her legs were cuttit off, she fought upon her stumps.

As with so many legends, how much is fact and how much fiction cannot be answered. But, knowing the women in my life, past and present, I like to believe this one is true.

Acknowledgements

Acknowledgements are due to the following for permission to quote copyright material:

The late Tony Birks for an extract from *Building the New Universities*, David and Charles, 1972.

Lancaster University.

RSPCA.

The Real Mary King's Close for an excerpt from their souvenir guide. (Skeletours is a fictional tour company and is no reflection of RMKC which is first and foremost about history.)

Barbara Dickson for her quote from *A Shirt Box Full of Songs: The Autobiography*, Hachette Scotland, 2009.

June Purvis for her quote from *Emmeline Pankhurst: A Biography*, Routledge, 2002.

Thanks are due to:

The Society of Authors and the Royal Literary Fund for keeping the wolves from the door during a very difficult year.

Simon Crowe of The Boomtown Rats for telling me what it was like on *Top of the Pops* during the 1980s.

Barbara Dickson for her songs and singing.

Adam Watters for bringing history alive and for his brave heart.

Wes Coleman for Canadian wine, Edinburgh, ghosts and his clan name.

Lancaster University for two degrees.

My Lancaster chums – VCP, RKP, Simon, Fo, Daz, Kev, John, Vince and Fylde College.

Amy Ford and her prayers-by-text.

My agent Broo Doherty.

My editor Lauren Parsons and all at Legend Press.

Cathie Hartigan and Margaret James for their first reads.

Mum and Don – for keeping things together on the home front.

Johnny, Eddy and Izzy – my bright stars.
Niall – from cider at the Sugarhouse to tea at the Ritz.

Finally, I have not strictly kept to the truth – this is a work
of fiction after all – so any mistakes or deviations are down
to me.

In loving memory of Siobhan and Helen Morris,
bright stars forever.

Come and visit us at
www.legendpress.co.uk

Follow us
@legend_press